VOLUP

Voluptuous Voyage

Lacey Carlyle

HEADLINE
Liaison

First published in 1995
by HEADLINE BOOK PUBLISHING

A HEADLINE LIAISON paperback

10 9 8 7 6 5 4 3 2 1

ISBN 0 7472 5145 2

Typeset by Avon Dataset Ltd., Bidford-on-Avon, B50 4JH

Printed and bound in Great Britain by
Cox & Wyman Ltd, Reading, Berks

HEADLINE BOOK PUBLISHING
A division of Hodder Headline PLC
338 Euston Road,
London NW1 3BH

Voluptuous Voyage

Chapter One

It was with a feeling of intense relief that Lucy sank breathlessly into her seat in the club car of the train and immediately ordered a champagne cocktail.

She'd only just made it.

Within a couple of minutes the steam train chugged its way ponderously out of the station on its overnight run to New York.

While waiting for her much needed drink, Lucy took out her enamelled and silver compact and smoothed the ruffled, deep-gold waves of her hair back into place, then dusted her nose with powder.

The steward brought her cocktail, effervescent and golden, and placed it in front of her. Lucy took an appreciative sip, felt the bubbles bursting on her tongue and against the roof of her mouth and swallowed gratefully.

She hoped that the drink would calm her down and cool the lingering remains of the sexual heat which had led to this afternoon's disastrous confrontation with her fiancé – now ex-fiancé – Boyd Stanford.

She also hoped that no one looking at her would guess that beneath the cool cotton voile of her demure, flower-printed dress, her silk camiknickers were still sodden with her female juices.

She crossed one silk-stockinged leg over the other, pressed her thighs together unobtrusively and wriggled slightly on her seat, hoping that the urgent pulsing of her sex would soon

1

abate. But the vibration of the train seemed to be arousing her even more.

Damn Boyd. In a few cold words he'd made it clear that she'd been living in a fantasy world as far as their physical relationship was concerned. She should have seen it coming, should have realised that there was something wrong, but since meeting him at her third debutante ball, she'd been besotted by his blond good looks.

He was so different from the boys she'd been brought up with, male cousins and the brothers of friends, who all seemed callow and gauche by comparison. Of course, it helped that Boyd was ten years older than her and American – his accent always sent tiny spirals of lust through her body – but she should have sensed that he had no interest in her sexually.

How could she have been so blind?

Since she was fourteen, enough men had made it clear they were physically attracted to her for her to be aware of her sexuality.

But she'd foolishly decided that the reason Boyd had never tried to make love to her was because he assumed she was totally inexperienced. He was therefore behaving like a gentleman and holding himself in check with difficulty.

It had been an unpleasant shock to discover, just a few hours ago, that this wasn't the case at all and the only thing about her he was attracted to was her money.

The champagne cocktail tasted good and she took a large mouthful. The icy effervescence of the sparkling wine meant it slipped easily down her throat, while the brandy left a warm, comforting glow.

Lucy felt that she could use all the comfort she could get at the moment.

Within seconds of her finishing the drink the steward appeared. 'Another cocktail, madam?'

'Please.'

He whisked the glass away on a silver tray and soon returned bearing another, expertly mixed in exactly the right combination of ingredients, the glass beaded with condensation. Lucy raised it to her full, discreetly reddened lips and took a sip while she considered the events of that afternoon.

After announcing her engagement to Boyd against some mild opposition from Aunt Sarah, her guardian, Lucy had travelled to America to meet his parents and stay with them on their country estate.

The visit had presented her with her first opportunity to spend any time alone with Boyd. Despite the fact it was the nineteen-thirties, Aunt Sarah had old-fashioned ideas about chaperonage and Lucy had made the outward voyage with her friend Faye and Faye's parents, until they'd reached New York where Boyd's mother supposedly took on the role of chaperone.

But Mrs Stanford had no objection to her son and his fiancée being alone together and Lucy had waited eagerly for the moment Boyd would pull her into his arms and make love to her, or appear in her room late at night and slip into bed beside her, hard and ready.

She'd tried every way she knew to indicate subtly to Boyd that she wanted him, and had been puzzled and perplexed when he'd apparently failed to get the message. She was tired of spending her nights alone, tossing and turning in the still, sultry air, longing for his lean, muscular male body.

That afternoon she'd decided she couldn't wait any longer – she wanted her endless arousing fantasies to become reality. She'd wait until they were out riding and then in some deserted spot, tell him what she wanted . . .

As she trotted along behind Boyd in the shade of the trees, the spreading branches casting blue-green shadows on the sun-baked earth, Lucy was in the grip of deliciously erotic anticipation.

The sight of his broad shoulders, firm, muscular buttocks and long legs was having its usual effect on her.

She felt her body gearing itself up; her nipples under her white silk camisole and the fine cambric of her shirt were ultra-sensitive and tingled demandingly. Every rise and fall on the saddle caused them to rub against the sheer silk, making them so hard and swollen that she was sure they must be visible through the two layers of fabric.

She imagined Boyd standing in front of her and deftly undoing the buttons of her shirt, dragging it impatiently down her arms, then pulling her camisole over her head to expose the hard points of her breasts. She saw him bending to take one taut, engorged peak in his mouth, sucking and licking until it was slick with saliva.

He'd peel her jodhpurs down her thighs, taking her camiknickers with them and revealing her golden floss, damp with her female juices. Falling to his knees he'd bury his face in the hot, steaming delta of her vulva, flicking his tongue into her, exploring her thoroughly before lowering her to the ground and . . .

Lucy's horse almost stumbled on a rabbit hole and she regretfully abandoned her fantasy to concentrate on riding.

Her camiknickers had worked themselves into the cleft of her buttocks and the soft folds of her private parts. The friction was wonderful, spreading waves of hot pleasure through her groin as she followed Boyd along the pathway leading to the open countryside. Despite the heat of the August afternoon, he began to gallop as soon as they reached the rolling pastures surrounding his parents' estate.

She urged her chestnut mare into a gallop too and gave herself up to the sheer exhilarating pleasure of the ride. At last

Boyd reined in his mount in the shadows of a knoll of trees and helped her dismount. The feel of his strong hands on her waist made her dizzy with lust.

She slipped into his arms and moulded her body to the hard length of his, pulling his head down to kiss him passionately.

Immediately he moved away and busied himself tethering the horses to a tree, then sank onto the grass and propped himself on one elbow.

Frustrated, but assuming that his gentlemanly streak was showing again, Lucy threw herself down next to him so that her thigh touched his. She was obviously going to have to come right out with it and tell him what she wanted – he really wasn't making this easy for her.

Maybe she should chat for a bit, then gradually lead up to what was on her mind.

'Are we doing anything this evening?' she asked casually.

'Didn't Mother mention it? The Randsomes are coming to dinner.'

Lucy tried not to let her dislike show. Of all the people she'd met while staying here, the Randsomes were her least favourite. Mr Randsome was in business with Boyd's father and talked incessantly about his plans to develop the area.

She didn't like him at all. He never missed an opportunity to fondle her and she found the way he stared openly at her breasts and legs very annoying.

Boyd cleared his throat and said, 'I've been thinking, there's really no reason why we should wait until spring to be married – why don't we bring it forward to the autumn?'

A great wave of joy swept over Lucy. Boyd was obviously finding it as difficult to keep a firm rein on his sexuality as she was, and this was his solution. She'd obviously picked a good time to suggest her own more immediate answer.

'Randsome and my father want to start work on their new

project as soon as possible,' he continued, 'so if we marry around October, I can go into partnership with them myself. If we don't marry until spring they'll have to find another partner.'

Her body on fire as she studied the hard muscles of his thighs encased in skintight breeches, Lucy wondered impatiently what this had to do with their marriage.

'How long will it take to transfer your money over here, do you think?' he asked.

Lucy was startled and found it hard to concentrate on the conversation due to the bubbling moisture gathering in her vulva in carnal anticipation.

'Why would I transfer my money over here? My trustees have it safely invested for me.'

'So I can buy into the partnership,' he told her patiently. 'You'll get a much better return on your money then.'

Lucy barely heard him. Why on earth was he discussing something so irrelevant when there were much more urgent issues at hand?

'Oh, Boyd,' she murmured, taking his hand and placing it on her breast, 'we don't have to wait until we're married. I want you now – I want to feel you inside me.'

He snatched his hand away and glared at her.

'You must have taken leave of your senses – you're behaving like a complete slut! Don't ever suggest such a thing again!'

Stunned, Lucy stared up at him.

'Don't you want me?' she asked.

'If you must know, I consider that aspect of our marriage to be purely to furnish me with heirs. Once you have done your duty in that respect I won't trouble you.'

His handsome face cold and closed, he turned away from her.

Suddenly Lucy's distress and disbelief turned to white-hot anger as she realised she'd been deluding herself all these weeks.

It wasn't her he wanted – it was her money.

Why hadn't she realised it sooner?

Leaping to her feet she stood over him and said furiously, 'If you think I'm going to settle for a marriage like that – you're wrong! Goodbye, Boyd – I'm going back to New York and I never want to see you again.' She untethered her horse and swung herself into the saddle.

Boyd rose to his feet and said distantly, 'Don't be ridiculous – you can't travel alone. We'll discuss this when you've managed to regain some measure of self-control.'

Ignoring him, Lucy urged her chestnut mare into a gallop and headed back to the house. The only train to New York left in the late afternoon and she'd no intention of missing it.

Once there she told Winnie, her maid, to pack a couple of bags while she changed, then she got one of the estate hands to drive her to the station.

Now, as the train slowed down to cross a bridge, Lucy stared broodingly out of the window. She knew it had been ill-mannered of her to leave so unexpectedly and without saying goodbye to Mrs Stanford, but she hadn't wanted to spend another moment there.

She'd left a hastily scribbled note and told Winnie to pack the rest of her cases and follow her on tomorrow's train.

Aunt Sarah would have a fit if she knew her niece was travelling across North America without even a maid but, after all, what possible harm could come to her on a train?

As she sipped her champagne cocktail, Lucy had no regrets. Thank goodness she'd found out what Boyd's real interest in her was before it was too late – even if she was still in a state of arousal which didn't seem to be abating as quickly as she would have liked.

She glanced around, seeing her surroundings for the first

time. The first-class section was luxurious in the extreme. Not quite as opulent as the private railway car she and the Stanfords had travelled out in, but much more interesting.

Her seat was upholstered in dusky-pink velvet and was as deep and comfortable as any armchair. The window next to her was draped with rose-pink damask curtains edged with gold tassels and held back by gold-embroidered loops of the same fabric.

All around her there was the muted conversation of wealthy Americans enjoying the cocktail hour before going to their compartments to change for dinner. Which was something she should think about doing herself – she could certainly use a shower.

She drained the last drops of her cocktail and rose to her feet.

Her compartment was compact and well appointed. The stewardess had unpacked her case and her toilet articles were laid out ready in the tiny shower-room attached to it. Lucy liked a lot of things about America, particularly the bathrooms.

Brought up in draughty, underheated houses where baths were usually taken in a few inches of tepid water in a freezing bathroom, she loved to luxuriate for hours in a deep, scented tub or stand languidly under a shower enjoying the stimulating spray of dozens of tiny jets of water.

She couldn't wait to take one now. Her camisole was sticking to her and her sodden camiknickers had worked their way into the hollows and furrows of her crotch again as she made her way through the train.

She stripped off her clothes, tossed them carelessly to the floor, and stepped in. Perhaps keeping the water fairly cool would go some way to alleviating her inconvenient state of arousal.

She gasped as the first needles hit her overheated skin and the water trickled and gurgled over her aching breasts to stream over her firmly rounded buttocks and her mound.

Taking the bar of carnation-scented soap she began languorously to soap herself, working up a lather over her rose-pink nipples, feeling the jutting hardness of them.

The cool water washed over the throbbing folds of her vulva, exciting her even more. She ran her hands down her body, across her belly and then stroked the slim curve of her hips.

Of its own volition one hand drifted between her legs. Her sex-lips felt engorged, slick with her lubrications, and she held them apart with her other hand so she could find the tiny sliver of flesh which gave her so much pleasure when she touched it. It felt hot and swollen and she gasped as she stroked it, an answering tingle of sensation jolting through her body.

Her eyes closed and her head tilted back against the wall of the cubicle, Lucy stood with her thighs wide apart and caressed herself, slowly at first then more urgently until she felt the wave of heat which always preceded her climax.

She cried out when she came and stayed in the same position with the water pouring over her until her legs stopped trembling.

In her compartment she dried herself off on a huge, fluffy towel, then opened the closet and looked at her reflection in the mirror on the back of the door.

There was a pink flush over the smooth ivory skin of her cheeks, neck and breasts. Her wide set, grape-green eyes stared back at her under dark winged brows as she studied her oval face and delicately curved body, wondering why Boyd hadn't wanted her.

Perhaps he liked a different type of woman – earthy brunettes with large breasts, or plump redheads with ample backsides.

Maybe he was one of those men who preferred his own sex. Or was he just cold?

Her reverie was interrupted by the stewardess tapping at the door asking if she needed any help dressing.

'No, thank you,' she called and decided not to dwell on it any longer.

The world, after all, was full of men.

She selected a cream satin suspender belt from the shelf holding her lingerie, fastened it and then perched on the edge of her wide bunk to roll a new pair of bone-coloured silk stockings up her shapely legs.

Despite the traumatic events of the day she was looking forward to dining alone in the restaurant car. All her life, like most young women of her age and class, she'd been accompanied almost everywhere and, although she'd lunched alone in public before, she'd never eaten dinner.

She pulled a cream charmeuse camisole over her head and shivered with pleasure as the cool silk shimmered down over her shoulders and breasts, catching briefly on her puckered nipples. A pair of matching camiknickers with inset panels of lace followed.

After a few moments consideration Lucy drew from its hanger an ecru *peau-de-soie* dress cut on the bias and stepped into it. Tiny seed pearls were sewn in a narrow band around the neckline and onto a belt of the same material. A strand of pearls and a matching pair of earrings completed her ensemble.

The restaurant car was abuzz with muted conversation as her fellow passengers sipped their aperitifs and studied the elaborate menu. The warm evening air was heavy with savoury smells mingled with cigarette smoke and perfume.

The steward led her to a table for one and asked what she'd like to drink.

'Champagne,' she said immediately. After all, she was

celebrating, wasn't she? Celebrating her lucky escape.

He brought her a bottle and removed the cork with just the faintest of pops, releasing a tiny swirl of aromatic vapour. After pouring her a glass he left the bottle in a silver wine cooler just next to her.

Lucy sipped the icy champagne while she covertly studied her travelling companions. She was aware she was attracting quite a lot of attention and hoped she looked the part of the sophisticated female travelling alone.

The women were all elegantly gowned and she was glad her aunt had encouraged her to buy an extensive wardrobe to visit Boyd's family. Her own dress, although deceptively simple, skimmed over her curves and clung to the slender lines of her body in the way that only a couture garment could.

She was unaccustomed to drinking much and the champagne quickly went to her head, leaving her feeling pleasantly distanced from her situation.

An amethyst haze, soon darkening to purple-grey, fell outside the window, veiling the countryside they were passing through until all she could see was her own reflection.

She could also see the group of people dining diagonally behind her. Theirs was a particularly glamorous party, the women, as far as she could see, sumptuously jewelled.

One of the men was just out of her field of vision, but she sensed his eyes resting on her quite often. She got the impression of a dark, aquiline-featured face and decided that a particularly deep voice with the trace of a foreign accent belonged to him.

The rhythm of the train was arousing her again, the vibrations spreading upwards through her body and causing her to shift slightly on her seat. She uncrossed her legs before crossing them again and pressing her thighs tightly together.

She enjoyed her meal though she didn't have much appetite,

merely toying with her cutlets and foregoing all the tempting puddings for a fresh peach.

She began to feel drowsy, lulled by the soporific movement of the carriage. She finished her champagne, then decided it was time to retire for the night.

But before she did, she'd make her way to the back of the train and go out to the observation platform. The heat of the day should have cooled by now and she could get a breath of fresh air before she went to bed.

She rose to her feet and walked gracefully, if a little unsteadily, past the glamorous group behind her, allowing herself only the briefest of flickering glances. The man she'd thought had been looking at her raised his eyes to her face as she went past, but she carefully avoided meeting them.

The observation platform was thankfully deserted and she closed the door behind her and leant over the waist-high wrought-iron railing.

It was much cooler than the interior of the train and she lifted the golden waves tumbling over the back of her neck so that the breeze could waft over her heated skin.

Her pelvis was resting against an intricate loop in the wrought ironwork and she could feel the cold, unyielding hardness of the metal through her thin dress and cami-knickers.

Dreamily she pressed her mound against it and shifted slightly, until she felt a protruding part of the design, a carved rose, make contact with the throbbing little bud of flesh she'd played with earlier.

The vibration of the train was instantly transmitted through her private parts and she gasped as hot waves of sensation washed over her. She rubbed herself against the rose and was taken aback by the sheer erotic excitement of it.

Holding the rail tightly, she began a voluptuous movement

of her pelvis to gain maximum stimulation and became lost in a gasping, carnal pleasure.

A slight sound behind her made her stiffen and cease her arousing movements, just as she was on the brink of a climax.

Biting her lip, Lucy kept her back to the door and heard it open fully, then someone stepped onto the platform behind her. There was a window in the upper half of the door and she hoped desperately that whoever had joined her hadn't seen what she was doing.

She caught a whiff of a lemony cologne with just a hint of foreign cigarettes and something else – leather perhaps – before she realised that whoever had come out was standing just behind her.

She jumped when a hand grazed slowly down over her silk-covered back and came to rest lightly on the curve of her bottom. She would have spun round and told the intruder in no uncertain terms to get off her, but another hand caught her by the back of her neck and kept her head from turning while a hard body was pressed against hers holding her captive against the rail.

Before she could call for help, a deep, male voice murmured, 'Shhh.'

Confused, Lucy realised her mound was being pushed back into its former position against the wrought ironwork and the delicious sensations she'd experienced before began again.

He slid a hand round in front of her to hold her by the waist while the other glided over her breasts. She knew she should be outraged, but somehow she wasn't. Her nipples stiffened expectantly, then she heard a sigh escape her parted lips as he began a sensual caress.

The situation took on the surreal quality of a dream as she leant forward over the rail staring unseeingly out into the darkness, a strange and unseen man fondling her breasts.

A dark, secret pleasure was uncoiling in Lucy's groin and spiralling stealthily throughout her body. She could feel warm liquid gathering between her already damp thighs and soaking steadily into the crotch of her camiknickers. She rubbed herself harder against the metal pressing her clitoris.

A cool hand slipped inside her dress and she gasped as it closed over the warm flesh of her bare breast and teased the nipple with two fingers, tugging at it gently.

In her highly excited state, particularly after the frustrations of the day, it was too much for Lucy. She moaned softly and arched her back cat-like.

The man stepped away from her but, although he was no longer holding her captive, she felt powerless to move. She started when she felt his hands graze over her well-rounded rump, trail lazily downwards, then lift her skirt.

One hand travelled up her thigh, lingered to caress the bare skin above her stocking top, then moved up the wide leg of her camiknickers. She couldn't stop herself parting her thighs slightly, half so she could rub herself even more intimately against the metal rose and half so his fingers could probe between her legs.

The touch of his cool hand on the hot, slippery outer folds of her labia was electric and even more exciting than the vibrating metal. Lucy bent forward, opening her legs abandonedly to him so he could reach the aching, tormenting bud of flesh.

She had to bite her lip hard not to cry out as he squeezed and manipulated the swollen sliver, then she felt a long finger slip inside her and commence a lingering exploration of her pulsing, velvet interior while his thumb remained on her throbbing bud.

A second finger joined the first and he rotated them within her, making her bear down on his hand, wanting more. His thumb continued to torment and manipulate her clitoris until a long-drawn-out moan escaped her as, in a convulsive, shuddering endless spasm of pleasure, she came.

The thumb continued to stimulate her bud, but in the seconds following her climax it was ultra-sensitive and she jerked away.

Immediately he wound an arm around her waist and pulled her back against his chest, dragging her dress up to the waist at the front. His other hand moved swiftly and delved down the front of her camiknickers to cup her mound.

She couldn't help herself, she parted her legs again, then gasped as this time he shoved three fingers roughly inside her, moving them in and out in a lewd, careless rhythm. She could feel his male hardness pressing into the small of her back, then he bent his legs so it was pushed into the cleft of her buttocks.

Lucy couldn't believe this was happening. She was permitting a total stranger to fondle her private parts and – even worse – she was enjoying it.

She came again; a hot, jolting climax which made perspiration form on her smooth skin. Unable to stop herself, she swivelled her hips and bore down to extract the last lingering pleasure, her head falling back against his chest.

She was jerked back to reality when she heard the door behind them opening again and felt him swiftly withdraw his hand and step away from her. She managed to close her legs but felt too weak and drained to stand upright and had to hold onto the rail. A middle-aged couple joined them on the platform, exclaiming about the heat inside the train.

'I'll be glad when September comes,' said the woman, turning towards Lucy. 'It's too hot for me at the moment and the restaurant car is unbearable.'

'It is, isn't it?' she heard herself replying automatically, then she managed to stand upright and turn around.

Whoever the stranger was, he'd gone.

Her camiknickers were soaking wet and she could feel a trickle of moisture making its way into her stocking top. She couldn't very well wipe it with her handkerchief with the middle-aged couple looking at her, so she murmured goodnight and was forced to walk the length of the train hoping it wouldn't reach the hem of her dress and become clearly visible.

It was strange making her way through the carriages knowing that one of the men watching her go by had only minutes before been handling her intimately.

The walk back to the sanctuary of her compartment seemed endless, but at last she pulled open the door, slammed it behind her and collapsed onto her bunk.

How could she have let a stranger lift her skirt on the observation platform of a crowded train and caress her so lewdly? The memory of it made her cheeks burn with warm colour.

But there was still a hot, smouldering pleasure between her thighs and just thinking about the encounter made her aroused again and she dreamily relived it while her hand strayed between her legs.

A long while later, she washed and slipped naked between the cool cotton sheets, unable to sleep for thinking about what had happened.

Who was her phantom lover and how had he known what she wanted? It was almost too exciting to contemplate what might have happened next if they hadn't been joined by other people.

It was a long while before Lucy fell into a deep sleep, her hand still clasped between her thighs, to spend a night tossing and turning tormented by dark, disturbing dreams.

Chapter Two

'Lucy Davenport – your Aunt Sarah will be furious,' commented Faye, pushing back her chestnut hair with one hand and then raising the teapot with a graceful gesture which made the sleeve of her draped, wrapover lemon-crepe afternoon dress fall back to reveal a shapely white forearm.

'No she won't – I could tell she didn't really like Boyd or the fact that he's American. She still thinks of America as a barely civilised colony.'

'Even so, she won't approve of you racing back to New York on your own without even your maid.'

They were having tea in the Art Deco splendour of the Waldorf Astoria the day after Lucy had returned to the city. Lucy had been in luck. The Faulkners were supposed to be visiting friends in Connecticut, but Faye's mother had succumbed to one of her frequent illnesses and she and her daughter were still in New York, while Mr Faulkner had gone up to Saratoga to look at a horse he was interested in.

Lucy shrugged and added milk to her tea.

'She needn't know.'

'Mother is sure to tell her.'

'Well, that's just too bad. There isn't much she can do about it after the event.' She picked up a small, perfectly iced cake and took a decisive bite. 'Anyway, I'm tired of America so I'm going home,' she announced.

'I don't think Mother will want to return just yet.'

'Then I shall travel alone.'

'You can't do that,' Faye pointed out. 'You'll just have to wait until she's ready to leave. Although I suppose someone else we know might be travelling back before that.'

'I'm going at the weekend – I shall book my passage tomorrow.'

Faye's large china-blue eyes became thoughtful. 'I wish I could come with you.'

'Why don't you? It would be so much fun travelling together.'

'I can't imagine Mother letting me – can you? She's so old-fashioned.'

'I'm not sure. Why don't you let me talk to her?'

'I wish you would – but I don't suppose it'll do any good.'

'Are you almost ready, my dear?' asked Andrei, entering Sonya's bedroom in their shared hotel suite.

Sonya was sitting in front of her dressing table, applying a slash of scarlet lipstick to her mouth. Her silver-grey eyes were accentuated by a skilful smudge of pewter eye shadow and her naturally pale complexion had been lightly dusted with translucent powder.

She had sable hair which was cut into a short, gleaming bob with a straight fringe, drawing attention to the perfect contours of her small, straight nose.

She had her back to Andrei so he was able to pause for a moment to take in the swooping, deep vee of her black gown which just skimmed the intoxicating swell of her slender buttocks. The smooth skin of her back was a cool ivory seductively framed by the dark material.

She met his eyes in the mirror. 'How much did you win?' she asked. He strolled up to her and placed his hands on her shoulders, then bent to kiss the white column of her neck.

'Enough to take us to Europe.' His hands slid down the

tight-fitting sleeves of her gown, caressing her arms through the stiff silk, then glided across to cup the points of her small, high breasts. Her lashes fluttered downwards to veil the excitement in her eyes for a moment, then she looked at him in the mirror again.

'It's been a while since we were there,' she murmured. 'Monte Carlo perhaps?'

'I have some business in London first but maybe Monte Carlo next month – before that it might be too hot and, unlike here, there won't be air conditioning.'

'Better too hot than too cold. Have you forgotten that we spent our entire childhoods freezing for most of the year?'

Andrei pinched one nipple and then pressed the palm of his hand against it, commencing a fluid, circular movement.

He was tall and slim with high cheekbones, aquiline features and heavy-lidded, yellow-green eyes. His thick, dark hair was brushed back from his face and was just beginning to show premature flecks of grey.

Sonya's head fell back against his groin and rested there for a moment.

'Will you fasten my necklace?' she asked when he released her. She picked up the glittering white gold and diamond necklace and passed it to him. His long, supple fingers made short work of the delicate clasp as he fastened it around her neck, pausing to kiss one bare shoulder blade.

'Were you able to amuse yourself while I was gone?' he enquired.

'As you can see,' she murmured.

Andrei turned to look at the figure spread-eagled on the bed, wrists and ankles lashed to the bedposts.

'And was he satisfactory?' he asked, amused.

The ice-blue eyes of Stephan, his valet-cum-bodyguard, were fixed on the ceiling and red marks on his wrists and ankles

19

where he was secured indicated how fiercely he'd strained at his bonds. There were also red stripes criss-crossing the tops of his thighs almost down to his knees.

'Stephan is always satisfactory,' purred Sonya, rising from the stool with sinuous grace and strolling over to the bed.

Stephan's member lay curled against the pale hair of his groin. He was a strikingly good-looking man in his early twenties with white-blond hair and pale eyebrows and lashes.

Sonya ran a scarlet-nailed hand lightly down his chest and he groaned. She flicked the glans of his penis with her forefinger and it stirred into life.

'Always ready,' she gloated. 'I shall leave him here until I need him again later.'

'Actually, my dear, I have a little errand for him, but it won't take long.'

'Very well – I'll have Marta release him.' Sonya picked up a small, intricately carved silver bell from the bedside table and rang it once. Immediately a door opened and a dark-haired woman in a severe navy-blue dress with a white collar and cuffs appeared.

'Yes, Princess?'

'You can let him go now,' said Sonya carelessly. She took Andrei's arm and together they left the room.

The scene at Pier 90 at the end of West 50th Street in Manhattan was one of orderly confusion as car after car disgorged passengers for the five day journey to Southampton on the SS *Aphrodite*.

Lucy and Faye stepped out of their limousine and gazed upwards at the huge, elegant liner, its gleaming paintwork dazzling in the strong afternoon sunshine.

'Look out!' Lucy pulled Faye aside as two longshoremen staggered past, struggling with a massive steamer trunk.

Faye could barely hear her friend for the noise. Above the babble of voices a band played, lending a carnival atmosphere to the proceedings.

They were conducted to their adjacent staterooms by an impeccably dressed steward and introduced to the stewardess who would look after them on the voyage.

'Not bad,' commented Lucy as soon as they were alone. She paused in front of the mirror to straighten the belt of her white-spotted, Wedgwood-blue, crêpe de Chine dress.

She liked her stateroom's uncluttered spaciousness, modern furniture and pretty chintzes. It had an adjoining black-and-white-tiled bathroom and double doors opened onto a small, private verandah.

She prowled around the luxurious room examining everything, while Faye sank gracefully onto the ivy-green satin quilt covering the bed and removed her hat from the perfect waves of her chestnut hair.

Lucy often thought that Faye looked like a doll with her small, cupid's bow mouth, round, pale-blue eyes and delicate tip-tilted nose. That afternoon her friend was wearing a white linen dress trimmed with navy braid and a matching jacket. The chic outfit subtly emphasised the curves of her hips and well-rounded bottom.

In a period when it was fashionable for women to have boyish figures, Faye was really too curvaceous for the current vogue, but it did her no disservice in the eyes of many men. She stretched happily and examined a tiny run in her pale stockings.

'What a blissful voyage this is going to be,' she remarked.

Her eyes were drawn to a mural on the wall above the bed in hazy shades of green, pink and blue featuring a shepherdess and her flock in a sylvan setting. She turned her head to study it and then said, 'She looks a bit like you, don't you think?'

Lucy came over to look at it and was struck by the expression on the girl's face – it seemed to her to be one of pure carnal gratification and reminded her of her own after her encounter with the stranger on the train.

She fully intended to confide in Faye and tell her what had happened, but hadn't yet found the right time. At some stage on the voyage the opportunity would undoubtedly present itself.

'I didn't think Mother would ever let the two of us travel alone,' went on Faye. 'I don't know how you managed to persuade her.'

Actually it had been easier than Lucy had anticipated. Mrs Faulkner had been laid low with a summer cold and was too weak to object as strongly as she might otherwise have done.

When Lucy had announced her intention of leaving on the next ocean liner bound for England, the older woman had made a feeble attempt to talk her out of it. But when it had become apparent that Lucy wasn't to be swayed, she'd fallen resignedly back against her pillows and agreed to let Faye accompany her.

Mrs Faulkner was slightly in awe of Lucy's Aunt Sarah and the prospect of having to explain to her just why she'd allowed the other woman's niece to make the crossing unaccompanied, except for her maid, had unnerved her.

She'd attempted to salve her conscience by finding out who else was on the passenger list. When she'd discovered that Amanda Derwent, a distant acquaintance and a second cousin of her husband, was travelling on the same ship, she'd sent her a note asking her to keep an eye on the girls.

Amanda had phoned her and assured her that she'd look after them. Mrs Faulkner had breathed a sigh of relief and told herself she'd done everything possible in an awkward situation. After all, what real harm could they come to?

Since her experience on the observation platform, Lucy had

been in an over-stimulated state. Colours seemed more vivid, scents more intense and her body seemed to be holding itself in a state of readiness for something – she wasn't sure what.

Five days of shipboard life seemed to present her with endless opportunities to live life to the full in a way previously denied to her.

On the outward voyage the liner had been caught up in a series of summer storms which had followed them across the Atlantic. Both girls had spent the entire time in their separate cabins praying for death as they succumbed to seasickness which didn't relinquish its terrible hold until they'd sailed into harbour.

It had been no fun at all and they both planned to make the most of the next five days of relative freedom.

'Let's go and explore while Winnie unpacks,' suggested Lucy. They were sharing her maid, no hardship on a liner renowned for the solicitousness of its staff and crew. 'We should decide on our table for dinner – we don't want to be stuck with a lot of dreary people,' she added.

They made their way to the first-class restaurant through the corridors thronging with passengers, the friends and relatives seeing them off and stewards struggling with cases and steamer trunks.

The chief steward had already allocated them places at a table given over to women travelling alone, most of them elderly. One glance at the names told Lucy all she needed to know.

'I don't think so,' she said firmly. She pored over the seating plan and then tapped it with one perfectly manicured fingernail. 'We'll sit here.'

'Who are we dining with?' Faye wanted to know as soon as they were out of earshot of the chief steward who was only half mollified by the generous tip Lucy had slipped him.

'I'm not entirely sure, but some of them had foreign names so they're bound to be glamorous. Whoever they are they've got to be more interesting than the old dears he was trying to seat us with.'

They wandered around the ship for a while trying to get their bearings, until they heard the gong signalling that it was time for people not actually travelling to leave the ship. They made their way up on deck and shortly afterwards watched Manhattan slip away as they steamed down the river.

When they returned to their staterooms to bathe and change, Lucy was surprised to discover that her room had acquired two bouquets of flowers. The smaller bouquet was from Faye's mother but there was no name on the massive arrangement of white flowers which Winnie had placed in the middle of the table.

The mingled scents of white roses, carnations and lilies filled the cabin with their voluptuous perfumes. There was something supremely sensual about the way the velvety roses nestled against the lace-edged petals of the carnations and the waxen trumpets of the lilies.

Lucy stood breathing in the mingled scents, idly admiring the perfection of the blooms. She slipped the tip of one forefinger into the half-opened flower of a lily and her nail was immediately covered by a fine dusting of bright yellow pollen.

Her reverie was interrupted by a tap at the door. It was a scarlet-jacketed bellboy delivering an invitation to a cocktail party Amanda Derwent was giving before dinner.

She left her stateroom and tapped on Faye's door which was opened by Winnie who was just finishing her friend's unpacking. An identical invitation to Lucy's lay unopened on the table.

Faye was soaking in a deep, scented bubble bath, her hair

24

protected from the steam by a towel wound turban-style around her head.

'Your cousin Amanda has invited us to a cocktail party,' announced Lucy, closing the door then perching on the edge of the bath. 'Will it be fun do you think?'

'I overheard Father telling one of his friends that she was fast,' said Faye. 'I thought it best not to mention that to Mother when she discovered that Amanda was travelling on the same ship.'

'Sounds promising then. What will you wear?'

'I'm not sure. Maybe the fuchsia silk, or the white crepe. What about you?'

Faye sat up, reached for the cake of fragrant pink soap next to her and began to work up a lather. Her breasts emerged from the steaming water, one coral-tinged nipple half-concealed by a tiny mound of foam. They were beautiful breasts and Lucy always found the sight of them enticing.

'I haven't decided yet. I'll see what Winnie has pressed.' She took the soap from Faye and murmured, 'Lean forward and I'll do your back.'

She began to work the rich lather into the smooth, slippery flesh of Faye's back in a circular movement.

'There's a huge bouquet of white flowers in my room,' she told her friend. 'And I haven't a clue who they're from. Your mother sent me a bouquet too, which was very sweet of her.'

'I have one from Mother, but that's all. How exciting – do you think you have an admirer?'

'I don't see how.'

Lucy began to lather Faye's creamy shoulders, allowing the tips of her fingers to stray down over the upper slopes of her breasts.

'Mmm,' sighed Faye, settling back in the water again, 'that feels good.'

Lucy allowed her fingers to trail lower until they brushed over one pointed, crinkled nipple.

'You have such beautiful breasts,' she breathed. She circled the nipple with a soapy forefinger, then covered the breast with her hand, feeling the hard nub of flesh hot against her palm.

For a while she caressed them dreamily, then her other hand slipped deep into the water between Faye's thighs.

Faye's eyes were closed but she parted her legs so Lucy could find the erect sliver of flesh which lay hidden in its soft delta.

There was silence in the scented, steamy bathroom – a silence broken only by the distant but incessant throb of the engines, the gentle lapping of the water against the sides of the bath and Faye's sighs of pleasure as she enjoyed her friend's ministrations.

At last Faye let out a long, soft moan and her body went rigid, her head tilting back and her back arching. Lucy withdrew her hand, then bent to kiss her friend. Their eyes met and they exchanged a look of perfect understanding before Lucy returned to her own stateroom to bathe and change.

Amanda Derwent's sitting room was crowded by the time Lucy and Faye arrived.

Lucy was wearing a favourite *eau-de-Nil* chiffon gown from Vionnet and had teamed it with a gold and jade necklace which intensified the green of her eyes. On one wrist was a bracelet in the same design and on the other a small cocktail watch with a mother-of-pearl face.

Faye was looking ravishing in a dress of fuchsia silk with a matching brocade jacket, beaded on the lapels. The dress emphasised her small waist and brought out the burnished sheen of her chestnut hair.

26

Amanda, a sophisticated, willow-slim brunette in her thirties, greeted them casually.

A long cigarette holder was held elegantly in one outflung arm as she brushed cheeks with Faye and then Lucy. She was wearing a stunning dress of emerald-green satin with a neckline that both Aunt Sarah and Mrs Faulkner wouldn't have hesitated to stigmatize as indecent. She introduced them to several of her other guests and then sashayed off to greet some other arrivals.

'Surely your mother can't know her very well,' giggled Lucy, accepting a martini from a steward.

They both watched with interest as one of Amanda's male guests seized her by the waist and kissed her with a passion neither of the girls was used to witnessing.

Lucy felt a frisson of arousal just watching them. Hurriedly she averted her eyes, took a *canapé* from another steward and munched it hungrily.

'Do you think he could be her lover?' asked Faye. Another male guest wound his arm around Amanda's slim waist and then let his hand slip downwards until it brushed over the swell of her satin-covered bottom.

'Which one? They both seem to be on intimate terms with her,' said Lucy, rather enviously.

Her attention was diverted as she suddenly became aware that she was the object of someone's unwavering scrutiny.

She turned her head slightly and her eyes met the sombre, yellow-green gaze of a tall, narrow-hipped stranger. His expression didn't change to acknowledge that she'd caught him staring, but he raised his glass in her direction before bending his head to listen to something his striking, dark-haired female companion was saying.

Lucy was immediately struck by the air of glamour which hung around the couple. She realised instinctively that they weren't English, but she couldn't have said how she knew that. She was vaguely aware that Faye's attention had been claimed by an immaculately uniformed ship's officer, but she was too interested in her covert observation to join in the conversation.

There was something about the man she found oddly unnerving, but she didn't know why. It wasn't just that he was undoubtedly very attractive – she wasn't the only woman looking at him, she noticed – but there was something *unsettling* about him.

Amanda Derwent paused for a moment to speak to Faye and Lucy took advantage of the fact to ask her, 'Who's that woman over there? The one in the steel-grey dress?' She didn't want to ask about the man directly, but hoped the information might be forthcoming anyway.

'Princess Sonya Behrs. And the man with her is Count Andrei Davoust. My dear, I don't know much about them – I met them at a house party last month. They're white Russians and they're supposed to be terribly wicked. Come along – I'll introduce you.'

'No, really – I'd rather not.'

She might as well not have spoken. Amanda seized one of her wrists in a vice-like grip and pulled her determinedly in her wake through the crush of people.

Princess Sonya was even more dazzling close up; rarely had Lucy seen features so haughtily perfect and so clearly defined. Every line of her exquisitely sculpted face might have been carved from pure ivory by the hand of a master.

The other woman's silver-grey eyes met hers, then Sonya smiled the smile of someone who has just been given a much-coveted present.

'I'm delighted to meet you,' she said softly. Her husky voice had a faintly foreign inflexion and something about it made a tiny shiver pass through Lucy's slender frame.

'You're very beautiful,' she blurted out, then could have kicked herself for sounding so gauche.

'And so are you, but in a very different style,' interjected Count Andrei. There was something familiar about his voice as he paid her the graceful compliment, then he took her hand, bent low over it and kissed it.

Lucy smiled at him politely. Her first thought on seeing him at close range was that there was something wolfish about him, her second that she'd met him before.

Amanda began to chat to Sonya and Andrei drew Lucy to one side.

'Have you had any caviar yet?' he asked, leading her over to the table where a wide selection of delicacies was fast being depleted.

'No – in fact I've never had any,' she replied. 'It always looks faintly off-putting.'

'Then you must try some.' She followed him round to the other side of the table where he used a silver spoon to pile a small mound onto a plate, then added a couple of wafer thin pieces of toast. He scooped up a heap of the glistening purplish eggs with one of the pieces and held it out to her. She tried to take it from him but he carried it to her lips so she felt compelled to take a small bite.

As Lucy's mouth closed she caught a faint whiff of his lemony cologne and suddenly she knew him.

It was her phantom lover from the observation platform of the train.

The caviar seemed to expand in her mouth and she had difficulty swallowing it. She managed to wash it down with a gulp of her drink as a fiery heat coursed through her body. Her knees went weak and she took a step backwards.

She'd never expected to meet him again and wasn't in any way prepared for such a confrontation. Aunt Sarah had made sure she had a thorough grounding in all forms of etiquette, but somehow nothing seemed to fit coming face to face with a stranger who had, on their one previous encounter, worked her to two heady, breathless climaxes in a semi-public place.

She steadied herself by clutching the edge of the table with one hand.

Of course, now she recognised him. He was one of the glamorous party who'd been sitting diagonally behind her on the train; the man with the dark, aquiline features.

But even as her face flooded with warm colour, she could feel her private parts unfurling like a sun-warmed chestnut bud. She was aware of a stickiness around her vulva which hadn't been there a few moments before and a tiny pulse began to beat high up in her hidden delta.

'It . . . it was you,' she stammered at last.

He didn't reply, but his heavy eyelids came down briefly and half-shuttered his eyes which gleamed an opaque, feral topaz in the rays of the setting sun lancing in through the window.

In the last few months Lucy had become very adept at flirting and it was her usual response to any attractive man she found herself talking to.

But how could she flirt with a man who'd had his hand buried in the velvet folds of her vagina, only seconds after they'd first met?

He held out another piece of toast-filled caviar and somehow she found herself opening her mouth and accepting it. Actually, she didn't much care for it – it was too crunchy and had a strong fishy taste where she'd expected something more delicate.

'Are you always as ready for a man as you were that night?' he asked.

Her mouth full of caviar, Lucy was unable to say anything,

but she looked wildly around in case anyone had overheard.

'Is your sex always so wet and open?' he continued in a low voice. 'Is it pulsing like that now, eager for stimulation . . . penetration?'

A slow surge of renewed heat flooded her body. It seemed to originate in her groin and washed upwards making her tremble.

'You have the most luscious derrière I've ever stroked . . . firm . . . yielding . . . peach-perfect. Had we not been interrupted I would have fallen to my knees and tasted it . . . tasted you.'

If her bottom had been a peach and he'd squeezed it, Lucy doubted if she would have run with more juice than she was doing now. She was hypnotised by his wolfish eyes and mesmerised by the sound of his low voice. She tried desperately to swallow the caviar but it took another large gulp of her martini to wash it down.

'Shall we go and watch the sunset?' he asked.

Although it was a question, there was nothing questioning about the firm grip he took on her arm as he opened one of the doors that led to Amanda's private verandah.

The setting sun had washed the horizon a deep, livid vermilion streaked with ochre and the cool breeze blowing was very welcome after the heat of the cabin.

Lucy gazed numbly at the sunset, feeling simultaneously wildly excited and completely at a loss. And Count Andrei wasn't exactly helping. He was leaning nonchalantly against the verandah rail, his head turned towards her appraising her silently, dispassionately.

'Did you receive my flowers?' he asked at last.

'They . . . they're beautiful. But how did you know I was travelling on this ship?' she asked, startled.

He didn't reply. Instead he reached for her hand, kissed it, then drew her index finger between his lips and sucked it lingeringly. A tremor like a jolt of low-voltage electricity shot from her hand, along her arm and straight to her sex. His mouth felt like hot velvet and immediately Lucy wanted to feel it elsewhere on her body.

Her nipples . . . her navel . . . her mound.

He let her finger slip from between his lips and placed her hand on his groin. Lucy tried to pull away, but he held it firmly in place over a hard, rapidly growing bulge.

'Undo my fly,' he ordered her softly. She wanted to refuse, but somehow she couldn't, she was in the grip of such a feverish excitement.

Her heart pounding, she slipped her fingers under his fly and slowly, clumsily, undid his buttons.

'Take it out.'

With trembling fingers Lucy reached inside and her hand closed over a warm, throbbing column. She drew it out and looked downwards, take aback by its beauty.

Long and slim, it had a large plum-like end which was a darker colour than the shaft. Thick, blue veins marbled the smooth surface and a drop of clear liquid was poised like a rain drop on the end.

She darted a glance back towards the closed doors leading into Amanda's cabin. At any moment they could be joined and unless he moved swiftly to cover himself, her reputation would be instantly in shreds.

But she was in the grip of a strange compulsion and her fingers explored the throbbing shaft with tentative pleasure.

She was cupping his heavy balls, weighing them in her palm, when she heard the door open behind them. She tried to snatch her hand away but his own moved like lightning to grasp her wrist and keep it firmly in place.

Lucy could do nothing except close her eyes and wait for

the moment when she would be denounced as a slut and from then on shunned by polite society.

Instead, there was a rustle of silk and they were joined at the rail by Princess Sonya.

'How lovely the sunset it,' she greeted them, standing next to Lucy and gazing out over the horizon.

Lucy couldn't understand it. It would be impossible for Sonya not to notice what was going on and that her travelling companion's penis was clutched in Lucy's hand, but she gave no sign of having seen anything untoward.

'Beautiful,' agreed Andrei, moving Lucy's hand caressingly up and down his shaft. 'See how the sea appears to be on fire.'

'There is so much beauty in the world,' sighed Sonya. 'Much of it on display for all to see, but too much of it hidden. Are your breasts as beautiful as your face, Lucy?'

Again, Lucy was starting to think she'd fallen asleep and must be dreaming. Otherwise how could she explain the fact that she was standing on the deck of an ocean liner, a penis in her hand, listening to such a calmly posed question by a woman she'd only just met?

'I . . . I don't know,' she stuttered.

Sonya reached across and began to undo the four small jade buttons which kept the bodice of Lucy's pale green chiffon dress closed. It had to be a dream because she seemed unable to do anything but stand acquiescently silent, while continuing to stroke Andrei's member.

Sonya finished undoing the buttons and pulled the bodice of the dress fully open, revealing Lucy's ivory satin camisole, held closed at the front by two tiny lace ribbons.

She tugged gently on the ribbons and the camisole fell apart, exposing the buttermilk swell of Lucy's breasts in all their pink-tipped perfection.

'Exquisite,' breathed Sonya. 'Don't you agree, Andrei?'

Andrei's heavy-lidded eyes surveyed them lingeringly and Lucy felt his penis twitch in response to the sight.

'Delectable,' he agreed.

The cool evening air made Lucy's nipples stiffen instantly. They stiffened even more when Sonya ran her smooth palm over them in a circular movement. Lucy found it intensely exciting, particularly when Sonya began to toy with her nipples, feathering over them with the tips of her fingers, then pinching them delicately between her finger and thumb.

There seemed to be a direct line from Lucy's nipples to her sex, because she felt herself getting wetter and wetter until the crotch of her ivory camiknickers was soaking and she could feel the soft floss of her pubic curls sticking together around her pulsing vulva.

She forgot where she was, forgot that there was a cocktail party taking place a few yards away on the other side of the door, forgot everything except that she was molten with lust.

It ended as suddenly as it had begun.

Andrei glanced at his watch and said, 'It's time we were leaving, Sonya, my dear.'

He removed his swollen shaft from Lucy's hand and buttoned it unhurriedly back into his trousers. Sonya gave Lucy's left nipple a hard pinch which made her gasp. Then, without a word, the two of them left her alone.

With trembling fingers Lucy fastened her clothing, her brain in turmoil, her body hungry and wanting.

Chapter Three

'What do you think?' asked Andrei as they strolled along the boat deck away from Amanda's suite.

'Perfect, absolutely perfect,' purred Sonya, her scarlet-tipped hand resting lightly in the crook of his arm. 'What about her friend? Did you get the chance to talk to her?'

'No. She's an unknown quantity, but she can soon be tested.'

'I shall enjoy that.'

Their eyes met for a moment as they continued with their unhurried walk, then Andrei said, 'Was Amanda agreeable to your suggestion for this evening?'

'Yes.'

'Does she know what to expect?'

Sonya ran the tip of her tongue along her lower lip as she considered her reply.

'Not exactly, but that should make it more interesting. After all, she's no innocent and she obviously finds you very exciting.'

They reached the furthermost point of the boat deck and paused to look out to the horizon. The last brilliant crescent of the sun was rapidly vanishing, dipping out of sight but leaving behind it an almost lurid glow of incandescent orange.

Even on such a calm, still evening the ocean was furrowed by deep, restless troughs and swells topped by ragged foam crests.

The sight was unsettling enough for Sonya to turn her back and lean against the rail to survey the acres of polished wood deck and the massive funnels and masts towering high above them.

She glanced around to check that there was no one in sight, then ran her hand over the cloth-covered bulge of Andrei's penis.

'Lucy has made you very hard – that is good. I'm tempted to put it to use here and now, but no – I mustn't be impatient, I must wait until later.'

She withdrew her hand and they began to retrace their steps.

'Does Stephan know what to do?' asked Andrei.

'Yes – everything is arranged.'

'What a pity it isn't Lucy who will be joining us,' he said pensively.

'One step at a time – you know that, Andrei. Though, with only five days, we'll have to take it fairly quickly. Perhaps later this evening an opportunity may arise. Shall we return to our suite?'

Faye was enjoying the party very much. Leo, the first officer, was a man very much to her taste. He had reddish hair, a broad-shouldered, burly frame and a fair skin made ruddy by frequent exposure to the sun and wind.

But the thing about him she liked best was his immaculate white uniform. She'd always been attracted to men in uniform and had lost her virginity to a guards' officer after seeing him on parade and being gripped by a heady, paralysing excitement at the sight of all that gold braid.

Leo made her feel much the same way. There was a delicious squirming sensation in the pit of her stomach and she felt slightly breathless, as if she'd just run up several flights of stairs.

She finished her martini and toyed idly with the plump, green olive skewered on a slender stick. They'd just finished discussing the merits of New York compared to those of London and she was hoping to get the conversation on a more personal basis.

'So, what are your duties on each voyage?' she asked, licking the olive delicately with the tip of her pink tongue. Leo's eyes were fixed on the olive and he watched while she drew it between her lips and slid it gently to the end of the skewer before taking a juicy bite.

'Sorry . . . what did you say?' he asked as she looked at him expectantly.

'I asked what you did on each voyage.' Faye swallowed and licked her lips, then accepted another cocktail from one of the attentive waiters. Leo ran his forefinger around the neck of his collar and went a slightly darker colour.

'I'm responsible for discipline,' he replied at last. A strange little *frisson* of pleasure rippled down Faye's spine and she shivered as she took a sip of her drink.

'What does that mean?' she asked quizzically.

'On any voyage there's usually a sprinkling of card sharps, confidence tricksters and gold-diggers. It's my job to spot them and stop them taking advantage of anyone.'

'That sounds intriguing – are they usually easy to spot?'

'Sometimes, but not always. I also make sure that all the passengers behave themselves and that there isn't too much rowdy behaviour. I keep an eye on unaccompanied ladies like you to make sure you aren't bothered by unwanted attentions and I ensure that there's no fraternization between officers and female passengers.'

'You're the ship's spoilsport then?' she murmured, looking up at him from beneath her thick, dark lashes.

'I prefer not to think of myself that way.'

'And what if there's a female passenger who wants to fraternize with a ship's officer?'

'It's against company regulations so I'd have to have a word with the lady in question and report the officer to the captain.'

Faye eyes him speculatively. She was *so* glad she'd been allowed to travel back to England with Lucy.

In fact where was Lucy?

The last time she'd seen her she was being fed caviar by a tall, wolfish-looking man and now both of them seemed to have vanished. The party was beginning to break up and people were drifting away, leaving behind them smeared glasses, smoke and the crumbling remains of half-eaten *canapés*.

At that moment Lucy threaded her way across the room to rejoin her friend. Faye thought that she looked flushed and there was an odd, feverish glitter in her eyes.

'Should we be making our way to the restaurant, do you think?' she asked.

'It would be my pleasure to escort you there,' Leo offered, 'then I'm afraid that duty calls again.'

Three decks high and almost three hundred feet long, the first-class restaurant was vast. The grand sweep of a massive staircase led down into it and Lucy and Faye paused at the top to survey the scene below them.

No one dressed for dinner on the first night, but even so the room glittered with the women's jewels and the bright and varied hues of their dresses. The animated sounds of conversation and the tinkle of glass and silverware drifted up the stairs towards them.

The coffered ceilings had indirect lighting which cast no shadows and bathed the whole restaurant in a soft glow. At each end of the room there were further lighting fixtures in the form of huge urns and the centre was dominated by a modern fountain-like sculpture with illuminated chrome tubes.

'Very intimate,' commented Lucy dryly as they descended the stairs. A steward conducted them to their table where there were still several empty chairs, but the people already seated were, for the most part, young and lively.

Faye, a great lover of good food, studied the extensive menu with interest. 'Look at this,' she said with delight. 'Blue Point Oyster Cocktail – I've never had that – *Squab en Cocotte*, Smoked Salmon – and that's just to start. There must be nearly twenty choices for each course.'

'We won't go hungry then,' replied Lucy absently, not really seeing the menu as she thought about her latest encounter with her phantom lover.

But he wasn't a phantom – he was all too real – and he was here on the same ship, where it would be difficult to avoid him.

But did she want to avoid him?

If she were being honest, she would have to admit that she didn't – she wanted to see him again very soon. And his travelling companion, the enigmatic and beautiful Sonya.

When Amanda arrived at Sonya and Andrei's suite some time later, she found the table sparkling with crystal and silver and Stephan serving drinks.

Amanda was already a little the worse for alcohol, but she accepted a drink and immediately began to flirt with Andrei while Sonya watched them, a slight smile playing around her scarlet lips.

Andrei was standing in the centre of the room while Sonya lounged elegantly on a small sofa, her legs crossed.

'Isn't anyone else dining with us?' asked Amanda, taking in the fact that the table was only laid for three. 'I would have brought someone to make up the numbers if you'd asked me.'

She looked disappointed, she'd hoped to monopolise Andrei and it would be difficult without another man to distract Sonya.

'We wanted you to ourselves,' said her host with perfect truth.

Dinner was brought to them on a succession of trolleys which were wheeled into the small service pantry. They took their places at the table – Amanda next to Andrei and Sonya opposite them – then Stephan served the first course, slices of fragrant honeydew melon and raspberries steeped in liqueur.

As he placed Sonya's plate in front of her she placed her hand on his groin and began to stroke it, causing an immediate and obvious reaction. Amanda almost choked on a raspberry and hastily took a gulp of wine as she looked at Andrei to see how he was taking it.

He appeared to have noticed nothing and continued to tell her about a recent party they'd attended.

Stephan stood immobile next to Sonya while she continued to stroke his bulging manhood, then she took his hands and placed them on her breasts. He moved behind her and caressed the small points lingeringly while she began to eat her melon as if nothing unusual was happening.

Amanda's eyes swivelled wildly from her to Andrei as he said, 'Sonya, my dear – what was the name of the German artist we met in Florence?'

'Helmut Berg – have you ever seen any of his work Amanda?'

'I . . . I don't think so,' stuttered Amanda, now unable to tear her eyes away from Stephan who was engaged in sliding the thin straps of Sonya's steel-grey gown down her ivory shoulders until her breasts were completely exposed. They were small, high and perfect, tipped by erect, prominent nipples the colour of milk chocolate.

Amanda looked away, took another gulp of her wine, then looked back as if she expected to discover that she'd imagined it and that Sonya was in fact fully clothed.

Having bared Sonya's breasts, Stephan remained behind her and fondled them expressionlessly, rolling the nipples between his finger and thumb, then covering them with his large hands.

Only when they'd finished eating the first course did he move away and begin to collect the plates. Naked to the waist but perfectly composed, Sonya asked Amanda about her recent stay in New York.

Amanda managed to stammer a reply, gulped most of her glass of wine and tried to act like this was an everyday occurrence.

'I loved New York,' Sonya told her, 'but it was extremely hot. The cool ocean breezes will be most refreshing, although it feels very warm in here tonight.'

As she spoke, she dipped her fingers into her glass, scooped up some wine and flicked it at her breasts where it ran over them and trickled down her alabaster cleavage.

Andrei rose to his feet, leaned across her and began to lick up the droplets, winding his tongue around one nipple, then licking his way down the pale valley between her breasts.

Amanda considered herself to be fairly sexually sophisticated – she'd had her share of extra-marital liaisons – so she was determined not to be thrown – whatever happened. She'd heard rumours about the two Russians so she wasn't totally unprepared.

As she watched Andrei's dark head move further down Sonya's belly, a prickle of sexual heat began to grow in her groin and her own nipples stiffened beneath the emerald-green satin of her dress.

Smiling slowly Amanda said, 'It *is* very warm tonight.' She raised her hand to the buttons holding her bodice closed and undid the top two.

'Allow me.'

41

Andrei's voice was that of a polite stranger as he moved behind her and unfastened the buttons to the waist. Amanda trembled with excitement, hoping he would touch her, then she flushed as Stephan came back into the room and began to serve the next course.

Andrei returned to his chair leaving Amanda's breasts half exposed, the nipples just visible at the edge of the deep vee of her gown. She managed to join in the casual conversation the other two kept going, while the manservant heaped their plates with food.

Stephan moved behind her to top up her glass, then suddenly dragged the wide straps of her gown down to her elbows, effectively pinioning her arms to the chair, and swiftly tied the straps together behind her.

Her enforced position made her full, naked breasts jut provocatively forward above the snowy tablecloth, the straps of her gown holding her firmly in her chair.

Stephan vanished back into the service pantry and Andrei and Sonya continued to converse as if nothing untoward was happening.

'Could I have some of my wine, please?' drawled Amanda, wondering how she was expected to eat. Not that she really cared – food was the last thing on her mind at the moment.

Andrei leaned across, picked up her wineglass and held it to her lips so she could take a sip. Then he cut a piece of her Dover sole, speared it with his fork and pushed it into her mouth.

She chewed automatically, then joined in the conversation, determined not to be disconcerted by the situation. It was really rather exciting and she was, after all, getting bored with her current lover.

Andrei continued to feed her bites of food while toying with his own meal. Occasionally his hand brushed her breasts, fondling them casually, rolling the engorged nipples between his finger and thumb.

A slow burn began to spread outwards from Amanda's groin, making her legs weak and her sex throb. She knew she was being exhibited for the sexual gratification of her host and hostess whom she sensed were both also in a highly aroused state.

The rest of the evening should be interesting to say the least.

The meal seemed endless and Amanda began to feel like a bomb about to go off. More than anything she wanted to be left alone with Andrei and have him make love to her, but something intuitively told her that wasn't going to happen – there was a darker and more complex game being played.

Whatever it was she was prepared to go along with it, welcomed it even.

At the end of the meal Stephan cleared away the dishes, then came back into the room holding a glass bowl of cherries which he gave to Sonya. He and Andrei stood on either side of Amanda and together they lifted her, on her chair, into the centre of the room.

Unhurriedly Andrei reached down and pulled Amanda's skirt up to the waist, revealing her black Milanese-satin cami-knickers and the matching lacy garters holding up her pale stockings.

When he picked up a knife and bent over her she had difficulty in suppressing a little mewing sound of apprehension.

He parted her legs and seized the crotch of her camiknickers, his fingers making brief, tantalising contact with the dark, wiry curls of her bush, then he pulled the damp strip of satin away from her mound. The knife slashed through the fine material and it fell apart exposing the full, luscious pout of her labia.

Amanda gasped, then gasped again as Andrei and Stephan stood on either side of her and carefully pulled first her outer sex lips apart, then the inner ones. The whole of her vulva was covered in pearly moisture, her clitoris a swollen nub of throbbing flesh.

Sonya stepped forward carrying the dish of cherries; it had obviously been in the fridge because condensation was forming on the glass. She placed it to one side, then knelt between Amanda's thighs.

Silently, her silver-grey eyes glittering, she slid a slender, scarlet-nailed forefinger straight into Amanda's moist, silken sheath.

Amanda's mouth fell open in an 'oooh' of surprise as Sonya pressed upwards against her slick anterior wall, then swivelled her finger thoughtfully around. Next, she picked a plump, dark purple cherry from the dish and inserted it slowly into the other woman's vagina.

The blood seemed to be pumping around Amanda's veins so noisily that she barely heard herself inhale sharply as the succulent, chilled fruit was pushed deep inside her. Whenever Sonya brushed her clitoris it twitched and Amanda could feel it throbbing demandingly.

One at a time the rest of the fruit followed until she was crammed with the juicy berries, their chill an exciting contrast to the heat of her internal flesh.

When Sonya began to stroke the shaft of her clit, Amanda felt white-hot with carnal pleasure, particularly as Andrei and Stephan began to fondle her breasts, their eyes never leaving her vulva.

A hot, tingling, tickling sensation began to emanate from the little bud which was the centre of her pleasure. It filled her groin and her belly, washing her in uncontrollable waves of excitement which made her moan and strain against her bonds.

Sonya turned her attention to the head of Amanda's clitoris, squeezing it between her finger and thumb, manipulating it expertly until the other woman let out a low-pitched, long drawn-out groan and climaxed convulsively.

The muscles of her fruit-filled quim contracted in a series of spasms which squeezed the cherries, and a slow trickle of dark purple juice ran from her, straight into Sonya's waiting mouth.

Sonya lapped at Amanda's private parts with a pointed cat-like pink tongue. She licked up every trace of juice, cleaning out each soft fold, slipping into every crevice.

Her tongue plunged into Amanda's channel and curled around a cherry. Skilfully, slyly, she eased it out and then swallowed it. She removed three more, one at a time then sat back on her heels, licking her lips.

'Your turn,' she said to Stephan. She took his place and helped Andrei hold Amanda open and ready for him.

His tongue was much bigger, blunter and rougher as he stabbed it into her and then jabbed it rhythmically against her bud.

It was too much for Amanda, she began to wriggle and squirm on the chair. Stephan started to ease the berries from inside her while Sonya and Andrei played with her breasts. Sonya's hand was much smaller and smoother than Andrei's but she handled the breast more roughly, pinching the nipple and raking it with her long nails.

The welter of sensations became confused as, with her eyes closed and head drooping backwards, Amanda gave herself up to the myriad sensations. At last Stephan ceased his oral ministrations.

'I think she is empty now,' he said, his accent much stronger than that of either of his employers.

Sonya and Andrei released the outer folds of her vulva and they settled back into position like a flower closing its petals at night.

They strolled over to the small sofa. Andrei sank down onto it and Sonya undid his trousers and drew out the heavy length of his penis. Then, while Amanda watched through lust-glazed eyes, she lifted her skirts to reveal that she wore nothing below the waist except her stockings. Amanda caught a glimpse of a neat triangle of dark silken hair, then Sonya lowered herself onto the waiting shaft.

Stephan undid the straps of Amanda's emerald-green gown and released her from her captivity on the chair. She barely had time to rub her arms before he pushed her forward over the table and flipped her skirt up over her waist. She could feel the severed crotch of her camiknickers dangling lewdly between her thighs as he positioned her with her legs wide apart, her pert, slim buttocks well up in the air.

Her inner thighs felt sticky and she could feel a renewed trickle of warm moisture as she waited impatiently to feel his member inside her. She turned her head to see him peeling off his trousers, his manhood hard and erect. Behind him she could see Andrei clasping Sonya's breasts, as she moved languidly above him.

Amanda felt the bulbous head of Stephan's penis nudging up against her sticky quim and she ground her bottom back against him impatiently. As he eased it slowly into her, she let out a heartfelt sigh of satisfaction.

His shaft was only of average length, but very thick and she felt herself being stretched to accommodate it. He grunted as he achieved full penetration and then commenced an unsubtle, but satisfying rhythm, gripping her hips and moving in and out, his heavy testicles slapping audibly against the ivory globes of her buttocks.

Amanda had lost sight of the fact that this was Andrei's manservant shafting her – she'd never had sex with anyone from outside her class before – and was so lost in the excitement of it all that only her pleasure seemed important.

By the time she convulsed into another heady orgasm, she'd forgotten that Andrei and Sonya were even in the room.

After dinner, Lucy and Faye had their coffee among the potted palm trees of the verandah café, seated on rattan chairs next to a foliage-covered trellis. The café was much more popular during the day and only three other tables were occupied.

Lucy decided it was the ideal moment to tell Faye about the first of her two encounters with Andrei and did so in a low, halting voice.

Faye's round china-blue eyes became even rounder, and her small cupid's bow mouth fell slightly open as she listened, mesmerised.

'I think that's the sexiest thing I've ever heard,' she breathed at last when Lucy had reached the end of her account. 'And you came – right there on the observation platform?'

'Twice,' confirmed Lucy.

'I wish it had happened to me,' said Faye wistfully, 'but I'd probably have run away.' She took a sip of her tepid coffee and grimaced. 'Damn – it's gone cold. I forgot to drink any of it, I was so riveted listening to you.'

Lucy glanced around the room and caught the waiter's eye. He came over immediately and poured them both a fresh cup.

'Who's the woman he was with at the party?' Faye asked.

'Princess Sonya Behrs. Amanda introduced us.'

'Isn't that her now – over by the door?'

Lucy glanced behind her. It was indeed Sonya, a tiny matching fur-trimmed cape which only fell to just below her shoulder blades, was now flung casually over her steel-grey dress. Just behind her Andrei and Amanda walked in and the three of them paused inside the door.

Amanda spotted them and waved in greeting, then the trio

walked over to them. Lucy felt a faint flush spotting her cheeks as she remembered that only a few hours before she'd held Andrei's penis in her hand while Sonya caressed her breasts. She hadn't had time to tell Faye about that little episode.

Amanda introduced Faye to them, then sank into a chair. Lucy thought that Amanda must be quite drunk, because there was an unfocused glitter in her eyes and her clothing looked slightly dishevelled.

Andrei ordered coffee and cognac for everyone while Sonya asked them if they'd enjoyed their meal. She and Faye began to discuss the standard of cuisine on the *Aphrodite* with only the occasional comment from the others.

When Andrei had finished his cognac he rose to his feet.

'Could I interest you two ladies in taking a stroll along the deck with me?' he asked Lucy and Amanda. 'We can leave Sonya and Faye to their discussion *gastronomique* and rejoin them later.'

Both Lucy and Amanda rose and each took a proffered arm. 'I'll see you in a while,' Lucy called over her shoulder to Faye.

Faye found Sonya a fascinating companion. The older woman made her feel unsophisticated and unworldly as she spoke of banquets and parties she'd attended in different countries around the world.

They were alone now in the verandah café – the other passengers had left to find somewhere more lively.

'I love good food,' said Faye, 'but I'm afraid to eat too much in case I put on weight. I'll bet you don't have that problem,' she added, glancing enviously at Sonya's slim frame.

'You have a beautiful figure,' said Sonya, 'gently curvaceous with a tiny waist.' She laid her hand on Faye's thigh as she spoke and looked into her eyes.

Faye felt as though she were drowning in the silver-grey pools. She could smell Sonya's exotic perfume and it wasn't one she recognised – she herself had tiny dabs of Chanel No. 5 on her wrists and behind her ears.

The other woman's scarlet lips were very close to her own and she could see the fine texture of her ivory skin and the faint rose-petal bloom of her cheeks. Sonya leant forward and kissed her softly on the lips. It felt like the caress of a butterfly's wings and Faye very much wanted her to do it again.

But Sonya sat back in her chair and took another sip of her cognac. Her hand remained on Faye's thigh as though she'd forgotten she'd left it there.

'Both you and your friend Lucy are such beautiful English roses,' said Sonya huskily, stroking the thigh under her hand. 'And your legs are so shapely.' She pushed the skirt of Faye's fuchsia-pink silk dress upwards and then leant forward to kiss her again.

Their lips met while her hand trailed lazily up Faye's leg under her skirt until it found the bare skin above her stocking top.

Her gentle touch sent liquid shivers of pleasure through Faye's body and, in involuntary response, she closed her eyes and parted her legs. Sonya's fingers brushed against the lace of her camiknickers and then fluttered against the strip of satin between her legs.

The sudden sound of a throat being cleared made Faye jump. Her eyes flew open to see Leo standing over them, his ruddy, fair skin brick-red.

Unhurriedly Sonya withdrew her hand while Faye hastily closed her legs and pulled her skirt down. She was mildly embarrassed that they'd been interrupted and glanced quickly at Sonya.

But Sonya didn't seem to be the slightest bit disconcerted. She picked up her cognac and sat elegantly back in her seat, surveying Leo from beneath her long, thick lashes, an expression of faint amusement on her face.

'Miss Faulkner – may I have a word with you?' he asked. 'In fact, perhaps I could escort you back to your cabin.'

Sonya rose gracefully to her feet, then stretched languidly, like a cat.

'I shall go and find Andrei. I'm sure our paths will cross tomorrow, Faye.' She turned on her heel and left them.

As Faye rose to her feet, Leo pulled her chair out for her. They left the café together and went out onto the deck where a stiff breeze was blowing. He cleared his throat again before saying, 'Miss Faulkner, I'm not sure how to say this but I think you'd be unwise to pursue that particular friendship.'

'Oh – why is that?' enquired Faye, who'd recovered her poise by now.

'Because I recognise the type, it's part of my job to do so. Both she and the man she's travelling with are adventurers and a well-brought-up young lady like you shouldn't be associating with them – it can only lead to trouble.'

'What sort of trouble?' she asked with interest.

'The captain takes a dim view of . . . of public indecency, and that woman had her hand up your skirt.'

Glancing at him out of the corner of her eye, Faye had a sudden intuitive feeling that coming across them like that had not just embarrassed Leo – it had aroused him too.

Interesting.

'What's wrong with that?' she asked innocently. She sensed rather than saw that his face went an even darker red as he weighed up her remark.

'It's . . . it's not the sort of thing you should be doing,' he replied lamely. She took his arm as they strolled along. There was nothing visible out to sea, just an ocean of unrelieved inky blackness.

'Would it have been alright if she'd done it in my cabin?'

'No it wouldn't! Miss Faulkner, please take my advice and don't have anything to do with either of them.' They walked along in silence until they reached her stateroom.

'Well, thank you so much for your advice, I'll give it some thought,' she told him, opening her door.

'Incidentally . . .'

'Yes?'

'How *do* you discipline female passengers?'

Leo swallowed, then swallowed again, his Adam's apple bobbing.

'Goodnight, Miss Faulkner,' he said and marched away, his back ramrod straight with disapproval.

Chapter Four

Lucy sat up in bed and stretched, then slid her arms into the ice-green satin bed jacket Winnie was holding out for her. She tied the ribbons at the neck into a loose bow and propped herself up against the pile of soft pillows.

The sun was streaming in through the curtains her maid had just opened, bathing the stateroom in brightness.

'Shall I ring for the stewardess, Miss?' asked Winnie, picking up the jade and gold jewellery Lucy had left on the dressing table and putting it away in a velvet-lined morocco leather case.

'Yes, please do – I'm starving, it must be the sea air.'

Winnie rang the bell which would summon the stewardess while Lucy studied the breakfast menu. It was as extensive and varied as last night's dinner menu and she hesitated over her choice.

'I'll take your jewels back to the purser's office, Miss, then I'll go and see to Miss Faye,' said Winnie.

Like most female passengers, Lucy had checked her jewellery in with the purser who kept it in his safe, releasing in the late afternoon whichever pieces she wished to wear that evening.

The stewardess arrived bringing with her the ship's newspaper which listed the day's events, and after a few more moments' deliberation Lucy ordered grapefruit juice, fresh figs, a croissant and *café au lait*.

As she sipped her coffee she thought about Andrei and Sonya

and wondered why she'd never before met anyone remotely like them. Boyd had seemed to be the last word in cosmopolitan sophistication, but the Russians made him look like a backwoods hick.

She was still deliberating when Faye tapped on her door and came in. She was already up and dressed in a lightweight heather tweed suit from Chanel, nipped in at the waist and tapering to a kick pleat at mid-calf. The supple tweed had moulded itself to her hips and thighs in a way that was subtly sexy.

'So, what do you think of our shipboard acquaintances?' asked Faye airily, sinking into a small, chintz-covered armchair and crossing her shapely legs.

'They're certainly intriguing,' said Lucy, finishing her coffee and pushing the tray to one side.

'I was warned off them last night,' Faye told her.

'Really? By whom?' asked Lucy, startled.

'The first officer. He said they were adventurers.'

'Goodness – I wonder what made him say that?'

'He came across Sonya kissing me,' said Faye, slightly self-consciously. 'He said that becoming friendly with them could only lead to trouble.'

'How very impertinent of him. I hope you told him to mind his own business.'

'Mmm. There's probably a better way than that of dealing with him.'

Lucy looked at her friend speculatively. 'It's the uniform, isn't it? Quite frankly I think that particular weakness of yours is likely to get you into more trouble than getting involved with Andrei and Sonya,' she teased.

Faye rose to her feet and crossed over to the window. 'It's a glorious day. I think I'll stroll around the deck, then I've an appointment with the hairdresser. Will I see you later?'

'I'll join you for bouillon at eleven.'

Amanda woke up around mid-morning feeling hungover, thirsty and still sexually aroused. There was no sign of her maid so she rang for the stewardess and ordered coffee, then shrugged into an oyster satin robe and went out onto her verandah. But the brilliant sunlight hurt her eyes and she retreated back inside.

She felt dazed and disoriented and couldn't quite believe that she'd let a servant have sex with her. It had been wildly exciting at the time, but today she felt humiliated.

If only it had been Andrei, or an officer, or any of the first-class passengers. Or anyone really except a servant.

She shuddered at the memory, but even so she was aware of a crawling little flicker of excitement as she remembered being exhibited for the sexual gratification of the others, first as she sat at the dinner table, then later tied to the chair. Why hadn't Andrei taken her and left Sonya to the manservant? *She* obviously had no such inhibition about her sexual partners.

There was a tap at the door and when she answered it a bellboy handed her a flat white box lavishly tied with silver and black ribbons and bearing the name of the ship's expensive shop.

Puzzled – she hadn't ordered anything – Amanda opened it to find an exquisite pair of lace-trimmed, black satin cami-knickers scalloped over the hips and fastening between the legs with two tiny buttons. A plain white card read 'To replace the ones I ruined. A.'

A smile on her face, she went into the bathroom and ran a deep bath, then threw a handful of rose-scented powder into the water before shedding her robe to sink into the milky depths.

While she'd been walking round the deck with Andrei and Lucy last night, she'd hoped the younger woman would leave them so she could invite Andrei back to her cabin. But Lucy hadn't been so obliging and, after one circuit, he'd wished them both a punctilious, 'Goodnight,' in the corridor, kissed their hands and vanished.

Amanda closed her eyes, put her head back on the edge of the bath and mentally replayed last night's strange scenario.

A knock on the door dragged her from her erotic reverie and made her start. Assuming it was her maid she called, 'Come in.'

'Just where did you get to last night?' demanded the voice of her current lover, Edward. Amanda's eyes flew open to see him standing in the doorway, tight-lipped and obviously angry.

When Sonya had visited her to dine with them yesterday evening, Amanda had simply not mentioned it to Edward because she knew he'd want to accompany her and she'd hoped to monopolise Andrei.

She'd been vaguely aware of Edward banging on her door late last night, but she'd been too befuddled by her alcohol-induced sleep to wake up and let him in. She knew he was aware she'd tired of him and he wasn't happy about it. Maybe at the end of the voyage it would be time to call it a day. She really wanted someone more exciting – someone like Andrei.

She cast him a dismissive look and drawled, 'And what does that have to do with you?'

'Everything I would have thought. You vanished after the party and then didn't appear at dinner. I searched the ship for you.'

'I was dining with those two fascinating white Russians.'

'Why didn't you invite me?'

'It wasn't my invitation.'

'You might at least have told me where you were going.'

Edward pushed a lock of tow-coloured hair back from his forehead and leaned against the doorframe, his hands pushed sullenly in his pockets. At twenty-six he was several years younger than Amanda and possessed the sort of boyish good looks that had made debutantes for eight seasons go weak at the knees.

Amanda found his looks rather appealing now. She lifted one slender leg in the air and began to soap it, massaging her delicate calf and working her way slowly up to the thigh. She was aware that Edward's eyes were fixed on her leg and the expression in his eyes was slowly changing from annoyance to lust.

She lowered the leg and washed the other just as languidly, then she sat up so her creamy shoulders and the full orbs of her breasts emerged from the water. She soaped her arms and then her shoulders and finally her breasts, lingering on the nipples with her long fingers.

Edward swallowed and his tanned cheeks darkened in colour. Amanda cast a sidelong glance at him from under her lashes and saw him half make a move towards her and then hesitate.

'Edward, darling – are you going to stay there all morning and sulk, or are you going to come over here and do the bits that I can't reach?'

Edward walked reluctantly across to the bath where Amanda reached out an indolent, soapy hand and unzipped his trousers. She took out his penis, squeezed it gently and was gratified when it immediately hardened.

She bent her head and kissed it, then licked her way around the crimson head – it felt hot and smooth as she explored it with a practised tongue – then flicked snake-like against the ridge running down from the glans.

Slowly, very slowly, she drew his shaft into her mouth, exerting pressure with her lips and sucking hard, making Edward groan and bury his hands in her hair.

She took it in as far as she could and then let it slip slowly out, an inch at a time. It was slick with her saliva as she lapped away, all the way down to where his testicles nestled closely against the base.

He took hold of the back of her head and held her face against his groin, massaging her neck. She reached up and undid his tie, then ripped his shirt open so that several of the buttons flew off and pinged against the tiled bathroom wall.

'S . . . steady on,' he stammered.

Amanda rose gracefully from the bath, the scented water streaming from her creamy, slender limbs. She stepped out and pressed herself against his tall frame, soaking his clothing.

'Make love to me,' she ordered succinctly.

His arms went round her automatically, sliding over her slippery, glistening back, one hand dropping to cup the pert swell of her bottom. Amanda opened her legs and he pushed his fingers between them from behind, massaging her vulva with the palm of his hand.

She bore down, rubbing herself abandonedly against him until his hand was wet with her juices. Conventional as always, he began to steer her towards the bedroom but she turned sideways and leaned back against the gleaming wall, panting slightly.

'Now,' she gasped. 'I want to feel your cock inside me now.'

He flushed at her crudeness but was obviously aroused by it. She reached for his shaft and rubbed the glans lubriciously against her clit, which hardened and swelled in response to the stimulating friction.

Amanda was suddenly assailed by a heady memory of Andrei and Stephan holding her sex-lips apart while Sonya slid a scarlet-nailed forefinger inside her. The image was so exciting and so vivid that she climaxed unexpectedly before Edward had even entered her.

She graspd his shaft and positioned it against the fleshy entrance to her hidden furrow, then bore down hard, engulfing his member in her warm stickiness.

He began to move in and out of her, trying and failing to keep any sort of hold on her slippery body as she thrust her hips in an answering rhythm.

It was a graceless and rather clumsy coupling. Edward's trousers fell down around his thighs and hampered his movements and the wet marble floor of the bathroom was treacherously slippery under foot.

Nevertheless, Amanda came again a few seconds before Edward gripped her tightly by the buttocks and convulsed into his own climax with a heartfelt groan.

When they separated a few moments later, Amanda let the tepid water out of the bath and refilled it, before climbing back in.

'Why don't you join me?' she invited him. But Edward was busy studying the damage to his clothing. His shirt only had one button left, his trousers were drenched and the sleeve of his jacket had a tear in it.

'I can't walk back to my cabin looking like this,' he said aghast. 'What will everybody think?'

'You worry too much about what people think,' said Amanda carelessly. 'Pass me a towel will you please?'

She stepped out of the bath, wrapped herself in the fluffy white towel and went back into the bedroom.

'That seems to have got rid of my hangover,' she commented. 'Drink?'

Dressed in a pair of wide-legged navy-blue linen trousers and an off-white silk-knit sweater, her golden hair held in place by a white-spotted navy silk scarf, Lucy strolled along the deck looking for Faye.

It was already hot, but the fresh breeze blowing off the Atlantic took the edge off the heat. The glare from the sea made her glad of her horn-rimmed dark glasses as she walked past the rows of padded reclining deck chairs, most of them occupied.

She and Faye had neglected to reserve any and those in the best positions had already been taken, but she eventually found her friend, her freshly waved hair the colour of a ripe conker, at the far end of the sun deck.

'Bouillon, madam?' asked the steward as Lucy stretched out on the deck chair next to her friend.

'I'm not sure – what's it like?' she asked Faye.

'Hot and salty.'

'Perhaps not – just coffee please.'

'The beauty salon's marvellous – I've booked a massage for this afternoon, I'm really going to pamper myself for the next few days.'

'I might have one myself – and a facial. I don't think sea air can be good for the skin.'

What Faye didn't mention was that she'd glanced at the appointments book and noticed that Sonya had booked a massage that afternoon so she had deliberately arranged to have one at the same time. She was intrigued by the older woman and hoped to get to know her better – despite Leo's warning.

Stretched out on the massage table, a warm pink towel her only covering, Faye was thoroughly enjoying the sybaritic pleasure of her massage at the hands of a petite Egyptian woman.

A lavish coating of perfumed cream had been applied and was now being massaged into every inch of her skin.

She'd sunk into a state of trance-like pleasure when she

smelt Sonya's exotic scent, then she heard her faintly accented voice saying, 'Well hello, Faye. How nice to see you again.'

Faye opened her eyes to see Sonya standing next to her, a pink towel draped around her slender form, her ivory shoulders slim and bare.

The Russian princess got lithely onto the adjoining massage table and stretched out. 'What do you think of the *Aphrodite*?' she asked, her husky voice a purr as the masseuse got to work on her shoulders. 'Andrei and I have not travelled on this vessel before.'

'She's a beautiful ship – not that I have a lot to compare her to. We came out on the *Ile de France*, but both Lucy and I spent the entire voyage being seasick.'

The two women chatted in a desultory way for a while and then, lulled by the gentle hands of their respective masseuses, fell silent.

When the Egyptian girl eventually reached her thighs, after working her way up from her toes, Faye began to find it arousing. Every touch seemed to be igniting a spark of desire deep inside her and she found herself pressing her mound furtively against the table.

When the girl's small hands began to glide over the generous swell of her buttocks, it was all she could do not to wriggle them upwards. But, after a few more minutes of attention to the area, it seemed that the massage was over because the masseuse murmured something about giving the cream time to sink in, covered her with a towel and left.

Deliciously drowsy and in a semi-erotic haze, Faye was quite happy to lie there, too lazy to resume chatting to Sonya. She must have drifted off to sleep for a few minutes because she woke up to find that her massage had started again.

If anything it was an even more sensual experience than earlier and was concentrated mainly on her derrière and thighs.

Her buttocks were gently kneaded for what seemed like hours and were held briefly apart between strokes, making her spread her legs slightly. Her arousal grew again, particularly when the girl massaged the insides of her thighs and her fingers brushed against the soft fronds of Faye's dark red fuzz.

The warmth in her belly grew as a fingernail was drawn softly down the cleft between her buttocks, making her wriggle deliciously on the table. It grew even more when she felt the tickle of a slender finger in the groove of her labia.

Unable to stop herself she parted her legs even further and sighed as gentle fingers massaged a dollop of cream into the slick, swollen tissues of her vulva.

It felt wonderful, simultaneously soothing and arousing. At first the fingers just glided over her outer labia, but then they drifted over her inner sex-lips and eventually into her cream-slippery furrow.

The first touch of her clitoris was electric, sending hectic messages of excitement coursing through her body. Faye forgot where she was, forgot everything except the all-encompassing pleasure she was experiencing.

The pad of a thumb settled on her swollen little bud and commenced a rhythmic stimulation while a longer finger slipped slowly into her velvety interior.

Faye couldn't help herself. She rotated her pelvis as a dark secret heat grew in her belly, making a faint film of perspiration break out on her smooth skin. The stimulation of the tiny nub of flesh grew more urgent and then, disconcertingly, another finger probed the tiny circle of her anus, and helped by the coating of cream, gained entry into the first quarter of an inch of the small aperture.

It felt like a somewhat rude intrusion and Faye automatically tensed her muscles, but the added stimulation increased her arousal and, as the finger made no attempt to penetrate further but merely swivelled backwards and forwards with a slightly scratchy tickling movement, Faye relaxed again.

A low moan escaped from her lips and she rotated her pelvis more urgently as a renewed wave of heat swept across her.

The pulsing, tingling, tickling sensation which had been building in her core exploded into a devastating climax which left her weak, trembling and, when she came back to earth, embarrassed.

What must Sonya and the other masseuse think?

Faye propped herself up on one elbow and glanced around her. She was surprised to see that the other massage table was empty.

Had she slept for ages and not the few minutes she'd thought? Had Sonya's massage finished?

She glanced back over her shoulder and was taken aback to see Sonya wiping her hands on a towel.

'Wh . . . where's my masseuse?'

'Gone to attend to another client, as has mine.'

Sonya had just caressed her to a climax?

She and Lucy often pleasured each other. It was something they'd discovered while at boarding school and, although both of them were adept at creating their own satisfaction, they agreed that to do it for each other was a different sort of delight.

But she'd only met Sonya the night before.

Sonya smiled at her, her eyes half veiled behind their thick, silky lashes.

'I always think of English ladies as cold, oh so cold. But not you Faye, *au contraire*, the blood runs hot through your English veins.'

Sonya laid her hand on the full curve of Faye's left buttock then pinched it hard. 'You have the most luscious derrière, it makes me think of the many things I would like to do with it . . . to it. Perhaps I shall.'

She secured her towel more firmly under her arms and then left from the room.

Lucy was surprised not to see Andrei anywhere on the ship all day. Although she told herself she wasn't actually looking for him, she would have expected to run into him *somewhere*. She did however meet several acquaintances and was invited to join them playing shuffleboard, which she enjoyed very much.

It was over cocktails with Faye that she saw him, part of a large, noisy group at the other side of the bar. He was standing rather apart from the others looking intently down into the face of a voluptuous redhead. Sonya had her back to them and was talking to a much older man who seemed to be hanging on her every word.

As it was the second evening at sea and the captain would be dining at his table in the first-class restaurant, everyone had dressed for dinner.

Lucy was wearing a gauzy white off-the-shoulder dress with so many flimsy layers to the skirt, it looked like a swirl of sea-foam.

She'd had Winnie fetch her platinum and diamond necklace and matching earrings from the purser's office, but other than that she wore no jewellery. Her waist was pulled in by a narrow silver belt and she was wearing silver kid shoes with a very thin heel and carrying a matching bag.

'Goodness,' commented Faye, who hadn't seen this particular gown before, 'Mainbocher?'

Lucy nodded. 'I couldn't resist it. It was an early purchase for my trousseau, but I might as well wear it now.' As she said it, she realised that she'd barely given Boyd a thought all day.

Good.

'It's lovely,' said Faye enviously, taking a sip of her Manhattan. 'I'll bet Mother wouldn't have bought that for me – she would have said it was too sophisticated.'

She glanced up and caught sight of Sonya for the first time. Lucy was surprised to see her friend blush and swiftly avert her eyes.

Was she embarrassed because the other woman had kissed her last night?

Surely not.

Lucy hoped that Andrei would come across and speak to them, but he didn't appear to have noticed their presence.

When, arm in arm, the two women descended the vast staircase for dinner they attracted even more attention than last night. It was the custom of the male passengers to keep an eye on the ladies descending the stairs and the appearance of any particularly alluring female was usually signified by the turning of heads.

When they reached their table they found to their surprise that Andrei and Sonya were already seated there, along with half a dozen other people. The steward held out a chair for her next to Andrei and Lucy slipped into it.

'What a perfect foil for your youthful beauty your dress makes,' he greeted her.

'Why thank you, Count Andrei,' was the best she could manage in the way of sparkling repartee. He crumbled a roll with his long fingers and studied the delicate swell of her breasts under the tight-fitting bodice.

'There can be few things more delightful than seeing a beautiful woman in a lovely gown,' he said softly.

As she looked at him, Lucy was struck by the thought that he was imagining her out of it, and the faintest tinge of colour crept across her cheeks.

He smiled at her, his yellow-green eyes opaque and unreadable. She thought again that there was something unsettling about him, something that heightened all her senses

65

and made her skin feel extra-sensitive.

She was very aware of the caress of silk on her body, the weight of her platinum and diamond necklace around the slender column of her neck and slight constraint of the belt encircling her waist.

She stirred uneasily on her seat, mentally searching her repertoire of small talk to find something light to say, but nothing seemed appropriate. His very presence seemed to have left her bereft of all the social graces so carefully instilled in her.

Fortunately, the steward came to take their orders and when he'd gone Andrei began to talk to the woman on his other side.

It was when they'd finished the first course – tender *primeurs à la Greque* for her, smoked sturgeon for him – that he suddenly looked at her again and asked, 'Does the lingerie you're wearing under that dress do it justice?'

Startled by the sudden salacious turn the conversation had taken, Lucy looked swiftly around the table, but everyone else seemed intent on their own chatter and no one was looking their way.

'Under such a gown you should wear only a wisp of silk or lace to caress the peach-mounds of your derrière and cover your hidden, scented delta just enough to render it additionally enticing,' he murmured. 'What could be more alluring than to see a woman dressed for a man's pleasure with only a thin strip of flimsy fabric between him and his desires. Tell me, Lucy, what are you wearing beneath that dress?'

Lucy's throat felt tight and dry. She took a gulp from her glass of Sancerre and tried to speak, but her voice came out as a croak and she had to turn it hastily into a cough.

He didn't give her chance to try again as he continued, 'And your silk stockings – what is holding them in position around your smooth, slender legs? Are you wearing a suspender belt . . . or garters perhaps? Confide in me, Lucy, because I wish to imagine how you look so that I may anticipate the pleasure of seeing you with my own eyes later tonight.'

Lucy was struck dumb by his deep mesmerising voice and the lewd things he was saying to her. A prickle of heat ran down her spine and her private parts suddenly felt congested and heavy.

The dining chairs on the *Aphrodite* were exceptionally comfortable and upholstered in Aubusson fabric with a geometric design, but suddenly the one beneath her felt hard and unyielding.

She looked at Andrei sideways from beneath her lashes, confused and uncertain. He gave her a wolfish smile, then she almost let out a yelp of surprise as she felt his hand run gently down her thigh under the cover of the tablecloth and come to rest lightly on her knee.

'I see I must find out for myself,' he told her. One by one, in a leisurely fashion, he began to lift the many gauzy layers of her skirt, and flip them back.

Lucy clutched her glass as if it were her only lifeline and waited for the inevitable moment when he would uncover her silk-clad knee. When he did, although his hand was cool, she immediately felt it burning into her flesh, branding her with sexual heat and making it difficult for her to breathe.

He began to stroke his way up her thigh, while he continued to talk of the things he planned to do with her in a matter-of-fact voice which made it sound, she thought, as if she had no say in the matter.

She wanted him to stop – this was far too public a place for such an exploration – but she also wanted him to continue, to touch her how he wanted, where he wanted.

When his fingers made contact with the band of smooth,

bare skin above her stocking top and discovered the ribbon suspender holding up the front of her stocking, he arched a dark eyebrow at her.

'A suspender belt or, as the Americans call it, a garter belt. I would like to see you in only that and your stockings – perhaps your shoes too.'

The tips of his fingers fluttered against the lace edging of Lucy's camiknickers and brushed against the thin strip of satin between her legs, then he pushed her thighs apart to allow his hand more freedom of movement.

When she automatically tried to close them, he forced them apart again and said in a low, authoritative voice, 'Keep them like that throughout the meal – wide apart so I may touch you whenever I wish.'

Numbly she obeyed him. She didn't know why, but she did. The fingers probed at the satin strip, then began to stroke it; delicate, arousing strokes which sent tingling tremors through her limbs and made a moist warmth envelop her belly.

The steward placed the next course in front of them and Andrei withdrew his hand and began to talk to the woman on his left. Lucy found her attention claimed by the man on her right, but her mind kept wandering as she toyed with her meal and tried to nod and smile in the right places.

Luckily her neighbour appeared quite happy with this response and didn't seem to expect or want anything from her in the way of conversation.

She was trembling slightly with anticipation. Her thighs remained wide apart under the cover of the starched linen tablecloth, waiting for the moment when Andrei would resume his covert caresses, as she was certain he would.

She found it exciting to sit like that – it wasn't a position she usually assumed – and there was something abandoned about it that appealed to her.

As soon as Andrei had finished his fish course – *he* didn't seem to have any trouble eating, Lucy noticed – his hand slid beneath the table and settled between her thighs to trace gentle arabesques over her vulva. The tiny bead of her clitoris had hardened and he circled it teasingly before caressing it through the satin until it quivered.

It was when he slipped a finger under the crotch of her camiknickers and stroked the slippery little sliver of flesh directly that Lucy gasped audibly. Her other neighbour who was still holding forth – she couldn't have said on what subject – stopped and looked at her curiously.

'I say – are you feeling alright?' he asked as she swallowed and then dabbed at her upper lip with her tiny lace handkerchief in an attempt to conceal her agitation.

'Excuse me – just a hiccup,' she managed to say. He started talking again while Lucy gripped the arms of her chair and struggled to keep her expression under control. The waves of carnal pleasure that Andrei's caresses were causing were making her feel faint.

She wanted to roll her head from side to side and close her eyes.

She wanted to bear down on his hand and rotate her pelvis.

She wanted to gasp and moan and pant.

But instead she had to sit apparently cool and poised while Andrei toyed wickedly and knowingly with her private parts.

A long finger began to probe the entrance to her sex-valley, tickling and stimulating her, dabbling in the warm juices which were beginning to trickle out. The finger probed further, slipping inside her, exploring the velvety walls of her hidden tunnel, making her want to wriggle around on her seat to get it further in.

It was a warm evening and despite the air conditioning a faint film of perspiration began to gather on her upper lip. She considered telling him to stop, but one glance at his implacable profile told her that the only way she'd get him to do that would be if she rose and left the table.

But she couldn't be certain that if she did stand up all the layers of her skirt would drop back in place. It would be terrible to walk the length of the vast restaurant and ascend the stairs with her dress in wanton disarray.

And anyway, she wasn't sure she wanted him to stop.

She had a respite during the next course. At least she thought it would be a respite but, as soon as Andrei had withdrawn his hand so he could attend to his *entrée*, he reverted to verbal stimulation.

'What beautifully soft, moist female parts you have, Lucy. So tight at first, then they unfurl gently like the petals of a peony on a warm summer's day. And your little bud – so shy and reclusive, hiding behind your sex-lips until coaxed out. How well it responds to stimulation – but too slowly. I promise you that by the end of our voyage together I will only have to look at you in a certain way and it will swell and harden, hungry for my touch.'

Afterwards Lucy couldn't have said what she'd eaten, or whether she'd enjoyed it, she was only conscious of a slow burn which felt like a fever. She became impatient with Andrei to finish eating – eager to have him caress her again.

At last when he did resume his expert attentions she let out a little shriek, then blushed scarlet when everyone at the table stared at her.

Andrei's hand was freezing cold, particularly in contrast to the hot, throbbing flesh he'd just touched. He must have had it wrapped around his glass of icy white wine just before touching her.

'S . . . sorry,' she stuttered, 'I . . . I bit my tongue by accident.'

Her eyes met Sonya's across the table and the other woman gave her a slow, knowing smile and, looking directly into her eyes, flickered the tip of her tongue over her scarlet lips.

It came to Lucy in a flash of insight, which belied her tender years and limited experience, that the Russian woman knew exactly what Andrei was doing.

She tried to dismiss the idea, but it took hold of her.

Hadn't they both behaved lewdly with her on Amanda's verandah? Sonya hadn't seemed a bit surprised to find her clutching Andrei's member – it was as if she'd expected it.

Was it some sort of game to them?

It was certainly looking that way.

But Lucy lost the power of coherent thought when Andrei commenced a rhythmic stimulation of her clitoris and a heavy, insidious pleasure began to build in her groin.

It was only when a fierce wave of heat washed over her that she realised too late exactly what he was doing – working her to orgasm in full view of everyone at the table.

Eyes glazed, rigid with the effort of not crying out, Lucy held her breath and tried without success to fight it. She was sure that someone would notice something and guess what was going on. But, just as she climaxed, Sonya knocked her glass of wine over and it was enough to cover Lucy's confusion.

A few moment later Andrei withdrew his hand and, while everyone's attention was distracted, sniffed his fingers and then licked them lingeringly, looking directly into her eyes.

Chapter Five

By the end of the meal Lucy had managed to smooth the layers of her skirt back over her knees so she was able to stand up without worrying if she looked dishevelled.

Andrei offered her his arm and they followed Sonya and Faye, who were chatting animatedly, up the staircase and out of the restaurant, where Sonya paused to speak to them.

'I've been telling Faye of the Russian vodka I like to drink sometimes after a meal. We're going to our suite so she can try a glass. Will you and Lucy join us?'

'Thank you but no – we're going to stroll around the promenade deck to enjoy the evening air. Perhaps we will see you later,' he replied.

He kissed Sonya's hand and then Faye's and Lucy thought she saw him exchange a swift, collusive look with his compatriot.

But she put it from her mind as they walked slowly along the deck where lamps cast circles of light and uneven shadows on the pale wooden floor.

Lucy was waiting for him to suggest that they go to her stateroom and, although she knew she should refuse, she didn't think it was possible for her to do so. The dangerous game he had played beneath the cover of the tablecloth had whetted her appetite for more and she knew he was aware of that.

In a shadowy corner at the end of the promenade deck he paused. Lucy leant against the rail and gazed out to sea, but all was inky blackness. She tipped her chin and looked up to where the stars shimmered high above them, too pale to cast any illumination over the ocean. A swathe of cloud glided from where it had been obscuring the moon, and pale rays of silver light slanted across the deck.

'Now I wish to see you,' said Andrei gravely. 'Raise your skirts for me so I may do so.'

'Wh . . . what here?' exclaimed Lucy, scandalised. Another couple strolled past them and nodded a greeting. 'You can't be serious – there are people about.'

'I am serious – very serious. Do as I bid you.'

Lucy looked from left to right – there was no one in sight. She didn't know why, but somehow she found herself raising her gauzy skirts and holding them above her waist while he stood and gazed impassively at her delicate pearl-white camiknickers and tiny matching suspender belt.

The fresh evening breeze swirled around her private parts, cooling them and flattening the pale satin against her belly.

When he lifted his hands to her waist and drew her camiknickers down to her knees she protested, but her words were ignored as he dropped to the deck and pressed a hard kiss on the pale floss covering her mound.

She found herself pushed back against the ship's rail and her arms automatically stretched out so she could grip it with both hands. He parted her legs as far as the constraining camiknickers would allow – which wasn't far – then with an exclamation of impatience pulled them down to her ankles and lifted one foot free of them.

The satin undergarment lay crumpled around her other ankle as, with the tip of his tongue, he licked delicately at the outer folds of her sex-lips. Lucy went rigid with shock as he traced his way along the rim, making the damp fronds of her floss even damper.

It was like nothing she'd ever experienced before, though

she'd imagined it often enough in her fantasies. Her legs felt unsteady and she gripped the rail harder, while his tongue found the bud of her clitoris and strummed it wickedly, sending wild sensations of undreamt of pleasure coursing through her limbs.

He circled around her swollen bud and probed his way between her inner sex-lips, pushing further into her until he found the hidden entrance to her quim. His tongue felt large and muscular as it swirled robust circles just inside her, then thrust strongly in as far as it would go.

He explored each crevice, licking and probing at every complex fold, leaving her weak with lust. When he began to strum her clit again, stabbing at it with his tongue, then pausing to drawn the tiny protuberance between his lips to suck; it was more than Lucy could stand and she moaned softly.

He resumed the strumming while a hot, heavy weight seemed to settle in her groin; a hot, heavy weight which threatened to explode at any moment.

By now she'd forgotten that they were on the promenade deck in full view of anyone who might walk past. In fact for all she knew people *had* been walking past – she was too far gone to notice.

There was a sudden rush of heat over her whole body and then a convulsive explosion of pleasure in her very core as she shuddered into an earth-shattering climax.

The stars above her head tilted dizzily and she closed her eyes, gasping and panting as Andrei rose to his feet and leant negligently against the rail beside her.

'Loath though I am to do so, may I suggest that you drop your skirts – some people are coming this way.'

Lucy hastily released her dress and the gauzy layers drifted slowly back around her legs. She kept her eyes averted as a group of people walked past, leaving behind them the whiff of expensive cigars and scent.

It was only when they'd vanished from sight that she remembered her camiknickers were lying obscenely around her ankle in clear view if anyone had happened to glance down. She was about to pull them up but an elderly couple came walking down the deck towards them and she froze in the act of bending over.

Andrei reached swiftly down saying, 'Lift your foot,' and swept them deftly into his pocket before the other people drew level with them.

'I take it,' said Lucy as soon as she regained the power of speech, 'that you have a particular weakness for railings – at least that seems to be where most of our . . . intimacy has taken place.'

He raised a quizzical eyebrow at her as she continued, 'There was the railing of the observation platform of the train, then the rail of Amanda's verandah and now the railing of the promenade deck.'

Andrei pulled her hand into the crook of his arm and began to walk along the deck.

'Believe me, my dear Lucy, railings aren't the only things I have a weakness for.'

The Russians' suite smelt of Sonya's exotic perfume and the dozen candles flickering there which cast long shadows on the wall. Sonya left Faye alone in the sitting room, saying she would only be a moment. When she returned she'd changed out of her elegant evening dress into a loosely belted satin robe printed with vivid jewel colours.

She was followed into the room by a stern-faced, dark-haired woman carrying a tray containing a dish of sweetmeats and a bottle and two glasses packed into the ice in an ice bucket.

Sonya lay back on a *chaise longue* and the woman placed the tray on a small table next to her.

'Will there be anything else, Princess?' she asked.

'Not at the moment thank you, Marta.'

'Andrei considers vodka as an after-dinner drink to accompany sweetmeats to be disgusting, but I find it an interesting contrast. There is a ritual to eating these sweetmeats and drinking this vodka which must be adhered to,' Sonya told Faye lazily. 'Are you prepared to do that?'

'Yes, of course,' said Faye, thrilled to be part of such a sophisticated, cosmopolitan scenario. Sonya looked so beautiful with her pale, perfectly sculptured features framed by her glossy, sable hair.

Her robe had fallen slightly apart revealing her delicate, alabaster ankles and her bare feet thrust into high-heeled, black satin mules.

'Come and sit here.' She patted the end of the *chaise longue* and Faye went obediently over and sat at her feet.

Sonya busied herself pouring drinks into the tiny glasses.

'Have you known Andrei long?' asked Faye diffidently. She was eager to know more about the enigmatic couple, but didn't wish to appear rude or intrusive.

'All my life,' she replied. 'We grew up together in St Petersberg, until we were forced to flee when the revolution came.'

A shadow crossed her face when she spoke, making Faye wish she hadn't asked the question. She didn't know much about the Russian revolution and didn't wish to appear ignorant of something which had changed the lives of so many so irrevocably.

'I was only twelve,' Sonya continued, 'and I knew nothing of the gathering clouds. Andrei was sixteen and a little wiser. Out of both our families we were the only survivors, all the others were murdered by the Bolsheviks.'

She passed Faye a glass of the clear spirit.

'But come – we won't speak of the past. Instead we will drink to the future. Be careful – this vodka is much more powerful than that customarily served.'

She raised her own glass to her lips, then tossed the contents straight down her throat. Faye would have liked to have done the same but she knew it would be a foolhardy act unless she wanted to spend the next fifteen minutes coughing and choking.

She look a tentative sip and immediately felt the searing burn of the fiery, powerful spirit as it coursed down her throat. She didn't actually like vodka very much – it was too dry for her sweet tooth – but she took another sip out of politeness.

Sonya picked up a sweetmeat from the bowl and purred, 'Life is full of such delicious contrasts – the sweetness of one of these after the dryness of the spirit. Shall I show you how I like to eat them?'

She drew the edges of her richly coloured robe apart to reveal that beneath it she was naked to the waist. A triangle of sable hair covered her mound, very dark in contrast to the marble whiteness of her thighs.

While Faye watched mesmerised, Sonya parted her legs so that the rose-pink folds of her outer sex-lips were on display.

With a brilliant smile the older woman picked up a piece of the sugar-coated sweetmeat and slipped it between her outer labia so it was held in position with just a corner pointing temptingly towards Faye.

'Come,' she said invitingly, 'you'll find it most enjoyable.'

Andrei led Lucy inside and along what seemed endless stretches of corridor until they reached her stateroom.

Once there he drew her into his arms and kissed her for what was, she realised, the first time; a deep prolonged kiss which started a demanding pulse high up in her sex. She pressed herself against him and rubbed her mound against the hardness of his groin like a cat scratching an itch.

He smelt wonderful, a subtle blend of lemony cologne, foreign cigarettes and just a hint of leather. His hands moved over her bare shoulders and then her back with a caressing circular movement.

He held her away from him just long enough to undo her dress and pull it down to the waist so that her bare breasts could thrust against the starched fabric of his shirt. It felt cool and smooth to her swollen nipples and she rubbed them feverishly against the fine linen.

Although she was in the grip of a carnal heat, Lucy was also nervous. She'd had a couple of hurried sexual encounters in the past, both of them unsatisfactory and both of which had left her frustrated and wanting more. She was afraid that Andrei would find her inexperience tiresome after the more sophisticated pleasures he must be accustomed to.

She suspected that the way she'd behaved with him to date had led him to believe she was far more experienced than she was.

He turned her around and undid her belt and then the rest of her dress, so that it fell to her feet and formed a drift of white around her. To her surprise he removed his shoes and jacket, then threw himself onto the bed and said sombrely, 'Don't move – I wish to look at you.'

In just her suspender belt, stockings and high-heeled silver shoes, very conscious of her bare bottom skimmed by the two narrow suspenders, Lucy kept her back to him and let him study her.

'Now turn around – slowly.'

She obeyed him, but one hand went down to cover her mound and an arm moved across her breasts in the classic gesture of concealment.

'Let me see you properly.'

Slowly she dropped her arms to her sides and her face began to burn as he studied every curve of her body and then her silken golden floss.

'Part your legs.'

Lucy stared at him in consternation. He should be holding her in his arms beneath the bed covers, preferably in complete darkness, not examining her like someone about to buy a slave and ensuring he was getting his money's worth.

But there was something compelling about his sober, gold-green gaze which made her obey him. Her face felt about the same colour as her deep-pink sex folds as she opened her legs and displayed herself to him.

She kept her eyes on the mural above her bed and thought again how knowing and sated the shepherdess looked. Perhaps she herself would look that way too by the end of the evening.

'Come here.'

She stepped out of the circle of her dress and walked across the room towards him, conscious of the movement of her small, high breasts as she went. He pulled her down beside him and said, 'Now you will look at me.'

He discarded his shirt to reveal a torso of staggering masculine beauty, marred only by the puckered slash of a scar. Lucy would have liked to ask what had caused it, but it seemed inappropriate to do so.

In the lamplight the planes of his chest were like those of a classical sculpture, leading down to a hard, flat belly. He left the bed and removed his socks and trousers, throwing them carelessly to the floor, then in one deft movement stripped off his undergarment.

Lucy had already seen and touched his male member, so she was able to look at it with reasonable composure – but had it been so big the last time? It seemed to rear up massively between his thighs. She felt a tremor of misgiving – would it hurt her? She wasn't sure she could accommodate all that.

He rejoined her on the bed and guided her hand to his chest. 'Sweet Lucy – caress me.'

Tentatively, Lucy flattened her hand against his skin and began a voyage of exploration. She stroked his chest, his shoulders and his arms, then traced the contours of his lean hips and muscular thighs.

She worked her way closer and closer to his shaft until she was circling it, then unable to help herself she touched it. It twitched and then throbbed as she closed her hand around it and she marvelled again at its smoothness.

Andrei grazed one nipple with the palm of his hand and Lucy shivered with pleasure. Her breasts had always been very sensitive and she loved to have them touched. He toyed with the nipple, rolling it between his fingers, then bent his dark head and took it in his mouth.

He sucked hard, the heat of his mouth searing her skin. There seemed to be a direct line from her nipple to her sex, which began to produce warm honey in eager anticipation. Andrei turned his attention to her other nipple and Lucy lay down on the bed, her head thrown back, one hand buried in Andrei's crisp hair, the other still holding his penis.

When he eventually raised his head, her nipples looked like small raspberries glistening with morning dew. His hand smoothed down over her belly and came to rest on her mound, cupping the silken covering of golden hair.

With infinite gentleness he coaxed her thighs apart and ran the tips of his fingers around the rim of her labia, dabbling in the warm moisture he found there. Her sex-lips felt slick and swollen as he teased and stroked them, easing further in until he found the entrance to her moisture-flooded inner chamber.

Two fingers slid inside her and began to probe and stretch

her velvety tissues, while his thumb found her throbbing bud and manipulated it skilfully.

The heat began to build inside her and in an answering rhythm Lucy squeezed his swollen shaft. Without pausing in his ministrations Andrei's other hand closed around hers and he murmured, 'Be still – I wish to come inside you and I'm already over-stimulated by what has passed between us tonight.'

She allowed his member to lie quiescent in her hand and resisted the urge to fondle it further.

She could feel her private parts opening like a flower as he caressed her internally and the sweet, tingling heat began to build in her groin again.

The thumb on her clit became more persuasive, then suddenly she spasmed into a climax, consumed by a wave of pleasure so intense that a choking cry was wrenched from her.

She was only half aware that he'd positioned himself between her thighs, but she felt his shaft probing her outer sex-lips and then her inner ones. She was still racked by lingering spasms of pleasure as he slid smoothly inside her, then she felt as if she were being stretched to capacity.

It wasn't painful but for a few moments she seemed uncomfortably full, until he began to move within her and then a new sort of pleasure transmitted itself to every nerve ending.

She couldn't help herself, her hips moved in time with his, and her internal muscles clutched him to her as a welter of new erotic sensation flooded her body.

This was what she'd been waiting for, for what felt like a lifetime.

This was what she'd wanted from him from the first moment they'd met – his hard body covering hers, his virile shaft inside her, creating a dark, secret heat.

Her legs went around his thighs and she crossed them, pulling him closer to her, drawing him in, wanting all of him.

She came again in a womb-wrenching, crashing tidal wave of pleasure just before Andrei's body went rigid and he jerked into his own convulsive, shuddering climax.

She must have dozed off because when she awoke she was alone.

She sat bolt upright wondering where Andrei was, then she swung her legs off the bed and caught sight of herself in the pier glass.

She was still wearing her suspender belt, stockings and shoes, but her suspender belt was twisted awry and her stockings laddered and snagged. Her dark-gold hair waved wildly around her flushed cheeks and her grape-green eyes looked huge and dark, but it was the expression on her face which really arrested her attention.

Now she looked even more like the shepherdess in the mural.

Andrei emerged from the bathroom drying himself on one of the huge fluffy towels.

'What time is it?' she asked, looking around for her clock – Winnie was always moving things. He found it on the dressing table and picked it up.

'Eleven-thirty.' He gathered up his discarded clothes and began to dress.

'Are you going?' asked Lucy, wishing she was still lying in his arms on the bed.

'I thought we would join Sonya, and possibly Faye, for a nightcap in the *fumoir* – I wish to play the tables for a while.'

The last thing Lucy wanted was Sonya's knowing eyes on her. She felt instinctively that the other woman would know how she and Andrei had spent their time and she wasn't sure she liked the idea. Faye would probably guess too and Lucy felt too dazed and pleasure-drugged to want to expose herself to any questions at present.

Much as she wanted Andrei to stay – he could after all have a nightcap here with her – she wasn't about to ask him. She shrugged into her silk robe and said casually, 'I think I'll take a bath.'

'Then I will see you tomorrow, sweet Lucy. *Au revoir.*'

Faye was in a daze as she made her way back to her stateroom. She shook her head, trying to clear it. That vodka had certainly been strong – although she'd only sipped hers it had been more than enough on top of a cocktail before dinner and wine with the meal.

She paused outside Lucy's door, but decided she would rather be alone. And anyway, Lucy could well be in there with the fascinating Count Andrei.

Her own evening with Sonya had been unbelievable. She wouldn't have thought it possible to experience such pleasure with another woman. The whole of her vulva was a hot, tingling mass of sensation. Her breasts felt swollen and her nipples were two hard thimbles pushing against the silk of her camisole. She was only sorry that it was over, but Sonya had gently hinted that it was time for her to leave, well before she was actually ready to.

'Miss Faulkner.'

In the act of unlocking her stateroom door, Faye paused and saw Leo making his way along the corridor towards her. She needed to sit down so she went into the room, leaving the door open behind her.

'May I have a word with you please?' he asked, standing in the doorway, his huge shoulders virtually filling the aperture.

'Certainly – come in,' she invited him, sitting hastily down on the bed before she fell over.

He stepped into the room, closed the door behind him and hesitated before saying, 'I just saw you coming out of the suite the two Russians are sharing. May I ask what you were doing in there?'

'Eating sweetmeats,' she told him giddily. 'Do you always interrogate passengers at the end of the evening?'

'Surely you can see what type of people they are. Do you think your parents would like you to associate with them?'

Faye didn't even need to think that one over. She knew that, had her parents been travelling with them, she and Lucy would have been confined to their cabins for the entire journey rather than be allowed to mix with the Russians and the crowd of people who made up their particular circle.

'No they wouldn't,' she admitted, 'but the same would go for about half the passengers travelling first class. Mother is very exclusive.'

'Then doesn't that tell you something?'

'Yes – that previously I've led a restricted life.'

She leant back, propped herself up on her elbows and studied the toe of one shoe. He really did look *terribly* attractive in that uniform.

'I must ask you again – please don't have anything to do with them. There are lots of other people on the voyage for you to socialise with.'

Faye began to move one ankle in slow circles and, glancing upwards, saw that Leo's eyes were fixed on her foot and the length of shapely calf emerging from her dress.

'Have you spoken to them as well as to me?'

'No, because it would do no good.'

In the grip of a sudden compulsion, Faye rose from the bed, went over to him and wound her arms around his neck. His hands automatically found her narrow waist, then he said in a strangled voice, 'I think you must have had a little too much to drink. I'll ring for the stewardess and she can help you to bed.'

'I'd rather you helped me,' she said daringly. As soon as the words were out of her mouth she couldn't believe she'd said them, but somehow found herself adding, 'Undress me and put me to bed – I'd like that.'

He tried to hold her away from him but she pressed herself against his burly body, her full breasts soft against his chest.

She wanted him to kiss her, she wanted him to do all the delicious things Sonya had done to her and more. Her whole body was on fire, her breasts aching for his touch, her sex eager for more of the stimulation it craved.

She felt his manhood hardening against her hip and caressed it through the stiff white fabric of his trousers.

'Miss Faulkner . . . Faye . . . please don't,' he garbled desperately.

But Faye ignored him and instead guided his hand to her breast and held it in position. She could feel the heat of his palm burning through the thin silk of her dress and her nipple hardened in response.

Slowly, tentatively, he stroked the ripe swelling, then, unable to help himself, slid his hand down the front of her dress and touched the firm, bare orb.

Faye heard him take a sharp breath as his hand closed around it and the slight grip she still held on her self-control gave way at that moment. She tore at the buttons holding his jacket closed while he tugged her dress from one shoulder, then fumbled at the waist for the fastening as she pulled him towards the bed.

They fell onto it in a clumsy tangle of limbs, then Faye knelt astride him and pulled her dress over her head to reveal her peach satin camisole, and camiknickers. He reached up to slip the shoe-string straps down her shoulders, exposing her full, ripe breasts, the coral nipples succulently swollen.

It was the work of moments for Faye to undo his trousers and release the thick, ramrod-hard shaft which had been straining against his clothing. It sprang eagerly upwards, heavily veined with a purple, plum-like end.

She undid the two tiny buttons holding the strip of satin in place over her vulva and took his shaft in her hand. He groaned as she guided it to her sex-valley and rubbed it licentiously against her pliable, engorged bud.

Sonya had paid a lot of attention to her bud, coaxing a response from it that even Faye herself had never come close to. The tiny sliver of flesh tingled in pure carnal acknowledgement of more pleasure to come.

Faye lowered herself onto the waiting column and gasped with delight as it filled her up. Leo grasped her by the waist and she began to ride him, slowly at first, her well-rounded hips moving in a voluptuous rhythm, then faster so her luscious breasts bobbed alluringly above him.

His blue eyes were riveted to her smooth-skinned orbs and his hips bucked in an answering rhythm as she bore down on him and used him shamelessly to satisfy herself. She enjoyed three tiny liquid climaxes before she felt a much bigger one starting to build. His shaft was stimulating her sex-lips and her honey-slicked core with every thrust, but it wasn't enough and she squeezed him demandingly with her plump, shapely thighs, desperate for release.

With a sudden athletic movement, Leo rolled her beneath him and buried his face in her breasts, showering them with kisses, then sucking eagerly at one firm, ripe nipple.

Faye locked her legs around his waist and strained against him, rubbing her vulva hard against the base of his shaft in an instinctive rocking movement. She trembled on the brink of a powerful climax and for endless seconds held her breath. Then with a low-pitched moan she let it wash over her, half oblivious to Leo, still pistoning away above her.

His own volcanic climax was swift to follow, and then he lay panting to one side of her, one strong leg still thrown over her.

Faye lay half asleep, cocooned in a deliciously drowsy warmth. She made a murmur of protest when he extricated himself from her velvety sheath and climbed off the bed.

From a great distance she heard him clearing his throat, then he said in a low voice, 'Miss Faulkner . . . Faye . . . please forgive me – I don't know what came over me.'

'Mmm?' Faye half opened her eyes to see him straightening his clothing, his face a deep, embarrassed crimson.

'I can only beg you not to report me to the captain, though goodness knows I deserve to be keelhauled for this. Please tell me I haven't hurt you.'

'Come back to bed,' murmured Faye drowsily.

Leo's eyes took in her bare coral-tipped breasts and the rumpled satin of her camiknickers which had ridden up to expose the full globes of her well-rounded bottom and he felt a renewed stirring in his member.

'I'd better go now,' he said, averting his eyes from the tempting sight. Hastily, before he could change his mind, he hurried from the cabin.

When Andrei entered the suite after an hour at the tables, he found Sonya alone, stretched out on the *chaise longue*, gazing at the night sky through the open curtains.

She pushed herself into a half-sitting position when he came in and asked, 'How was you evening with the lovely Lucy?'

'Everything I could have hoped for,' he replied. 'I thought I might see you in the *fumoir*.'

'I didn't feel like gambling tonight.'

'Did you amuse yourself with Faye?' He sat on the *chaise*

longue and lifted her legs over his lap so she was half lying across him. He began to caress her calves, kneading the muscles with his strong fingers.

'Very much. I believe she will do whatever we wish, though I would suggest that I have one more session with her alone. What about Lucy?'

Andrei looked reflectively into the candle burning in a silver holder on the small table in front of them.

'She has an independent spirit. I don't think she will like the involvement of others.'

'Good – that will make it even better – and more interesting.'

'Tomorrow then?'

'Tomorrow.'

Andrei's hands moved slowly up Sonya's bare legs, caressing her thighs, then slowly drew her robe open until the silken triangle of her fleece was revealed. With a sudden rough movement he buried his hand in her crotch and thrust three fingers inside her. She moaned and pushed herself hard against his hand.

'Shall I ring for Marta?' he asked, massaging her vulva with the palm of his hand.

'Yes!' she gasped.

He picked up a small silver bell from the table and rang it. After a few seconds, Marta appeared in the doorway.

'Yes, Count Andrei?'

'Prepare the bedroom please – we will be ready in about five minutes.'

'The leather straps?'

Andrei looked at Sonya who nodded.

'The leather straps. Oh, and the blindfold I think.'

Chapter Six

Stretched out side by side on padded deck chairs, the morning sun beating strongly down, the salt breeze in their faces, Lucy and Faye were lost in their respective thoughts.

Lucy was thinking about her lovemaking with Andrei and how wonderful it had been, but she hadn't liked the fact that last night he'd left her to go for a nightcap with Sonya instead of staying for a while.

She'd received a large bouquet of white orchids from him that morning, which was very gratifying, but she wished that he'd stayed with her instead. She was already aching for him to take her in his arms again and touch her . . . kiss her . . . penetrate her.

Just the thought of it made warm moisture gather in the velvety folds of her sex.

She was unaware of the exact nature of the relationship between the two Russian aristocrats, but she knew intuitively that it was far more subtle and complex than anything she could imagine. She wondered if it would be possible to detach him from Sonya, but she felt instinctively that it wouldn't and, anyway, she wasn't sure she wanted to.

Sonya herself exerted a powerful fascination on Lucy and she wanted to spend more time with her. She wondered what had happened between Sonya and Faye last night. Faye hadn't said anything and appeared to be slightly hungover, but other than that she looked happy enough – contented even.

Lucy was sure that she'd tell her eventually – hadn't they

always shared their secrets? But for now she was perfectly happy to remember every erotic moment of her evening with Andrei, and how he'd pleasured her in undreamt of ways. She could barely wait for the moment that they could be alone together again.

Next to her, Faye took a reflective sip of her bouillon and wished her head would stop aching. She stretched like a cat and wondered if any other woman on the ship had enjoyed herself as much as she had last night. The time spent with Sonya had been sublime. Somehow the Russian princess had known all the secrets of her body and used her knowledge to great effect.

And then after that, Leo.

Faye couldn't stop herself giving a delicious little wriggle and then glanced sideways at Lucy to see if she'd noticed. But Lucy's eyes were closed and, if her expression was anything to go by, she was indulging in erotic daydreams of her own.

Actually, Faye was a little embarrassed about the way she'd thrown herself at Leo, but she'd been indisputably the worse for drink and it had just been too tempting. The few previous sexual encounters she'd enjoyed had been initiated by the man – she'd never made the running before – and she wasn't sure she could bear to look Leo in the face now.

But the same drink-induced recklessness which had led her to seduce him – because that was what she'd done – had led her to mount him rather than taking the passive role and she'd found it an exhilarating experience. It had given her a heady feeling of power she'd never had before and it was a power she'd enjoyed wielding.

Both women were jolted from their reveries by the appearance of Amanda and Edward, strolling arm in arm along the sun deck.

'Darlings, you look pretty much the way I feel,' trilled

Amanda, sinking onto the foot of Faye's deck chair. 'You met Edward at my little party, didn't you? And just what have you two been doing with yourselves?'

Amanda looked stunning in a clinging butterscotch linen suit which emphasised her pencil-slim figure. Her glossy dark hair was held back by a silk scarf and her eyes were hidden behind dark glasses. She was smoking a cigarette through a tortoiseshell holder which she waved affectedly around as she spoke.

'Hello, Amanda, what a gorgeous suit – Lanvin?' asked Faye enviously. Although she had a wardrobe full of expensive clothes they had all been chosen by her mother who had fixed ideas about what was suitable for a debutante in her first season. She yearned for something more sophisticated.

'I saw you both getting chummy-wummy with those two delicious Russians at dinner last night, then you all vanished,' Amanda continued. 'I hope you weren't having a party without little me.'

'Sadly, there was no party. How was your evening?'

'I lost money gambling in the *fumoir* – rather a lot too – then we looked in at the dance in the main lounge. Are you feeling alright, my dear, you look a bit green around the gills. *Mal de mer* or over indulgence?'

'The latter I think.'

'Then what you need is a nip of champagne. Why don't you both come along with us to the terrace grill and we'll see what we can do.'

'What do you think, Lucy?' Faye appealed to her friend, 'should we?'

'Why not?' said Lucy lightly. Amanda strolled down the deck, talking to Faye while Lucy fell in step with Edward. He was really rather attractive, she thought, in his blazer and white flannels, but surely he was years younger than Amanda.

And where was Amanda's husband? Was he on the ship? Had they been introduced to him at the party? The liaisons she'd observed recently were a far cry from the rather austere respectability prevailing in the circles Aunt Sarah and the Faulkners moved in.

'Is this your first voyage on the *Aphrodite?*' Edward asked her.

'Yes, we went out on the *Ile de France* and other than that I've never been on another liner.'

Lucy found him very easy to talk to and they strolled amicably along the spacious sweep of the deck past the towering masts and funnels to the terrace grill.

The grill had a curving wall of windows at one end from which a series of broad decks descended like steps to the sea. From their table by the windows they had a stunning view of the deep-green ocean bisected by an arrow of boiling, broad white wake which stretched into infinity.

'Champagne, ladies?' asked Edward when the bar steward came to take their order. They all nodded, although Faye asked for some orange juice with hers, and Edward ordered a whisky and soda for himself.

The icy champagne tasted unbelievably refreshing and made a perfect late-morning drink. Faye, who'd been unable to face anything to eat for breakfast, began to contemplate the possibility of lunch with a reasonable degree of enthusiasm.

It was a lively meal, even if each of the three women did keep glancing round to see if there was any sign of Andrei and Sonya. Only Edward remained happily oblivious to the fascination the Russians exerted on his female companions.

After lunch Edward went off to do some clay-pigeon shooting while Amanda went for a nap before her visit to the beauty salon.

Lucy and Faye returned to their deck chairs and told

each other about their respective evenings.

'Goodness!' exclaimed Faye when Lucy had finished her rather halting recital of her amorous activities. 'That makes my evening sound fairly pedestrian.'

'Hardly,' Lucy replied, 'I'm astonished that you actually seduced someone. I know you're susceptible to men in uniform, but to actually ask him to put you to bed! Have you seen him today?'

'No,' answered Faye, blushing slightly. In fact she'd spotted Leo talking to another passenger on the promenade deck and had hastily turned round and walked away before he'd noticed her. She knew she'd have to face him sometime, but this morning had seemed too soon.

'Talking about it has made me feel really excited again,' said Lucy dreamily. 'I wish Andrei would appear and take me back to my stateroom. I know I'll probably see him at dinner but I don't think I can wait until then.'

At that moment they were approached by a handsome blond man in his early twenties. He paused at the foot of their deck chairs and, looking from one to the other, said in a heavy foreign accent, 'Miss Faulkner?'

'That's me.'

'I bring you a message from Princess Sonya.' With a small bow he handed over an envelope, then turned on his heel and left them.

'Who was that?' Lucy wanted to know.

'He must work for Sonya and Andrei,' said Faye opening the envelope. 'Sonya has invited me for tea – how thrilling.'

'Lucky you,' said Lucy enviously, wondering why she hadn't been invited as well. She suddenly felt edgy and frustrated. 'I think I'll go for a walk – work off that huge lunch. I'll see you later, enjoy your tea.'

* * *

Faye spent a long time choosing what to wear and eventually settled on a silk chiffon afternoon-dress in gentian blue with scalloped edges oversewn in a darker shade of silk. The dress was cut on the bias and clung alluringly to her hips and thighs as she walked.

She made up her face carefully and repainted her nails with clear pink polish, then brushed her chestnut hair until it gleamed like burnished copper.

She was shown into Sonya's bedroom by the stern-faced maid she'd seen before and found Sonya propped up against a pile of pillows on her bed wearing a pair of black satin lounging pyjamas with scarlet lapels.

The room was decorated in a different style from her own which was furnished with modern Art Deco furniture and pretty chintzes. Sonya's furniture was lacquered black wood with inlaid marquetry and her quilt and curtains were a vivid scarlet. They were the perfect setting for her exotic dark beauty.

'Faye – welcome,' Sonya greeted her. She patted the pillows next to her and rather self-consciously Faye sat on the bed, kicked her shoes off and swung her legs up.

'You look very beautiful today,' Sonya complimented her. 'What a lovely dress.' She put out her hand and smoothed the chiffon over Faye's hip, then bent across and kissed her on the lips.

A strange bubbling noise made Faye turn her head. There was an unusual metal urn with steam coming out of it on a tray by the bed.

'It's a samovar,' explained Sonya. 'This is how Russians make their tea. It will be ready in a little while. My beautiful Faye, I thought about you much today and how I enjoyed touching and caressing you last night.'

Faye felt a flush creeping across her cheeks at the memory.

'I think I've embarrassed you. Life is a fleeting thing, Faye

– who knows what awaits us next week, next month, next year. It seems only sensible to take any pleasure which comes our way, because for all we know this ship could sink tomorrow and there will be no more pleasure for any of us. Embarrassment is a pointless and futile emotion – I banished it from my life years ago.'

'I'm not embarrassed,' protested Faye, not altogether truthfully. 'I loved the things you did to me yesterday.'

'Would you like me to do some more?'

'Yes, I would – very much.'

It was true. Just smelling Sonya's exotic perfume made Faye's nipples feel tender and her sex moisten.

'I think today I will introduce you to a different sort of pleasure, one you have probably never experienced before, one which may well be beyond anything you have imagined. But you must put yourself in my hands completely. Will you do that?'

'Oh yes,' said Faye fervently.

'Good. First we will have tea.'

For once Faye had no appetite for the wafer-thin cucumber sandwiches and tiny cakes Marta brought in. She was in the grip of a suppressed excitement which affected her appetite, although she ate a few mouthfuls out of courtesy.

When Marta had removed the tray, Sonya rose gracefully from the bed and drew the gauzy white inner curtains closed so that the sunlight streaming in through the portholes became hazy and diffused.

'First we will remove this lovely dress.' Deftly Sonya undid the tiny buttons and placed the garment carefully over the back of a chair, leaving Faye clad in her slip, camiknickers, and cream stockings held up by garters. Her lingerie was of the palest blue silk, lavishly embroidered in the same colour.

Sonya picked up a long, white feather and began to glide it

over Faye's bare arms and shoulders. The sensation was delicious. When Sonya slid her shoulder straps down her arms and caressed her naked breasts with the tip, it felt wonderful and Faye leant back against the pile of downy pillows like a cat being stroked by its mistress.

Just a touch on her nipples made them tingle demandingly and ripples of pleasure ran down her belly as Sonya teased her navel.

'Turn onto your stomach,' Sonya directed her softly. Faye's back and shoulders were given the same treatment, then the pale strip of flesh above her stocking tops. Sonya unbuttoned Faye's camiknickers and eased them down around her thighs, drawing the feather over her curvaceous bottom in fluid circular movements.

Faye felt herself parting her thighs without having made a conscious decision to do so. The feather brushed over her pubic curls with a touch so light that it was like a wayward current of air, then tickled her clit with a tantalising, teasing pressure.

It was a voluptuous sensation, having her vulva stimulated by a feather in the languid afternoon heat.

'To enhance what I am about to do you must remain in exactly the same position, so I'm going to bind your wrists and ankles with silk scarves,' murmured Sonya.

She rearranged the bed with the pile of pillows in the centre, then made Faye lie over them with her slip bunched up around her waist, her bottom high up in the air and her thighs wide apart. She tied her wrists together with one scarf and secured them to the bedhead, then tied each ankle to the posts at the bottom corners of the bed.

Faye felt a little uneasy at the unexpected turn the afternoon had taken. There was something humiliating about having her backside so high in the air and her legs so wide apart. She felt suddenly vulnerable and exposed and wished she hadn't agreed to this.

But her misgivings vanished when Sonya picked up the feather again and caressed her buttocks lingeringly. She felt a tiny trickle of moisture dampening the soft curls of her reddish floss and relaxed again. The feather teased its way along her outer sex-lips, tracing every soft fold, then drifted along the rim of her inner sex-lips to explore the cleft of her flesh valley.

When Sonya tickled the tiny swelling of her clitoris Faye sighed and the little sliver of tissue hardened in response.

The tickling became more insistent, but it wasn't a strong enough stimulation to bring her the release she was beginning to crave.

Perhaps soon Sonya would use her hand or her mouth to make her come. There were ripples of excitement in her belly and she started to feel a build up of tension in the swollen tissues of her sex.

Sonya began to speak to her in a husky, persuasive voice.

'I love the pleasure of contrasts, don't you? A swim in cool water on a hot day; the sweetness of sugar stirred into a glass of lemon juice; dark, bitter coffee drunk as an accompaniment to the richest chocolate truffles. Well, the same is true of sex, but more so. You are enjoying the pleasure my touch is giving you, but think how much more you would enjoy it after you have experienced a little delicious pain.'

Faye didn't like the sound of that at all. She stirred uneasily on her pile of pillows and wished that she wasn't in such a vulnerable position. But Sonya kept on teasing her clit, keeping her in a state of intense arousal, without ever applying the additional stimulation which would be necessary to send her over the edge into the abyss of pleasure.

'Are you enjoying what I am doing?' enquired Sonya softly.

'Y . . . yes,' admitted Faye.

'But you wish I would touch you like this . . .' Sonya slid the tip of her finger along the shaft of Faye's bud and stroked it rhythmically. It was almost, but not quite, enough to give her the release she wanted.

'Yes,' she gasped.

'And so I will, after I have spanked you, so you may experience for yourself how wonderful the ecstasy of release is when your luscious bottom has enjoyed quite a different stimulation.'

Spank her?

Faye had never been spanked in her life. Even her nanny had confined her discipline to making her stand in a corner when she'd been naughty.

Even so, there was something about the idea of Sonya spanking her which seemed very exciting.

And after all, what harm could it do to try it?

At that moment Faye would have agreed to almost anything to be rid of the unbearable frustration that had her in its grip.

'Would you like me to do that?'

'Y . . . yes.'

Sonya's finger found Faye's clit again and rubbed it with a sure, deft touch. Faye could feel how wet and slippery it was as the other woman increased the pressure of her finger. She felt perspiration breaking out on her skin as her excitement mounted.

'*Aaah!*' she cried out as she spasmed into a blissful, satisfying climax. She strained at the scarves, unable to move, when what she wanted to do was writhe around on the bed and press her thighs together to hold onto the sensations inside her for as long as possible.

All too soon it was over and then she felt Sonya's cool hand stroking her bottom, gently squeezing her flesh as if trying to decide where to begin.

'You must not cry out, however much you want to, or half the ship's officers will come crashing in,' Sonya warned her.

A sudden surge of excitement raced through Faye's body at the thought of Leo throwing open the door and finding her bent obscenely over a pile of pillows, her naked bottom in the air, her vulva on full display and Sonya spanking her.

What on earth would he think?

The next second the flat of Sonya's hand smacked sharply down in the middle of her left buttock, making her gasp with shock. The smack was swiftly followed by another in the identical place on her right buttock. She couldn't honestly say that it hurt, but it certainly stung.

There was a pause and then several slaps rained down in rapid succession on her left side, each one slightly overlapping and a little lower than the one that preceded it. The last one on the underhang of her buttock stung most of all and she felt her rump beginning to glow.

There was a pause and Sonya laughed softly.

'Another contrast – how pink the marks I'm making look against your white skin.'

She slapped the underhang on the right side of Faye's plump posterior and then followed it by several more smacks in rapid succession, each one a little higher.

Faye felt her backside beginning to glow in earnest. The heat from her punished derrière somehow transmitted itself to her sex and made her feel molten inside. She ground her pubis against the pillows but they were too soft to stimulate her.

Sonya landed several blows across the damp cleft between her buttocks, then smacked her way down to the tops of Faye's thighs.

Faye began to writhe and strain at her bonds. She wasn't sure why, but the spanking was acting like a powerful aphrodisiac, making her desperate for another climax. She could feel the heat filling her vulva, making her tissues swollen and slick with her juices.

Sonya's last slap caught her squarely across her flesh-valley making her jump, then the other woman thrust two long, slender fingers high up into Faye's velvety chamber and swivelled them rhythmically.

'It has made you wet and ready as I thought it would,' she whispered, probing further.

Faye tugged desperately at the silk scarves holding her so firmly in position, desperate to bear down on Sonya's hand to feel it even further inside her. But they held her secured to the bed as the other woman withdrew her fingers and then played with Faye's vulva, opening her wide with both hands and toying with her sex-lips.

When she circled the hard, throbbing knot of Faye's clitoris with the tip of her finger, Faye couldn't stop herself pleading, 'Sonya – please.'

Her bottom was still glowing with a fiery heat and there was an itch in her clitoris which was making her feel almost faint, it was aching so strongly for stimulation.

She felt a cool finger on the bead-shaped head of her clit and then Sonya squeezed it between her thumb and forefinger. Almost immediately, Faye convulsed into a climax so strong she almost blacked out. It felt as if it was wrenched from her very core and transmitted itself to every nerve ending, particularly the hot, fiery burn of her recently spanked backside.

She cried out, a strangled almost animal cry which led Sonya to clap her hand over Faye's mouth and hiss. 'Shh!'

Sonya moved away across the room and went out through the door leading to the suite's sitting room.

'Sonya!' Faye called weakly after her, 'aren't you going to untie me?'

There was no reply, so she had no alternative but to stay in her obscene position, her slip bunched up around her waist, her camiknickers lying in a crumpled heap beside her, her pink-splodged bottom on lewd display.

The door opened again and Sonya reappeared.

'The cocktail hour is almost upon us,' she said brightly. 'Tell me, Faye – what is your favourite cocktail and I'll have Marta make it for you.'

'A sweet Manhattan. Sonya – will you untie me now please?'

In reply, Sonya sashayed over to the bed, her satin pyjamas making a seductive swishing sound around her long legs. Her cool hand smoothed over the curves of Faye's still burning derrière and then she flicked Faye's bud with her forefinger. The bud quivered in an instant response.

Sonya laughed softly. 'Oh, I don't think we've finished here yet.'

'I'm uncomfortable – I want you to untie me please.'

'What is a little discomfort after such pleasure?'

Sonya left the room again and Faye pulled desperately at the silk scarves, but they held her firmly in place and she had to face the fact that, until Sonya chose to let her go, she was a helpless captive.

She could call out and maybe someone would hear her, but the humiliation of anyone else seeing her like this was too awful to contemplate – she'd rather stay tied up all night.

The door opened and Faye turned her head, about to plead with her captor. To her horror, Marta came into the room carrying a silver tray holding cocktails and placed it on the table by the window.

Faye couldn't believe that Sonya had exposed her to this humiliation. The maid didn't even glance at her, just deposited the tray, then silently left the room.

Worse was to follow.

When Sonya glided back into the room Faye burst out, 'How *could* you! How could you let your maid see me like this! Let me go at once!'

In reply Sonya picked up the silver cocktail shaker and began to shake it, before saying, 'Andrei will be joining us for a drink.'

'*What*! You can't let him see me like this! Untie me!'

When Andrei appeared in the doorway a few seconds later, Faye let out a low moan and buried her face in the bedcover. She was unable to think of any moment in her life as utterly, completely humiliating as this one.

As soon as she was free she would have no alternative but to throw herself over the side of the ship.

'Good afternoon, Faye,' Andrei greeted her, then he sank into an armchair and stretched out his long legs in front of him.

Faye could tell by his voice that he was directly behind her and so would have a clear view of the full, white globes of her bottom and the exposed folds of her labia and sex-valley. To add to her total degradation it would also undoubtedly be obvious that she'd recently been spanked.

Faye kept her crimson face buried in the satin bedcover and willed herself to die, right there on Sonya's bed.

'Your Manhattan will be just a moment, Faye,' said Sonya, then she crossed the room and stood beside the bed.

'Here you are, lift your head and I will hold the glass to your lips.'

Faye refused to raise her burning face, then jumped when she felt Sonya's hand, cold from its contact with the cocktail shaker, on her bottom.

'Doesn't Faye have a beautiful derrière?' said Sonya to Andrei. 'So full and round, so plump and ripe – it was such a pleasure to spank it.'

'I envy you and I only wish I had been here to witness it – I would have enjoyed that very much.'

'Perhaps Faye would like me to do it again with you

watching. Or perhaps she would prefer to have you spank her yourself this time, Andrei, while I watch.'

Sonya toyed carelessly with Faye's clitoris, and Faye couldn't help herself moaning as a quiver of reluctant response passed through her body.

She felt faint with the humiliation of the situation but, even so, as Sonya stroked and squeezed her tingling bud, she could feel herself moistening and the soft tissues of her vulva swelling in a shaming response.

'Come lift your head – a drink will make you feel better,' Sonya murmured.

The thought that she might be able to drown her degradation in alcohol was too tempting. Faye raised her head just enough for Sonya to hold the glass to her lips and then she gulped down most of the cocktail in one go.

The icy liquid coursed down her throat and spread an immediate warm glow through Faye's body. It also seemed to fill her vulva with renewed heat and she was aware that Sonya's skilful caresses were arousing her again to the extent that, against her will, she let out a low moan.

Sonya slid two fingers inside her and said conversationally to Andrei, 'Inside she is like the finest quality velvet, and so warm and moist. I can feel her soft folds engulfing my fingers, drawing them in. She wishes me to pleasure her again and perhaps I will. Is that what you want, Faye?'

Faye didn't reply and Sonya ran the tip of her finger along the shaft of Faye's clitoris, then squeezed it rhythmically. Faye was horribly aware that she was on the brink of another orgasm. How could she bear to climax with Andrei's eyes fixed on her exposed private parts?

But how could she bear not to with Sonya manipulating her bud so deftly between her finger and thumb?

The pleasure she was experiencing blotted everything else

out, particularly as the cocktail had now hit her. With one last knowing squeeze, Sonya brought Faye to another gasping, choking climax which made her go rigid and wrench convulsively at her bonds as pleasure exploded through her body.

'So responsive,' gloated Sonya. 'Pour her another drink, Andrei.'

Again Sonya held the glass to her lips and Faye gulped down the potent cocktail.

'It will be time to bathe and change for dinner soon,' observed Sonya. 'But I think we have time for Faye to be spanked and pleasured one last time before I release her. Do you wish to do it, Andrei, or shall I?'

'I think we should let Faye choose.'

'Very well – which of us shall it be, Faye? I think it only fair to tell you that Andrei is just as adept at pleasuring a woman as I am.'

The thought of dark, enigmatic Andrei spanking her bare bottom, then dabbling in her overheated private parts with his long, elegant fingers, suddenly seemed like the most desirable thing on earth to Faye.

To her horror she felt the unmistakable wetness of female juices gathering in her sex and then overflowing to trickle down her thigh and into her stocking top. She was humiliatingly aware that, as both Andrei's and Sonya's attention was obviously riveted on her private parts, neither of the decadent couple could have failed to notice it.

'There's your answer, Andrei – I think Faye chooses you.'

Her face still buried in the quilt Faye felt Andrei's hand, larger and warmer than Sonya's, on her silken posterior and heard him say, 'Would you like me to do that – would you enjoy it?'

Trembling with anticipation Faye said in a choked voice, 'Yes.'

Without warning his hand cracked down across the crown of her bottom, making her buttocks bounce. He didn't spank her hard, not even as hard as Sonya, but he spanked her thoroughly and for what seemed like a long time.

It took a minute or two before Faye realised that she was awaiting each slap with eager anticipation, welcoming it even. A hot, carnal glow suffused her punished backside and spread to her vulva, making it itch and pulse greedily.

She began to push her bottom demandingly upwards as far as her bonds would allow her to, then gasped as he slipped his other hand under her belly and slid it over her mound until his probing fingers could reach her sex-valley.

Faye didn't think she'd ever experienced anything as exciting as Andrei burying three fingers high up in her sex and moving them rhythmically up and down as he continued to spank her.

Each smack landed well away from the one that had gone before, so she was never sure where the next would come, adding to the excitement. His slaps were really little more than pats, but each one left a tiny stinging glow which swiftly spread outwards in ever-increasing waves of hot, wanton pleasure.

His thumb worked on her swollen bud, driving her wild. Faye pushed her face as far into the quilt as she could and bit her lip in a Herculean effort not to cry out.

Three last, flat-handed slaps rained down across the cleft between her buttocks. The first across the fleshy crown, the second across the underhang and the third squarely across her flesh-valley.

At the same moment his thumb squashed her clitoris with a circular movement and she gave a muffled scream and convulsed into the strongest, most earth-shattering climax she'd ever experienced. Hot waves of pleasure racked her body leaving her weak, trembling and barely aware of where she was or what had happened.

She was only dimly conscious of her wrists and ankles being freed and then she was turned gently on her side and the pillows were removed from under her and placed behind her head. Sonya clasped her in her arms, petting and caressing her while Andrei spread a cool, soothing, rose-scented cream into her burning rump.

She lay on the bed between them, her camiknickers now back in place, her slip decorously around her knees, and let Sonya give her tiny sips of a freshly mixed drink.

She was suffused by a sense of wellbeing, and she felt more languorous and relaxed than she could ever remember feeling in her life.

She felt she could lie here for ever with Sonya gently stroking her hair and Andrei holding her hand and dropping occasional kisses on it.

Eventually Sonya said, 'We're giving a party in the pool room this evening. We hope that you'll come, there will be an invitation waiting for you in your cabin.'

'I'd love to,' murmured Faye.

'Now you should dress and go and take a bath and a nap. We'll look forward to seeing you later.'

Chapter Seven

Lucy was dressing for the evening when the phone rang. She'd just been to the hairdressers and her hair rippled around her heart-shaped face in becoming, old-gold waves.

Winnie put down the dress she was holding and went to answer it.

'It's Count Andrei Davoust, Miss Lucy,' she said, holding out the receiver.

'Hello.'

'Lucy – how are you today?'

The sound of his deep, seductive voice made her stomach turn circles, but even so her voice was cool in the extreme as she replied, 'Fine, thank you.'

He'd had all day to seek her out, so why had he left it until now?

'I have something for you. May I come to your stateroom?'

'I'm dressing.'

'Even better. I'll be there in a couple of minutes.' He replaced the receiver before she could say anything further.

Lucy turned to her maid, 'I don't need you any longer, Winnie – would you go and see if Miss Faulkner wants any help please?'

Winnie left the room and Lucy continued to fasten the tiny pearl buttons on her oyster satin Molyneux gown. Diagonally cut, with a draped *décolletage* and gently flared skirt, the gown clung to her slender figure and emphasised every curve.

When Andrei arrived she took her time about opening the

door and then greeted him fairly distantly. The sight of him, lean and tanned, leaning casually in her doorway, made her stomach lurch with a surge of lust so strong it took her breath away, but she was determined not to let it show.

'Would you like a drink?' she asked. 'Oh, and thanks for the flowers by the way.' She waved her hand carelessly in the direction of the orchids, carefully arranged by Winnie in a crystal vase.

He shook his head and strolled over to where she'd seated herself in front of the dressing table.

'I came to give you this.' He proffered a white envelope and a narrow white box tied up with a pale green ribbon. Lucy took them from him, put the box to one side and slit open the envelope to find it was an invitation to a cocktail party in the indoor pool room.

She picked up the box and held it aloft by hooking a loop of the bow over her forefinger.

'What's this?' she enquired, arching one dark eyebrow.

'The obvious answer to that, my dear Lucy, is open it and see.'

Inside the box, nestling on a bed of moss-green satin, was a gold brooch in the shape of a leopard. It was a beautiful piece of work, skilfully crafted and with two emeralds for eyes.

Lucy examined it appreciatively and placed it regretfully back in its box. She stood up and handed it back to him.

'It's lovely, but you must know I can't accept it.'

'Why not?'

'Surely you know the form? Flowers, scent and chocolates are acceptable gifts for a young unmarried woman from a man – nothing more expensive.'

Andrei moved close enough to Lucy for her to smell his lemony cologne. His hands glided over her hips, smoothing over the rich fabric of her dress, then he pulled her close to him. The feeling of his tall, hard body against hers made her tremble slightly and she was aware of a stabbing little pulse high up in her groin.

'Even when the man and woman in question are lovers?' he said softly.

His words made Lucy stiffen. Although she was aware that that was exactly what they were – or at least had been last night – she was surprised how uncomfortable the thought made her.

She knew that in the circles in which she moved there were certain unwritten rules regarding liaisons. Young, unmarried women weren't really supposed to have them, although she knew that girls often went to bed with their fiancés, or why else would there be at least a couple of weddings a season arranged in a hurry, almost invariably followed by the birth of a child seven or so months later?

She presumed she and Faye were unusual in that both of them were possessed of a thirst for sex which sometimes led them to behave impetuously.

Married women, on the other hand, once they had done their duty and produced an heir, were very likely to start looking around them for the opportunity of dalliance.

Look at Amanda, openly travelling across the Atlantic with her lover, though as a sop to convention they had separate accommodation.

'That doesn't make any difference,' she said at last in reply to Andrei's question.

He pulled her closer so she could feel the hard, arousing bulge of his manhood. One hand travelled slowly down her back to smooth over the firm thrust of her bottom and caress it lingeringly through the oyster satin.

She could feel her sex-lips spreading softly like camellia petals on a warm day. The dewy moisture gathering high up in her hidden folds created a slight tickling sensation as, in response to the pull of gravity, it began to creep slowly downwards.

His other hand slid inside her gown and found her breast. She gasped at the touch of his fingers on her bare skin and had to clutch his arms because her legs suddenly felt weak.

Her mind fogged over as she was overcome by a surge of desire so strong it made it difficult to breathe. When Andrei drew her panelled satin gown up over her thighs, stroking them through the sensual slippery material, she rubbed herself against him cat-like, her eyes closed, her head thrown back.

He held her gown around her waist and caressed her bottom, belly and thighs through the whisper-fine Chinese silk of her pearl-grey camiknickers.

His fingers slid over her mound and circled her triangle of golden floss, rubbing the silk tantalisingly against it. He slipped his hand between her legs, coaxing them gently apart and then massaging her vulva through the crotch of her camiknickers.

She could feel her juices soaking into the fabric, making it damp and sticky as he explored her sex-valley and probed it as deeply as he could, until the silk was stretched virtually to ripping point. It filled her with hot, carnal pleasure to have his silk-sheathed fingers moving inside her, massaging her internally and making her clitoris harden in eager response.

He unfastened her camiknickers and drew them slowly down her thighs. She stepped out of them and was surprised when he buried his face in the damp silk, breathing deeply.

'The scent of a woman is truly one of the most potent aphrodisiacs in the world,' he murmured, laying the delicate undergarment aside.

Without warning he seized her by the hips and bent her forward over the padded chair in front of the triple-mirrored dressing table. She caught a glimpse of her flushed, surprised face and then her gown was thrown upwards and he held her in position with his thighs while he ripped open his trousers.

Lucy could only gasp as she felt his hot, ramrod-hard penis thrusting into her, burying itself in her aching core.

He paused when it was embedded right up to the hilt and bent over to free her breasts from the front of her gown, then he clasped her hips and began a lewd, vigorous pumping. The friction worked on her velvet tissues to send hot spikes of pleasure shooting through her body.

She managed to grip the edges of the chair, giving herself some leverage, and thrust back at him so she was meeting every arousing movement with one of her own.

It was a rough, exciting coupling. Lucy could feel the tops of her thighs getting wetter and stickier as she felt a mounting heat in her quim and her juices flowed freely. She began to pant as she felt her release remaining elusively out of reach.

She felt his hand slip around to her mound, then it dropped so that his fingers could find the hard knot of her clitoris and commence rapid, rhythmic stimulation.

The results were immediate and electric. Within seconds she shuddered into a hot, wrenching climax and she felt her body jerking against his as he pressed her harder against the chair.

He grunted something and then emptied himself into her in a series of convulsive thrusts, which pushed her so far over the chair that her head made contact with the padded seat.

The position was far from comfortable and she tried weakly to straighten up as soon as she regained the use of her limbs. Andrei's hand buried itself in her hair and turned her face towards the triple mirror of the dressing table.

'Open your eyes and look at us,' he urged her softly.

She was shocked by what she saw, a dozen images of them

both frozen in their obscene position were reflected remorselessly back at her.

Her golden hair had fallen wildly around her face and her eyes were enormous and glowed with a dark emerald fire. The skirt of her gown lay in rumpled folds around her back, leaving her thighs and bottom very much on display.

It was an image of herself she was unfamiliar with and the fact that Andrei was part of it, still penetrating her, made it even more disturbing.

Slowly he drew her upright and turned her to face the mirror, his shaft still deep inside her. Her firm, high breasts had been drawn free of her low-cut gown and the deep vee formed a lewd frame for them. They looked very pale in contrast to the deep-pink of her nipples, which jutted provocatively out like small chunks of rose quartz.

Andrei covered one with a tanned hand, then opened his fingers so the nipple protruded through. He tugged it gently and Lucy felt an answering response in her velvety sheath so that her internal muscles flexed around his member.

He withdrew from her slowly and said, 'Come, it's time to go to the party. But first . . .' He picked up the emerald and gold brooch and pinned it to the front of her dress. Still dazed by their coupling, Lucy made no objection.

She picked up her crumpled camiknickers and went into the bathroom to wash and tidy her clothing. When she emerged Andrei was standing on the small half-moon of teak which was her private verandah, smoking a pungent foreign cigarette.

The expression on his face was bleak and distant and as she watched him unobserved for a few moments, she wondered what he could be thinking about, then he turned round and stepped back into the stateroom.

As they walked along the corridor together, her hand under his arm, he asked, 'Do you gamble, Lucy?'

'Not really – the opportunity has never arisen. I'm pretty good at several card games, but I've never played for money or been in a casino in my life.'

It had been the custom among her friends at boarding school to play cards after lights-out and Lucy had had a natural facility for all the games they'd played. One of her friends had once joked that she must have sold her soul to the devil for all the winning hands she seemed to be dealt.

'After dinner we thought we might visit the *fumoir* and try our luck – will you join us?'

It sounded rather exciting. Perhaps she'd play a little herself – she might even win.

Lucy had swum in the outside pool on the sun deck, but she hadn't yet visited the one indoors. In the corridor just outside the door the tall blond man who'd delivered Faye's summons to tea with Sonya was collecting the invitations. Andrei spoke to him briefly in Russian and then they passed through the double doors.

'Who's that?' asked Lucy.

'Stephan, my valet.' Lucy thought that he didn't look much like a valet – he had the physique of a man who did a hard physical job and, although his face was expressionless, she got the impression that his cold blue eyes were carefully assessing her.

The pool room was modelled on classical lines and tiled in deep-blue mosaic inset by niches at regular intervals, each holding a statue of a Greek god or goddess. Creamy, finely textured marble covered the floor and a flight of shallow, curved marble steps led into the pool.

The lighting came through frosted panels in the ceiling and bathed the room in a soft, unreal glow. The pool was lit from beneath by porthole lamps which made the water shimmer, and a fountain played at one end, sending a constant spray of tiny drops up in a graceful arc which spattered musically down onto the water.

Lucy would never have thought of throwing a party in such a venue, but she had to admit that it made the perfect background for the lavishly dressed guests to mingle and sip drinks. The sounds of animated conversation and ripples of laughter echoed around the room as Sonya stepped forward to greet her.

'Lucy – I'm glad you could come.' Sonya took her by the arm, detaching her from Andrei, and led her to where a waiter was loading his tray with freshly shaken cocktails.

Sonya looked stunning in a tight black taffeta skirt which was split from her ankle all the way up to mid-thigh. She was wearing it with a short, vividly printed Chinese jacket with a mandarin collar. The vibrant hues of peacock, scarlet, amber and emerald combined in a glorious riot of colour on the rich satin and made a perfect foil for her sleek sable hair, pale face and crimson lips.

'What will you have to drink?' she asked Lucy.

'Vodka martini with a twist please.'

Drinks in hands, the two women strolled over to a cushioned marble bench set in an alcove behind the fountain.

'The voyage is half over and we have not yet spent any time together,' commented Sonya, running the end of her crimson-tipped forefinger around the top of her glass in a voluptuous manner.

Lucy refrained from pointing out that Sonya could have invited her to tea as well as Faye. She realised with a little stab of resentment that she was jealous of the way her friend and Sonya seemed to have become so close so quickly.

But then, Faye could well be thinking the same about herself and Andrei.

The party seemed to be hotting up very quickly. Already

the laughter had become more demonstrative and several couples were openly embracing. A group of people were dancing with a sexual provocativeness not seen at the dances in the main lounge and there was a louche air to the proceedings which Lucy found extremely stimulating.

In front of them a dark, sultry-looking woman whom Lucy knew to be South American, suddenly leapt onto the parapet of the fountain and began to undulate sinuously to the music pouring out of the gramophone. Her movements became wilder and more explicitly sexual as the minutes passed.

Sonya draped one arm negligently along the back of the marble bench and began to stroke Lucy's hair.

'How well she dances,' she conceded. 'How hotly the blood must flow through her veins. She makes me feel cold as ice in comparison. And what a beautiful, lithe figure she has. Do you find her attractive, Lucy?'

'Yes, very,' Lucy admitted frankly.

'I admire her lack of inhibition, the way she revels in the admiration of all watching.'

The woman obviously began to find her tight skirt too restricting because, without missing a beat, she undid it and let it slither to the floor, then kicked it to one side.

Her endless legs were clad in dark, sheer silk stockings held in place by lacy scarlet garters. To Lucy's surprise instead of the more concealing camiknickers customarily worn by women, her sex was barely covered by a tiny scrap of scarlet silk which fastened on each hip with ribbons tied into bows.

Lucy found that her eyes were riveted on the scarlet triangle. She'd never seen such immodest lingerie – it barely concealed the woman's soft, dark fleece and she could actually see several tendrils of curling hair escaping.

To her amazement, one of the male dancers, also South American, fell to his knees on the parapet and, grasping the woman by the buttocks, buried his face in her provocatively swaying delta.

Lucy glanced swiftly around and saw that in the time she'd been watching the dancer, several other guests had discarded much of their clothing and had begun to dive and wade into the pool.

There were no ship's officers present and the two waiters circulating were not in the ship's uniform and were therefore presumably in the employment of one of the guests. She realised now that Stephan had probably been posted in the corridor to keep out anyone not invited and that all the guests were the ones for whom fast living was the norm.

She found it really thrilling to be part of such a decadent scene and tried to look blasé, as if she attended parties like this all the time.

On the other side of the room she saw Amanda leaning back against one of the fluted marble pillars while a man Lucy didn't recognise was openly massaging her mound over her skirt, his face buried in her neck.

'How warm it is in here,' said Sonya, slowly unbuttoning her Chinese jacket. She was wearing nothing underneath and she casually parted it at the front to reveal her small, high breasts, the nipples large and prominent and the colour of milk chocolate.

Unable to stop herself, Lucy caressed them fervently, running her fingers over the tautness of the crinkled aureoles and then gently pinching the large nipples until they hardened in swift response. She covered one breast and then weighed it in the palm of her hand before stroking the fine alabaster skin.

Sonya watched her through her thick lashes, her silver-grey eyes glinting in the diffused light.

The slit in Sonya's skirt gaped invitingly open and Lucy slid her hand into it and up the other woman's silk-clad thigh.

The skin above her stocking top was cool and smooth and Lucy caressed it lingeringly. Sonya's breathing had quickened and Lucy could feel a hectic pulse beating on her inner thigh.

She couldn't resist exploring further and her fingers brushed the lacy edge of Sonya's camiknickers.

'Touch me,' Sonya murmured and bent to kiss Lucy softly on the lips. The Russian woman leant back against the marble bench, her breasts on full display for anyone to see, and slowly parted her legs as far as she was able to in the tight skirt.

It was enough for Lucy to wriggle her fingers upwards until they made contact with the damp satin between her legs. She rubbed it with the tips of her fingers and felt a sense of power when Sonya sighed and her eyes fluttered closed. Under her delicate caresses the strip of satin soon became soaked through.

She was half aware that several people were watching them, but she really didn't care. She eased the strip of satin away from Sonya's vulva and slid her fingers under it, where they made immediate contact with the swollen kernel of her clitoris.

Sonya's response was electric, her back arched and her head dropped back as if the slender column of her neck wasn't strong enough to support it. Lucy's feeling of power increased and she massaged the kernal in a circular movement, squashing it with the pads of her fingers.

She could feel warm moisture gathering, making it difficult to keep the nub of flesh under her control. She kept losing it as her fingers slipped off and into the intricate folds of Sonya's sex-lips.

She wanted to explore the other woman's dark, secret inner chamber, but Sonya's skirt was too tight for her to open her legs any further and Lucy could only get the tips of her fingers inside her.

She returned her attention to the engorged kernel, squeezing it and rubbing it along the sticky shaft the way she liked to rub her own.

It wasn't just Sonya who was getting wetter and wetter. Lucy could feel her own dewy juices trickling steadily into her pearl-grey camiknickers, which were already damp after her earlier bout of lovemaking with Andrei. She hoped the moisture wouldn't soak through the seat of her oyster satin gown – that would be too embarrassing for words.

The rhythmic rubbing had its inevitable effect and Sonya let out a low moan and her thighs closed convulsively around Lucy's hand, effectively trapping it as she shuddered into an urgent climax.

Someone clapped, bringing Lucy back to reality with a bump. She was briefly conscious that she and Sonya were the centre of attention at that end of the room, then someone noticed that the two South Americans were now copulating frantically away on the edge of the fountain and everyone turned to watch them.

Andrei came up carrying two more vodka martinis. Lucy hastily tried to withdraw her hand from between Sonya's legs but it was held trapped in place. With all the social poise she could muster she smiled at him and accepted the drink.

The icy liquid felt wonderful and she gulped down at least half of it as Andrei said, 'Are you enjoying the party?'

'Very much,' she managed to say. Sonya, the waves of her climax at last receding, relaxed her muscles and Lucy was able to pull her hand free. Andrei took it and, looking straight into her eyes with his yellow-green ones, placed her fingers between his lips and sucked hard.

It was an arousingly erotic gesture which made Lucy tremble with lust while, completely composed, Sonya sipped her own drink and glanced around her to see what everyone else was doing.

'I don't see Faye anywhere,' she commented, 'do you?' Neither of the other two could see her either. 'Perhaps she's still taking a nap,' suggested Sonya. The two exiles exchanged a brief, knowing glance and Lucy had the uncomfortable sensation of being excluded from something.

They must have sensed her feelings because Andrei said, 'Come – we will swim. It will give us an appetite.' He didn't say whether the appetite would be for food or sex.

'There are several of our guests I must speak to.' Sonya rose elegantly to her feet and wandered off, glass in hand, to join a group of people who were chatting at the other end of the pool. Like Sonya, two of the women had their breasts exposed and one was naked from the waist down, except for her stockings.

Most of the men had discarded their clothes and many of them sported erections. Lucy found her eyes drawn to the various male members and marvelled at how different from each other they were. Some were short and thick, others long and slender and some simply huge. One man sat, legs apart, on the edge of the pool, while in the water a plump red-haired woman performed fellatio on him.

Andrei began to strip off his clothes.

'You'd better remove your lovely gown – I can't think immersing it in salt water would do it any good.'

Lucy unfastened the buttons and slipped off the dress, placing it carefully over the back of the marble bench. She hesitated for a moment and then removed her stockings and suspender belt, but nothing would make her actually remove anything else in front of all these people.

In her pearl-grey camiknickers and camisole, she allowed Andrei to lead her to the top of the marble steps and then hand-in-hand they descended into the tepid water. He was completely naked and a sidelong glance revealed that he had a magnificent erection rearing up between his thighs.

It was a strange feeling to be swimming in her silk underwear through the softly lit water, surrounded by people disporting themselves in various imaginative ways. Lucy followed Andrei to the far end of the pool and paused when she saw Faye coming in through the door.

Faye's eyes widened in shock as she took in the debauched scene. Lucy thought that was pretty much the way she'd feel herself if she'd just arrived. She swung herself out of the pool and waved to her. As soon as she left the water she became aware that the thin silk of her lingerie had gone virtually transparent in the water and had moulded itself to every curve and hollow like a second skin.

'Hello, Faye – I'd have a drink if I were you,' she greeted her friend, 'or it might seem a bit much to take.'

Faye looked glowingly beautiful in a parchment-silk jersey dress with a beaded neckline. Her chestnut hair was gathered in at the nape of her neck which made her look older than her eighteen years. Long cream silk gloves covered her shapely forearms and she carried a tiny beaded bag.

'Have I missed all the fun?' she asked faintly. 'I drifted off to sleep and only woke up half an hour ago. What's this – the fall of Rome?'

'Just another boring party,' teased Lucy. Faye gazed around her awed.

'It reminds me of our last school dance,' she said at last. Lucy laughed out loud and then Edward, Amanda's lover, came to join them.

His eyes roamed appreciatively over them both, then he said, 'Would you like to dance, Faye? I think we're the only two people with our clothes still on.'

Lucy went back to the pool and sat on the steps up to her waist in the water watching Andrei forge his way towards her doing an athletic crawl. He joined her on the steps and said, 'I think I'm ready to eat – shall we dress and move on?'

Lucy suddenly realised that she couldn't very well pull her dress on over her dripping lingerie, but she had nothing else to put on. In the changing room she stripped off the soaked camiknickers and camisole and dried herself before rolling her stockings back into position and fastening her suspender belt around her narrow waist.

As she clipped the suspenders closed she thought she'd just have to make her way back to her cabin wearing the dress over her virtually naked body, then she could don some more underwear.

Andrei however had other ideas. 'The thought that you are virtually naked under that dress excites me,' he told her as they left the pool room. 'I wish to take you to dinner like that.'

'I don't think so,' said Lucy firmly. 'What if I slipped descending the stairs into the restaurant? It would be too awful for words.'

'I will keep a firm hold on you.' He stopped in the corridor and turned her to face him, his eyes holding hers. 'Do it for me, Lucy.'

She wavered for a moment but then she remembered that he had left her last night to return to Sonya and he hadn't been near her all day.

It was time to make it clear that he couldn't always bend her to his will.

'No, Andrei – it would make me very uncomfortable not to be properly dressed.' Despite his protestations she insisted on making a detour to her cabin where she pulled on another set of lingerie before they went for dinner.

In the casino atmosphere of the *fumoir*, passengers on the *Aphrodite* who wished to do so could gamble the evenings away. As she wandered around the tables with Andrei, Lucy was gripped by a heady excitement as she tried to decide what to try first.

She eventually decided on roulette, which seemed simple enough, and bought some chips. She bet hesitantly at first, backing black and red alternately, but she seemed to be on a winning streak and won almost every time.

She was just as lucky when she decided to pile everything she'd won so far on one number and after some deliberation chose thirty-six.

Unbelievably it came up.

'I've won! I've won!' she cried, clutching Andrei's arm. It was a substantial amount but, as she was already a wealthy woman, the money meant less to Lucy than the thrill of actually winning it.

Leo, the first officer was mingling with the passengers and watching the proceedings.

'Congratulations, Miss Davenport,' he said as she collected her winnings. 'Would you like me to take all that to the purser's office for you and lock it in the safe?'

'Oh no, I don't think so. The night's still young, I'm going to try cards next.'

Andrei smiled down at her.

'He's right, Lucy – you should stop now while you're on a winning streak. Why not let him put your money in the safe? Roulette is just a matter of luck, but playing cards requires skill.'

Nettled, Lucy retorted, 'I'm good at cards – at least the games I can play.'

'Nevertheless you would be no match for any experienced player.'

'Why on earth not?'

'Believe me, you wouldn't be. Why not give your money to the first officer and then come and watch me play.'

124

'I want to play myself. I'll bet I can beat you.' The words were out of her mouth before she realised what she'd said, but she didn't regret it. She knew she was being reckless, but it was intensely irritating to be treated like a child by a man who'd previously treated her as a woman.

'I doubt that.'

'Then we'd better have a game.'

'I would not care to take advantage of you in that way. Come, let us have a glass of champagne and watch Sonya play *chemin de fer*.'

'I want to play you at cards,' she said stubbornly. 'Just one game.'

'Very well, but only one game and we'll play for low stakes. I'll go and see if there's a table free.'

He went off and Lucy was surprised to have Leo take her to one side.

'Miss Davenport. I really must advise you not to play with him.'

'Why ever not?'

Leo's pleasant face was troubled as he tried to voice his misgivings diplomatically.

'Because he may be setting you up. It happens all the time, I'm afraid.'

'You heard him – we're only going to have one game and the stakes will be low.'

'It won't stop there. Let me tell you what will happen. You'll win the first game and want to continue, he'll feign reluctance and you'll find yourself insisting. Somehow the stakes will get higher and higher and he won't stop until he's taken you for everything he can.'

Lucy stepped back from him, her grape-green eyes glinting furiously. 'What a deeply insulting insinuation to make. I won't listen to any more of this.'

She strode away from him and across the room to where she found Andrei skilfully shuffling a deck of cards. Leo followed her and struck up a conversation with some passengers standing nearby. It was obvious to Lucy that he was going to monitor the proceedings and it made her angry.

Andrei tried to set the stakes very low, but she overruled him. He dealt them both a hand and Lucy studied her cards carefully, her brow furrowed in concentration, then the game began.

At one point she thought she was going to lose, but she was lucky in the additional cards she was dealt and shortly afterwards the game ended with her victorious.

Sonya came to watch the end and applauded when Lucy lay down her winning hand in triumph.

'You are lucky tonight,' she commented. 'It's not often Andrei loses and I've never known him lose to a woman before – you must have had some good cards. Don't I beg you, play him again – your luck can't possibly hold.'

Irritated that everyone seemed to assume she was just lucky rather than good at the game, Lucy shuffled the cards and dealt them.

'The best of three I think,' she said determinedly.

'If you insist – but let us just play for the fun of the game, not money,' suggested Andrei.

Lucy tossed a large wad of notes onto the table.

'There's my stake,' she said coolly.

A small crowd gathered as she won the second game and lost the third. She raised the stakes again, determined to win a substantial enough amount of money from him to prove that he'd been misguidedly patronising.

Leo tried twice to persuade her to stop, but she ignored him. She won over and over again until she felt drunk with exultation.

At last Andrei said ruefully, 'I'm going to have to call a halt to this – you've virtually cleaned me out.'

Lucy shot a triumphant glance at Leo, but he still looked worried.

'Just one more game,' she begged.

'Very well – but only one.'

It was then that she began to lose.

She couldn't understand it. Each hand that was dealt seemed to be worse than the one that went before and however carefully she played, she didn't seem to be able to win. Several times Andrei suggested that they stop, but she was determined to emerge the victor. By midnight she'd not only lost everything she'd won at roulette – she'd also lost a good deal of her own money as well and scribbled at least a dozen IOUs.

A terrible suspicion that Leo may have been right when he'd told Faye that Andrei and Sonya were adventurers, began to take hold of her.

Had she been ridiculously naive?

Was this what they'd really wanted from her all along?

Had the sex just been a smokescreen, or an added bonus depending on which way you looked at it?

The really humiliating thing was that to get hold of this amount of money she'd need the agreement of her trustees, as her capital didn't become hers to spend as she wished until she either married or reached the age of twenty-one.

How on earth was she going to explain this away? And what if her trustees refused to release the money? She wasn't sure that a gambling debt was legally enforceable and it would be mortifying to have them refuse to honour it.

Andrei stretched out his long legs and looked at her with his opaque gold-green eyes, his face expressionless.

'I think I'm going to have to call it a day,' she said, trying to speak lightly. 'I'm also going to have to ask you to give me time to pay – I don't have that much money on board with me.'

He glanced at the pile of notes and the IOUs, then signalled for a waiter. 'Two cognacs please.'

The people who had been watching began to drift away, only Leo remained, his face troubled.

'I'd like to speak to Miss Davenport alone,' Andrei said to him. Leo looked at Lucy who nodded. He moved a few yards away but, although he was out of earshot, he kept glancing in their direction.

The waiter brought their drinks and Andrei swirled his around his glass before taking a gulp.

'I don't want your money, Lucy,' he said at last. 'Keep your roulette winnings and tear up your IOUs.'

Her face flamed. Now he really *was* treating her like a child.

'I'll pay you what I owe you,' she retorted stiffly.

'No you won't. I don't take money off young girls who get carried away.'

'I always pay my debts.'

'Then pay me some other way.'

'H . . . how?'

The expression on his aquiline face became wolfish.

'I'll consider the debt fully discharged if you become my sexual plaything for the remainder of the voyage.'

Her face flamed again and a little dart of lust jabbed upwards through her belly.

Become Andrei's sexual plaything?

Accommodate his desires for the next couple of days?

The idea was so exciting that she felt short of breath for a few seconds and her mouth went dry.

'Wh . . . what will that entail?' she asked, stalling.

'That you make yourself sexually available to me and do everything I ask you to without question, however aberrant it may seem.'

'And that will wipe the slate clean of all this?' She gestured at the money and IOUs on the table. 'At least take the cash – it wouldn't be right for me to keep everything.'

'I don't think so.' He put the slips of paper in an ashtray and set them alight, they flared briefly, then shrivelled into ash within seconds. He pushed the money across the table to her. 'Give that to the first officer who I see is still hovering a few yards away. He'll put it somewhere safe for you until the end of the voyage.'

'I won't take it.'

Impulsively Lucy scooped it up and crossed the room to where Sonya was still playing *chemin de fer*.

'Andrei won't take this so I insist that you do. Use it to stake you for the rest of the evening.'

Sonya looked over her shoulder to where Andrei was still sitting and raised an enquiring eyebrow at him. He shrugged in reply.

'Very well.' Sonya took the notes and turned back to the game. Leo intercepted Lucy on her way back across the room.

'I hope you're satisfied now,' she said coldly. 'You saw him burn my IOUs and he wouldn't keep the money, so I've given it to Sonya.'

The expression on Leo's face told her that he realised there was more to it than that.

'If you run into anything you can't deal with, don't hesitate to come to me,' was all he said.

Chapter Eight

The wind had freshened and a great gust of salt-laden air hit Amanda in the face as soon as she opened the heavy, watertight door which led out on deck.

There were very few people around, but as she passed one of the lifeboats she heard a muted murmur of voices coming from the shadows behind it, then a hastily suppressed moan and the unmistakable rustle of clothing.

Amanda smiled to herself and waited until she was well out of earshot before she leant over the rail to look at the black, boiling sea. It was much rougher tonight and the spray had turned the deck slippery underfoot.

She had made the crossing between New York and Southampton several times and sometimes she thought she'd like to spend her life in transit.

People behaved differently when they were travelling. Everyone knew that the journey would be soon over and they would go their separate ways, so they tended to behave with less restraint. Friendships and relationships which would have taken weeks or months to form on dry land were often forged in days.

Amanda was in no hurry for the voyage to end. It was true she was slightly bored with Edward, but it wasn't really his fault – it was just that at times his youth and inexperience showed.

At first it had been very exhilarating to have attracted a man so many years her junior. She'd been both envied and censured by her friends and she'd enjoyed being the centre of so much gossip, but now she was ready to move on.

She'd briefly hoped to replace Edward with Andrei – that would really give her social circle something to talk about. But it hadn't taken her long to realise that although Andrei might take her to bed, his life was too entwined with Sonya's for him to fulfil any meaningful role in her own.

She was also aware that in London her husband was waiting for her to come home. It was almost time for them to spend a few weeks with his parents in their ghastly, freezing castle in Scotland.

On the whole her husband didn't make too many demands on her, but he was adamant about her attendance at the annual shooting party given by his father.

The people invited were always anathema to her. All they wanted to do was tramp over rain-swept moors all day slaughtering things, then in the evening drink whisky and dance highland reels.

It was always so cold up there too. The rooms were invariably arctic and her parents-in-law considered the idea of a fire in the bedroom decadent in the extreme. And she wouldn't manage a decent bath in weeks as the water was nothing more than a tepid trickle.

Amanda shuddered at the prospect and continued to pace along the deck, pulling her brocade wrap more closely around her. It really was getting rough and the ship was rolling around in a way that threatened to become uncomfortable.

She wondered what she was doing outside. The smoky atmosphere in the *fumoir* had suddenly seemed uncomfortable, so she'd thought she'd get a breath of fresh air, but it really was quite chilly tonight and she'd have enough of that over the next few weeks to last her a lifetime.

Her reverie was interrupted by the approach of a sailor.

'Captain's compliments, ma'am, but he wants all passengers off the open decks – we may be running into a storm.'

In the soft orange glow from one of the overhead deck lights Amanda could see that he was a strapping dark-haired youth with the sort of muscles that threatened to burst out of his uniform.

'I was just going in,' she told him. 'I hope it isn't a bad storm.'

'The captain's changing course in the hope of avoiding it. Would you like me to escort you back inside?'

'There's no need, but thank you.'

With a slight smile Amanda continued along the deck towards the nearest door. She'd gone about fifty yards when the ship suddenly pitched into a deep trough and she lost her footing on the slippery deck. She began to roll towards the rail just as a massive wave crashed down next to her, drenching her with its spray.

She was going to be swept overboard!

She scrabbled at the deck with her nails, but there was no purchase to be found on the smooth wood. She screamed but the sound was lost in the howling of the wind.

Another wave crashed over her and dragged her several yards further towards the rail. She could see a lifeboat over to her left – if she could just make it that far she could hold onto one of the ropes.

A burly, barrel-chested figure suddenly appeared from out of the darkness and dragged her to her feet, then wound a muscular arm around her waist. She dimly recognised the sailor who'd spoken to her a few minutes earlier and clung thankfully to him as he steered her towards the door.

But the strength of the wave which broke over them a few seconds later was too much, even for him, and they were knocked sprawling against the side of the lifeboat. A huge, hairy hand clamped around her wrist and then he lifted her bodily and shoved her into the lifeboat under the cover of a tarpaulin. Dazed and drenched, Amanda crawled completely under cover and heard him scramble in behind her.

In the darkness she heard the sound of his ragged breathing and then he asked, 'Are you alright, ma'am?'

'I think so – thanks to you.'

Above their heads the storm raged and crashed while torrential rain hammered down on their canvas roof. She tried to wriggle herself into a sitting position but her skirt had become caught on something on the rim of the boat. She crouched on all fours and reached behind her trying to free it.

A sudden flash of lightning illuminated the scene and she saw that the sailor was struggling to secure the edge of the tarpaulin, which was flapping wildly in the wind and allowing icy spatterings of rain inside.

The lightning was followed by three more flashes in quick succession and she saw that he'd frozen in the act of struggling with the heavy canvas and his eyes were riveted on the firm swellings of her buttocks. She realised that her soaked champagne silk camiknickers had gone completely transparent and she might as well have been kneeling on all fours naked from the waist down.

She tugged hard but her skirt remained stubbornly caught.

'I can't free my skirt – it's caught on something,' she said into the pitch darkness which followed the lightning.

'I'll see to it, ma'am.'

She heard him moving behind her and then a large hand brushed against her wet, silk-clad bottom. The hand withdrew as swiftly as if she'd been red-hot.

'I can't reach it,' he mumbled.

Exasperated, Amanda jerked hard at the material, but it remained obstinately caught. She was kneeling on the base of the lifeboat, unable to turn over and sit down and the position was rapidly becoming uncomfortable.

'Please try again.'

He crawled closer and reached blindly for her skirt, just as she raised her backside in the hope of lifting the material enough to ease the tension which was holding it so firmly in place.

She felt his hand on her thighs and gasped. He groped at her feverishly for a few moments, rubbing and kneading her rump, then pressing roughly between her legs.

The results were electric. Amanda forgot about her considerable physical discomfort as a fire swept through her loins, leaving her burningly, painfully aroused.

She wanted this hulking sailor's shaft inside her now. She wanted him to take her and fill her up with his maleness, to pump in and out of her in a hot animal coupling which owed nothing to finesse.

He fell back with a groan saying, 'I'm sorry . . . I didn't mean to . . . I'll lose my job now . . .'

'Fuck me!'

The words were out of her mouth before she realised she was going to say them. There was a thick, heavy silence for a few seconds, even the wind and rain abating as her words echoed around under the tarpaulin.

'Didn't you hear me?' she demanded. 'I want you to fuck me!'

She reached awkwardly behind her and made contact with the soaking canvas of his trousers. Her hand closed over the massive, rock-hard bulge of his manhood and caressed it. He let out a low growling noise, gulped and then grabbed for her. He bent over her from behind, groping and fondling her breasts and bottom, his canvas-covered erection pressed painfully into the cleft between her buttocks.

He backed away long enough to tear her flimsy camiknickers

from her with a damp ripping sound and then shoved his hand against her vulva and massaged it hard. She pressed down, already excited almost to the point of orgasm.

There was no room for manoeuvre, no hope of adopting a more comfortable position, just his muscular body bent over her slender one, her rump held high up in the air by her trapped skirt.

He rubbed away at her dripping sex, pushing two fingers inside her and moving them clumsily around. Amanda was panting so hard that she became dizzy. His huge hands encircled her thighs and parted them, then he fumbled with his trousers and she felt the swollen end of his shaft nudging up against her. He moved it up and down then jabbed it wildly against her sex-valley.

She shifted position slightly and felt it slide over her dripping membranes until it found her hidden entrance. Two hard, bucking thrusts and it was inside her, making her feel as if her eyes were bulging from her head and her tongue was about to hang out of her mouth as it filled her completely.

It was a rough and frantic coupling as he bent over her, pumping vigorously in and out, the rough hair on his thighs scraping abrasively over the silken skin of her posterior. He clutched and squeezed any parts of her he could reach, clamping his great hands on her breasts and hips and squeezing greedily.

She came quickly; a heavy, almost painful climax which felt wrenched from the very depths of her womb. She could feel her dark hair whipping wetly against her cheeks as he drove away at her, impaling her distended, dripping furrow, almost splitting her in two with great rolling waves of pleasure.

He erupted volcanically inside her, his body racked by long-lived, jerking spasms. She felt him about to subside as she was on the brink of coming again and grabbed his hand. She shoved it between her legs and worked herself against it for a few seconds, then spiralled into another dizzying, jolting orgasm.

He slumped heavily over her back and at last her skirt gave way under the weight. She collapsed onto the bare boards on the floor of the boat and he sank heavily down beside her. They lay in gasping silence for a few minutes and Amanda made a move to separate from him. Unbelievably she felt his huge organ swelling again and a hairy arm clamped around her waist.

He was gentler this time, stroking her breasts and murmuring in her ear, but the same hot, burning excitement swept over her and she goaded him on to greater efforts, forgetting for once that she was a lady and using obscenities she wasn't even aware that she knew.

The wind and rain had stopped by the time they sat up and he threw aside the tarpaulin to let in the light from the deck lamps.

He fastened his trousers while Amanda tried dazedly to repair her appearance. He leapt out of the boat and held out his arms for her to slide into, reverting to being a respectful sailor. Amanda clutched her brocade wrap closely around her, grateful for its enveloping folds as he escorted her to the door leading back inside.

'Would you like me to take you back to your cabin, ma'am?' he asked, keeping his eyes averted.

'I'll be fine from here, thank you.'

She was horrified by her appearance once she reached the sanctuary of her stateroom. Her silk stockings hung in tatters around her legs, her hair was wet and tangled and streaks of dirt covered her arms, face and clothing.

She ran herself a deep bath and slipped dreamily out of her ruined clothes. The warm water felt wonderful as she immersed her aching limbs and tender private parts.

Humming to herself, she soaped her legs voluptuously. It

was only then that she remembered she'd left the tatters of her champagne silk camiknickers lying in the lifeboat.

The ship seemed to be rolling and pitching a lot as Lucy and Andrei left the *fumoir* and made their way along the corridor. Lucy kept one hand on the handrail and held onto Andrei with the other as they lurched along, struggling to keep their balance.

'I hope it doesn't keep this up long,' said Lucy dubiously. 'I was seasick for the entire voyage on the way out.'

'I think it was worse while we were playing cards,' he replied, 'but we were too engrossed to notice. I suspect that it will have subsided completely soon.'

They were on their way to the Russians' suite and Lucy was torn between erotic anticipation and nervous apprehension. What if he wanted her to do something she found distasteful? But it was too late to start thinking about that now – she'd entered into an agreement and she'd have to stick to it.

They arrived at the lift doors and paused while they waited for it to descend. As soon as they were inside Andrei turned to face her and drew her breasts out of the low-cut front of her gown.

'Andrei – what if someone else gets in!' she exclaimed.

'That's the last protest I wish to hear from your beautiful lips,' he said, bending his head to flicker his tongue wickedly over her nipples. 'If you object to anything else I choose to do, you will have broken our agreement and I will have to punish you.'

His words made a *frisson* of something dark and shivery ripple down her spine.

She stood, pressed back against the wall, while her nipples were sucked and licked, torn between enjoyment at what he was doing and terror that the lift would shudder to a halt and someone else would join them.

When the lift did stop at the deck on which his suite was situated, she made an automatic gesture to push her breasts back inside her dress, but he stopped her by seizing her wrists and holding them behind her. She struggled but he tightened his grip.

'Andrei! Let me go! *Anyone* could be in the corridor,' she hissed as the doors slid open. Thankfully it was deserted but she was uncomfortably aware that the door of one of the cabins could open and someone emerge at any moment.

'I don't think you have completely grasped the extent of our agreement,' he told her as he propelled her out of the lift. 'If I wish to take you on our table in the restaurant with everyone watching, I will do so. Now for arguing with me we're going to walk to my suite with your breasts on full display.'

Lucy bit her lip to stop herself saying anything else, thinking that if anyone saw her she'd die.

The walk along the corridor seemed endless and it was with a sense of great relief that they reached his suite and he paused to put his key in the lock.

He held the door for her and she walked in, then stopped dead in horror when she saw Stephan tidying some papers on the other side of the room. Her hands would have flown up to cover herself, but Andrei still retained a firm grasp on her wrists.

She went a vivid pink as the valet's cold blue eyes surveyed her impassively. Then he looked at Andrei and asked, 'Shall I fetch some refreshment, Count?'

'Cognac.'

To Lucy it seemed to take forever for the man to arrange a decanter and two glasses on a tray, carry it across the room, and place it on the lacquered coffee table.

It got worse.

As Stephan poured two shots, Andrei reached across and carelessly fondled her breasts until she felt so degraded she could scarcely resist leaping to her feet and bolting from the room.

She heaved a sigh of relief when he eventually said, 'That will be all, Stephan. I'll ring if I want you.' The man bowed and silently withdrew. Andrei turned to look at Lucy. 'You have much to learn,' he told her sombrely.

'That I'm no good at cards, for example,' she retorted, unwilling to let him see how affected she was by his shaming treatment of her in front of the valet.

'I think you've already learnt that.'

He leant back and stretched out his legs.

'Now you will pleasure me with your mouth.'

Lucy bit her lip and hesitated. Although she found the idea quite exciting, she'd never done such a thing before and wasn't sure how to go about it.

'I . . . I'm not sure what to do,' she admitted.

He raised a surprised eyebrow at her.

'Take out my penis and do what comes naturally – I'll direct you if I find what you're doing doesn't please me. No, leave your breasts on display,' he added as she made a movement to pull her dress over them.

She knelt beside him and slowly unbuttoned his trousers. His member sprang out, hard and ready, the glans dark and engorged. Tentatively Lucy kissed the end and was rewarded when it twitched appreciatively. She kissed her way delicately down the shaft, then used her tongue to inscribe swirling circles around his testicles.

His manhood felt hot and heavy in her hand and two drops of clear liquid had formed on the glans. They tasted salty when she licked them.

He groaned softly and murmured, 'Take it in your mouth.'

Obediently she slipped the first couple of inches between her lips and began to suck gently. He groaned again and she felt a stirring of power that she could have this effect on him. He buried his hand in her hair urging her to take more of him in.

There was the sound of a key in the lock and, in alarm, Lucy tried to look up, but his hand kept her head firmly between his thighs.

She could tell by the rustle of taffeta that it was Sonya before she even heard her voice saying, 'Hello again, you two.'

'How was your evening?' asked Andrei, raising his hips slightly to encourage Lucy to continue.

'Good. Lucy, you'll be delighted to know that your money brought me luck and I almost tripled it.'

Lucy managed to wrench her head free and cried, 'Andrei – surely you can't want me to carry on with this while Sonya is in the room!'

'You pleasured Sonya earlier this evening in front of a room full of people – why do you now object to doing the same for me in front of her?'

'It . . . it's embarrassing,' she said lamely.

'I'm not embarrassed. Are you embarrassed, Sonya?'

'On the contrary, I should enjoy watching very much if Lucy will permit me.'

She sank into an armchair across the room and put her feet up on a small table in front of her.

'Please continue, Lucy – just forget I'm here.'

Reluctantly Lucy bent her golden head and began again. She was horrified when she heard Sonya ring a bell and knew that Stephan would soon answer the summons. She was also aware that there was absolutely nothing she could do about it, so she continued with her task, keeping her face buried in Andrei's groin.

She heard Stephan come in and Sonya ask for a liqueur, then he took his time about taking it to her, before he left the room again.

Lucy sucked, licked and flicked at Andrei's throbbing column for what seemed like an eternity, exploring every inch of it. She experimented with different ways of getting more of it into her mouth and was rewarded by his grunts of pleasure. At last he told her to stop.

She raised her head to see Sonya, her skirt pulled up around her waist, her camiknickers around her thighs, elegantly masturbating as she watched them. Her crimson labia had a provocative pout which Lucy found arousing and she sank onto the sofa beside Andrei to watch the other woman touch herself.

It was only a few hours ago that she'd stroked those swollen, velvety folds herself. She found it intensely exciting to watch the skilful way Sonya caressed herself, until eventually her eyes fluttered closed and her head dropped back as she enjoyed her climax.

'I shall go to bed soon,' Sonya said, yawning and showing the tip of her pink tongue. 'It's been another exciting day. Andrei, will you need Stephan again tonight?'

'I don't think so.'

'Then I shall make use of him for a while. Goodnight.' She pulled her camiknickers back around her waist, let her skirt fall, then left the room.

Andrei reached across and rubbed Lucy's mound carelessly. 'I hope you aren't tired yet – it's going to be a long night.'

Faye couldn't sleep.

The storm had ended as swiftly as it had begun, but she'd found the pitching of the vessel disturbing and lay wide awake, half expecting it to start up again.

Eventually, in the early hours, she got out of bed and pulled her hyacinth-blue satin dressing gown on over her white lace nightgown. The dressing gown was a favourite of hers and was edged with piping of a deeper blue, with her initials embroidered on the pocket.

She went outside and saw that an almost full moon had risen and was throwing a corridor of shimmering silver across the sea directly to her verandah. The sight soothed her and she rested her arms on the rail, trying to count the dazzling array of tiny stars which were scattered across the inky sky in far greater profusion than she'd ever seen at home.

This voyage was certainly turning out to be more enjoyable than the outward one. She already felt that in a few short days diverse, unimaginable pleasures had opened out for her. Her brief couplings in the past seemed meaningless now that she'd been introduced to much more decadent gratification by Andrei and Sonya.

And she'd seduced Leo. That had been enormously enjoyable too. She felt a little shiver of secret carnality whenever she thought about all the different experiences she'd had over the last few days.

What a pity it would all come to an end so soon.

She'd be staying with her married sister, Emily, until her parents returned from America – but maybe that wouldn't be such a bad thing. Emily was completely taken up with her children and unlikely to expect her to account for every minute of her time. Perhaps with some careful planning she'd be able to arrange some erotic interludes.

There were several dashing officers of her acquaintance she wouldn't mind seducing. She knew she should really be looking for a husband, that was what was expected of her, but at the moment the idea of broadening her experience seemed much more attractive.

She supposed that once they reached London she wouldn't

see Sonya and Andrei again, unless they were staying in the city for a while, but she thought she'd heard them talking about the South of France. How wonderful it must be to travel around, going wherever you liked, doing whatever you wanted.

Although it must be awful to be exiled from your own country and never be able to return there however much you wanted to.

Her thoughts turned to that afternoon in Sonya's bedroom and she felt herself blushing in the darkness as she remembered being tied to the bed, her legs spread-eagled and her bottom high up in the air.

Who would have thought it would be so enjoyable to be spanked? Though whether the spanking itself would have been as stomach-churningly exciting without the antidote of being brought to a climax before and afterwards, she wasn't sure.

It had been deeply humiliating to have Andrei come into the room and see her like that, her backside glowing from Sonya's slaps, unable to move or cover herself up, but it had also been tremendously arousing.

Faye pressed her thighs together and felt a lewd little tingling in her groin as she remembered how he too had spanked her, his elegant, well-manicured hand rising and falling over the full globes of her posterior already made tender by Sonya's stinging slaps.

She reached down and squeezed her own bottom experimentally. It didn't feel particularly sore now and the marks had faded by the time she'd woken from her nap, but it would be a long time before the memory faded.

She'd seen Lucy leave the *fumoir* with Andrei and wondered whether she was back in her stateroom yet. She hadn't heard her moving around. Maybe she should go and tap on her door.

Perhaps even now Andrei was spanking her. Lucy's pert buttocks were much smaller than her own ample ones, so there would be less to smack. Did that mean it would hurt more or less?

There was still a drowsy lingering pleasure between her thighs and she wished she wasn't alone. The voyage was too short for her to waste any of it.

She went back into her cabin and then out into the corridor. She knocked softly at Lucy's door but there was no reply. She knew there was no hope of sleep, at least for a while, so she decided to go for a walk.

The ship appeared to be deserted. She wandered along the corridors and through the main lounge without seeing anyone. She might have been alone on an abandoned ship with only the throbbing of the engines and an echoing throbbing in her sex to keep her company.

She strolled through the huge double doors leading into the first-class restaurant and then paused in the shadows at the top of the sweeping flight of stairs when she heard a noise.

The room was lit only by a single cluster of Lalique lamps to the left of the foot of the stairs. On the table next to the lamps, amid the silver cutlery and crystal, three people moved in a synchronised rhythm, like swimmers performing a well-rehearsed routine.

She recognised the sultry South American beauty she'd seen in the pool room earlier that evening, but now she was with two men. She was flat on her back across the table, her skirt around her waist and her tiny scarlet panties around one ankle. Her long, tanned legs were wound around the waist of her earlier dancing partner as he shafted her in a vigorous erotic rhythm.

Her head was flung back and her mouth open to receive the penis of the other man who was standing just behind her head. His member moved in and out of her parted lips to exactly the same rhythm.

It was a wanton scene and it made Faye gasp in shock. She stepped back into the shadows so they wouldn't see her and watched avidly. What a marvellously salacious scenario it was. She wondered what it would feel like to have two men penetrating her simultaneously.

The man who was pumping in and out between the woman's thighs was caressing her hips and flanks, while the other was fondling her large, olive-tipped breasts.

Faye wondered what they would think if she glided down the stairs to join them. Would they welcome her or would her presence be an intrusion?

She tried to imagine lying across the table, the starched white linen of the tablecloth stiff and cool underneath her, her legs spread, perhaps with her knees bent and her feet on the edge of the table.

Maybe before the two men entered her, one would kneel between her thighs to explore her with his tongue and make sure she was wet and ready, probing every moist crevice, savouring the taste of her.

Perhaps the other man would kiss her face and neck before fastening his mouth to hers and flickering his tongue between her lips. Then he'd . . .

A sound behind her made her jump and she spun round to see Leo walking towards her. She moved hastily across to him, reluctant to have him find her watching three other people at their licentious play.

'Miss Faulkner . . . Faye!' he exclaimed. 'What are you doing up at this time of night?'

'I couldn't sleep,' she told him truthfully, 'so I thought I'd go for a walk.'

Dressed as always in his immaculate white uniform, Leo looked infinitely desirable. She felt a renewed stirring high up in her sex at the sight of him. It was as if the two of them were alone on the high seas, with all the vast expanses of the ship as their erotic playground.

'Leo . . .' she murmured, moving close to him and winding her arms around his neck.

'Faye – please don't,' he begged her. 'I was very wrong to . . . to do what I did last night. I took advantage of your innocence and . . . temporary inebriation and I can't apologise enough.'

'Don't apologise,' breathed Faye. 'It was wonderful.'

She pressed herself against him and was gratified to feel a distinct hardening of his groin.

A sudden crash from behind made them both start and he moved swiftly away from her to the top of the stairs leading down into the restaurant.

She gathered from his muffled exclamation that he'd seen what was happening below. She went to stand beside him, but he hustled her back away from the stairs before she could see anything.

'What is it?' she asked innocently.

'Nothing you should see,' he told her, steering her across the room and then down the corridor. 'There are things that take place on board this ship no lady should ever be exposed to. I'm afraid that we have some particularly raffish passengers aboard for this crossing – and they all seem to be friends of those white Russians. I warned Miss Davenport not to play cards with Count Andrei – or whatever he calls himself.'

'But he wouldn't take Lucy's money, even though he won,' protested Faye.

'There's more than one way to take advantage of youth and inexperience,' retorted Leo grimly. 'I'd clap him in irons if it were up to me.'

They were walking past the library and Faye took his hand and pulled him inside. In the muted light of just a couple of lamps the large room was full of shadowy corners. The chestnut-panelled walls held row after row of shelves crammed with leather-bound books. Dark blue Wilton rugs were laid at intervals on the polished parquet floor and leather covered armchairs were arranged in groups.

'Why are we coming in here?' asked Leo. 'I'll escort you back to your cabin and then there's something I have to attend to.'

Faye knew he meant the trio in the restaurant, but she had a mission for him which was much more urgent than spoiling someone else's fun. She wound her arms around his neck and pressed her full breasts against his tunic. He tried to disentangle her arms saying, 'Please . . . don't do that.'

But Faye had a wanton heat between her legs and she was determined to overcome his scruples.

'You don't really mean that, do you?' she murmured, letting one hand slide down over his chest to his groin. She caressed the rapidly growing rod she found there, and then sank to her knees and undid his fly.

'Faye . . . I can't let you – aaah!' he moaned as she drew his semi-erect shaft from his trousers and took it in her mouth. He was silent after that, except for a few barely suppressed groans, while she worked on him with more enthusiasm than expertise. But it had the desired effect because almost immediately he became ramrod hard.

When she was satisfied that he was well past the point of no return, Faye rose to her feet and led him to one of the leather-topped writing tables. She sat on the edge and lay back, then reached out for him.

Like a man in the grip of a tropical fever he covered her body with his own, kissing her frantically and stroking her breasts over the hyacinth satin of her robe. He pushed it impatiently apart to reveal the white lace of her nightgown, her heavy breasts semi-visible through the open weave of the delicate fabric.

With a groan he fastened his mouth to one pebble-hard nipple over the lace and began to suck. Faye could feel the strength of his erection digging into her hip and rubbed herself demandingly against him.

He pulled the front of her nightgown down, paused to stare greedily at her naked, coral-tipped nipples and then caressed one while sucking hard on the other.

Faye felt as though her nipples must be joined to her sex by taut but delicate strands of wire, because every caress evoked an answering response in the hidden depths of her female parts.

He dragged at the belt on her robe, untying it so it lay in a pool of deep-blue satin around them. He pushed her nightgown up her thighs and fumbled between her legs, making her gasp and open them wide for him.

The flesh-groove of her labia was slick and sweet with her juices, which had been forming steadily for a while now. He dabbled his fingers in her distended folds, then thrust them high up inside her, grunting with satisfaction when he felt how wet she was. She moved against him, hooking her thighs around his, her nightgown up around her waist.

The leather beneath her felt cool and smooth against her bare bottom and she wriggled voluptuously, driving Leo wild. He mounted her and plunged his shaft deep into her core, then began to ride her, already at full gallop.

It felt wildly abandoned to be coupling on a table in the deserted library, aware that they could be interrupted at any moment by another insomniac passenger.

It was a short, breathless ride, but it didn't last long enough for Faye. It was only a couple of minutes before Leo emptied himself into her and they lay quietly, his face buried in her breasts.

She stroked his hair and then, when he began to feel heavy, she murmured, 'That was good – now it's going to be even better.' He raised his head to look at her questioningly. 'I haven't finished even if you have – shall we go back to my cabin?'

Chapter Nine

Lucy awoke as the cool light of dawn filtered through the curtains in Andrei's bedroom. He was lying on his side with one arm flung over her, a hand on her breast. He looked younger in sleep, much more relaxed, the planes of his face less harsh.

She felt stiff and sticky, but there was still a faint, throbbing heat between her legs, reminding her of just how she'd spent the early hours of the morning. She stretched tentatively and winced as the muscles in her thighs shrieked in protest.

She glanced at the clock on the bedside table and decided she'd better return to her cabin. She daren't risk Winnie arriving to find her bed hadn't been slept in. She could gossip to the other servants at some stage and Aunt Sarah might get to hear of it. Besides, she could do with a few hours more sleep and she had no wish to be served breakfast in bed by Stephan.

She slipped from under the covers and looked around for her dress, but it was nowhere in sight. She found it in the sitting room and stepped hurriedly into it. She managed to regain the sanctuary of her cabin without seeing anyone and hastily rumpled the sheets and punched the pillows before running herself a deep, warm bath.

She lay back in it while the scented bath salts she'd tipped in soothed her aching limbs. She felt languid and sated as she allowed vivid images of last night – or rather earlier this morning – to flit across her mind. She caressed her own breasts, toying with her swollen, slightly sore nipples. When she gently touched herself between the thighs, her clitoris still felt like a tight little knot protruding fleshily between her outer sex-lips.

She'd just climbed out of the bath and wrapped herself in a huge, snowy towel when there was a knock on her door.

'Who is it?' she called.

'Andrei.'

Lucy opened the door and stepped back. He must have awakened as she left because he'd obviously had a shower – his hair was still wet – and he was fully dressed in flannels and a white shirt with a sweater knotted casually around his neck.

'I was just about to catch up on some sleep,' she told him, yawning drowsily.

'Later. Now we're going for a stroll around the deck – get dressed.' He sprawled on the bed while she looked vaguely through her wardrobe, wondering what to wear. He came to stand beside her and watched while she flicked through the clothes.

'This dress I think,' he told her, taking it from its hanger and examining it carefully. It was a printed black and white silk day dress with a square neckline and elbow-length sleeves. It buttoned down the front with large black buttons and had a tightly belted waist and flared skirt.

Lucy selected a camisole from a drawer and was about to drop it over her head, but Andrei stopped her.

'No underwear.'

She looked at him in dismay – the dress was only of thin silk and she was almost certain her nakedness under it would be obvious, particularly if the light was behind her. But something in his expression warned her not to demur, so she buttoned up the dress and sat on the edge of the bed to roll her stockings up.

She was about to secure them in place with two black lace garters when he said, 'Now this.'

He produced something from his pocket which looked like

nothing she'd ever seen before – a sort of girdle or bridle in supple black leather – and held it out for her to inspect. It was a few moments before she noticed that it had four small suspenders dangling from it, but it didn't look anything like a suspender belt.

'What on earth am I supposed to do with this?' she asked in bewilderment.

'Lift your dress around your waist and I'll show you.'

Nonplussed, she did as he asked and then watched in horror as he held the leather girdle for her to step into.

'I'm not wearing that,' she said faintly.

'Yes you are – remember our agreement?'

Slowly, reluctantly, she stepped into it and allowed Andrei to draw it up her silk-stockinged legs and fix it into position, while she watched in the mirror.

There was a narrow strip around her waist and another strip which ran from it down the cleft between her firm buttocks.

Just below the small circle of her anus the leather split into two and went forwards then upwards to rejoin the band around her waist at the front, about four inches from the centre on either side. Four small leather suspenders dangled from it adding to its obscene appearance.

The effect of the girdle was to hold her outer sex-lips wide apart so her inner lips and clitoris were boldly on display. Her clitoris stood stiffly to attention, dark and swollen and covered by a slick film of moisture. Her pale fuzz of pubic floss framed it like some sort of lewd halo.

'That . . . that looks depraved,' she whispered as she looked at her reflection in the mirror.

'I agree. Delightfully, lusciously, licentiously depraved.'

He kissed her neck, then fastened the suspenders to her stocking tops, his hands lingering on the soft skin above them. He ran his finger under the strip running down the cleft between her buttocks, then tightened it slightly until it practically vanished into the groove.

'Let's take that stroll. You may lower your skirt.'

Lucy looked anxiously at her reflection. The skirt was fairly full and fell in folds around her legs. As long as they didn't get too close to anyone, perhaps no one would notice.

It was cool out on deck, but the early morning sun was already strong enough to take the edge off the chill. With Andrei's arm around her waist, Lucy walked along beside him, thankful that the deck was deserted.

The strip of leather running down between her buttocks worked its way deeper and deeper into her cleft, the friction of it, particularly against the bud of her anus, stimulating her against her will.

They stopped by one of the funnels where, sheltered from the wind, Andrei slowly undid the buttons at the front of the dress from the waist down to the hem.

'We will walk further.'

To Lucy's horror, as soon as they left the shelter of the funnel, her skirt was caught by the breeze and blew up around her waist. She shrieked and made a grab for it, hastily smoothing it back down.

'Don't touch it again, or I will tie your hands behind your back.'

'Please, Andrei – I can't bear to have anyone see me like this.'

'You can bear what I tell you to bear. Now release your dress.'

Somehow Lucy found herself obeying him and it immediately blew up at the front, but remained around her calves at the back. They recommenced their walk with her sex and buttocks sometimes on blatant display and sometimes hidden among the swirling folds of her skirt. She clenched her teeth every time they rounded a corner in case there should be anyone about.

They reached the prow of the ship where the breeze was particularly playful and Andrei paused again as her skirt was whipped up around her waist.

Without a word he ran his forefinger along the slippery grooves between her inner and outer labia, feeling how heavily engorged they were. She shivered but remained motionless as he inserted the finger deep inside her and slowly rotated it.

Despite the cool, gusty breeze which blew along the deck she felt hot and her velvety walls clenched around the intrusive digit. She could feel her hot juices beginning to trickle slowly from her and squirmed as he probed and explored her dripping quim.

He circled her clit – taking full advantage of the way the girdle made it jut out – and came teasingly close to it, but didn't actually touch it. Lucy could feel perspiration breaking out on her brow as she mentally urged him to stroke the responsive little nub of flesh into the blissful release of a climax.

Her skirt blew back around her legs again and he removed his hand.

'You may button your skirt now,' he told her. Heaving a sigh of relief, Lucy fastened it with clumsy fingers. They continued with their walk and a few minutes later she saw to her utter terror that another couple were walking their way.

Her hands fluttered down to keep her dress in position and Andrei said, 'If you touch that skirt again you will not enjoy the consequences. Come – we will lean against the rail while they go by.'

Trembling with nervousness, Lucy leant back against the rail by Andrei's side. The breeze was blowing straight at them and thankfully it flattened her skirt against her legs. She knew it was less likely to blow up while the buttons were fastened, but even so it was still a risk.

As the couple drew level, Lucy recognised them as two of Andrei's friends. They were both still in evening dress and obviously hadn't yet turned in for the night. Behind her, she could feel her skirt whipping upwards, but it remained taut against her thighs at the front. She almost let out a yelp when she felt Andrei's hand running up the back of her thigh to linger on the bare flesh above her stocking top.

She was shocked when he hailed them and began a conversation, while pushing his fingers between her thighs from behind and toying with her slippery, swollen private parts. The way the girdle held her open made it easy for him to touch her, even though she tried to press her thighs together.

She felt like a creature, an object, as he impaled her on two fingers and moved then stealthily up and down. He was enjoying her embarrassment, her shame, as he fondled her for his own degenerate pleasure.

She kept her eyes fixed on a distant point on the deck and took no part in the conversation, convinced that the couple could see what he was doing to her. She was certain that if she met their eyes they would be knowing and amused.

Andrei began to circle her clit again, sometimes just touching the shaft lightly, sometimes avoiding it. Her sex-lips felt so distended in the restricting girdle that it was almost painful. The desire for satisfaction was unbearably strong, so much so that if they'd been alone she would have darted her hand between her legs and given the throbbing sliver of flesh the stimulation it needed to bring herself to a climax.

She could feel herself on the brink, and was torn between wanting to come immediately, regardless of the other two, and wanting him to hold off until they'd gone.

It was with a great sense of relief that at last they said their laughing goodbyes and walked away.

'You absolute *bastard*,' said Lucy feelingly.

She felt that she would pass out if she didn't climax soon, but the couple were still in view. Just at that moment her skirt blew up at the front, revealing the girdle in all its obscene glory.

Moving slightly closer to her so that his body blocked the sight of her exposed vulva should they turn round, Andrei grasped the strap running between her buttocks with one hand and pulled it upwards. Immediately her outer lips were dragged even further apart. At the same time he squeezed the head of her clitoris and she let out a tiny cry as her body jerked convulsively into orgasm.

She sagged against the rail, aware that her release was even stronger than usual, fuelled by the dark, depraved pleasure of the situation.

Her dress fluttered back down over her thighs so that as an elderly man passed a few moments later, he saw nothing untoward.

'All this fresh air has given me an appetite,' remarked Andrei. 'Shall we go and eat breakfast together?'

Lucy knew that it wasn't really a question.

Amanda woke up feeling hungry. It was an unaccustomed feeling for her so early in the morning, usually coffee and a cigarette were all she could manage. She rang for the stewardess and ordered grapefruit, scrambled eggs, grilled tomatoes, mushrooms, toast, marmalade and coffee.

She was just spooning a chunk of chilled grapefruit in her mouth, wincing pleasurably at its acidity, when Edward arrived.

He looked clean-cut and handsome in his immaculate tweeds – a far cry from the hulking sailor she'd had the night before. He helped himself to coffee and then sat at the foot of her bed to flick through the ship's daily newspaper, reading any items of interest aloud.

'It's the captain's gala dinner tonight,' he reminded her. 'I suppose that means you'll be spending all afternoon at the hairdresser.'

'I may not be able to get an appointment,' she said, tucking into her eggs with great enjoyment. Edward looked at her admiringly. She was wearing a peach satin robe and her dark hair fell to her shoulders in a series of glossy waves. Her brown eyes looked huge in her delicate face and without her make-up she looked younger.

'Do you really have to go up to Scotland as soon as we arrive back in England?' he asked abruptly. It had been on his mind for most of the voyage. Since their affair had begun some months previously they'd not been separated for more than a few days and when in London usually managed to see each other several times a week.

'I must, I'm afraid – Charles absolutely insists. It will be a month of sheer purgatory as far as I'm concerned. Lucky you being able to stay in London.'

'I don't want to be there if you're not. Can't you wangle me an invitation somehow?'

'Not really – if it were anyone but the parents-in-law I might manage it, but they always invite their own set.'

'Well, is there anyone else with a house in the area I might be able to stay with?'

'Not that I know of. I'm sorry, Edward, but we're just going to have to put up with it.'

Edward's pleasant, even features became sullen.

'Tell Charles you're not going.'

Amanda sighed and spread a piece of toast lavishly with butter. 'Must we keep going over this? You're being very boring about it.'

'The voyage will be over in two days and then I won't see you for ages. And we haven't exactly spent much time together while we've been at sea, have we? When you're not at the hairdresser, you're with those two Russians. Where did you get to last night? You vanished again and I spent over an hour looking for you.'

Amanda shot him a bored glance from under her lashes. Really, Edward was never happy unless they were joined at the hip. Whatever made him think that she was answerable to him? Even Charles didn't demand that she account for every moment of her time.

'As a matter of fact I had quite an adventure. I went on deck for a breath of fresh air just as the storm was getting up and I was nearly swept overboard by a massive wave.'

'What! Why didn't you tell me?'

'I'm telling you now. I really thought my number was up, but some big, brawny sailor came to my rescue. He tried to help me to one of the doors leading back inside, but another wave knocked us both over. He managed to get us to one of the lifeboats and we crawled under the tarpaulin and waited it out there.'

Amanda considered for a moment hinting about what had taken place, but dismissed the idea out of hand. No, no one must ever know about that. It really was beyond the pale to have done such a thing and she was almost, but not quite, ashamed of herself this morning.

But it had been tremendously exciting – the sort of hot, dirty sex that would have shocked Edward. This really had been quite a voyage so far. First she'd allowed Andrei's valet to have carnal knowledge of her and then she'd practically begged a sailor to take her on all fours like an animal.

Maybe up in Scotland there'd be some ghillie or tenant farmer she could seduce.

'What would you like to do this morning?' asked Edward, interrupting her reverie. The expression on his face indicated what he'd like to do, his eyes were fixed on her creamy cleavage and she didn't have to look to tell that beneath his tweed trousers would be a tell-tale bulge.

'I thought I might go and write some letters in the library.'

'Let's do some clay-pigeon shooting – that would be more fun.'

'For you, you mean. I'm going to see enough of men pointing guns at things in the next month to last me a lifetime. Why don't you run along and find someone else to play with?'

It wasn't often that she spoke to him so dismissively and his face darkened. He rose abruptly from the bed and left the cabin without a word, leaving Amanda to stretch voluptuously and relive her shameful coupling of last night over a third cup of coffee.

After they'd eaten breakfast, Andrei allowed Lucy to return to her cabin to catch up on some much-needed sleep. It was lunchtime when she awoke and by the time she'd dressed in a light-biscuit tweed suit worn with an ecru silk blouse, it was late enough for her to hurry as she made her way to the restaurant.

She found Edward sitting morosely over his soup but he brightened up when he saw her.

'I say, will you join me, I hate eating alone.'

'Where's Amanda?' she asked as the steward threw a starched, straw-coloured napkin over her knee and handed her a menu.

'I've no idea.' His tone indicated fairly clearly that he cared even less, or at least that was what he was trying to convince himself.

Lucy studied the menu abstractedly. She was hungry but

160

couldn't concentrate on it. 'What are you having?' she asked Edward.

'Soup, steak-and-kidney pud and jam roly-poly,' he told her. She shuddered and rejected the idea of ordering whatever he was eating to spare herself the trouble of making a choice.

'Melon, cold smoked duckling and a green salad,' she eventually decided. Edward poured her a glass of hock and she sipped it thoughtfully. She wondered where Faye was – she hadn't seen her today. A couple of times she'd thought she'd heard movement from her cabin, but when she'd tapped on the door there had been no reply.

'Are you going to the captain's gala dinner tonight?' Edward asked her. It was a rhetorical question – it was rare that anyone missed it.

'I imagine so.'

She hoped Andrei didn't have plans which meant she'd have to forego it. She was well aware that for now she was his plaything, her life not her own to direct, and the idea was unsettling.

What if he had something even more shaming in store for her than the obscene girdle he'd made her wear that morning? Although there was no point in worrying about it really, she'd find out soon enough.

But although she'd found wearing the girdle and being paraded around the deck in it degrading, she was uncomfortably aware that she'd been reluctantly aroused by it too. So much so that she was beginning to wonder if she had some dark, secret streak of perversion buried deep in her psyche.

It was almost a relief to be with someone as patently open and wholesome as Edward for a while and she found him pleasant company. He seemed to shake off whatever it was that was bothering him – something to do with Amanda no doubt – and became quite entertaining.

After lunch he suggested a stroll along the deck, then coffee in the verandah café.

It was a hot afternoon and the sun was directly overhead, beating mercilessly down. Lucy removed her jacket but was still much too warm in her tweed skirt.

It was while they were heading back towards the café that they saw Andrei and Amanda on a deserted part of the deck. Their heads were close together and they had the air of conspirators. While Lucy and Edward watched, Amanda pulled Andrei's head down and kissed him deeply, her hand sliding down his back to stroke his flannel-covered thigh.

A few seconds later they walked away, arms around each other, towards the section of the ship where Amanda's cabin was located.

Lucy glanced at Edward and saw the hot flush mottling his cheekbones. He clenched his fists and thrust his hands deep into his pockets, before turning on his heel and heading in the opposite direction. He stopped when he reached the end of the deck and waited for her to catch up.

'Let's go for a drink,' she suggested. 'It's too hot for coffee.'

They sat in the terrace grill and Lucy sipped another glass of chilled white wine while Edward drank whisky. She didn't know for certain that Andrei was about to bed Amanda, but it certainly looked that way and Edward obviously thought so. She wondered how soon after leaving the other woman Andrei would come to look for her to make sure he got the rest of his pound of flesh.

She'd better make sure he couldn't find her.

At least not until this evening and the later the better.

'It's very hot,' she murmured. 'Why don't we go and find a secluded corner of the deck and sunbathe?'

'Good idea,' he said listlessly. They separated to change into bathing costumes and then Lucy led him to a little-frequented corner of the second-class sun deck. She was well aware that nobody looking for her would ever think of searching the second-class quarters of the ship.

Edward didn't even seem to notice they'd left the first-class section. He'd just downed three whiskies in swift succession on top of the alarming amount of wine he'd consumed at lunch and he was showing it.

They found a couple of deck chairs and stretched out in the sun.

'Amanda's going to give me my marching orders – I just know she is,' he said suddenly, his voice gloom-laden.

'Have you known her long?' asked Lucy after a pause, rubbing cream into her thighs.

'A few months. She's the most wonderful woman I've ever met, even if my parents do disapprove. She's so beautiful – don't you think she's beautiful?'

'Yes she is,' replied Lucy truthfully.

'I love her but she doesn't take me seriously. I want her to leave her husband and marry me, but she won't.'

Lucy could see why not. There was still a stigma attached to a divorced woman which, for some reason she couldn't fathom, was never attached to a divorced man.

'I've never made love to a woman like her, she's fantastic in bed, so soft and warm and responsive.'

Lucy was startled – this wasn't the sort of thing well-brought-up men said to well-brought-up women. On the other hand Edward knew she'd been seeing a lot of Andrei and that she'd been present at the debauched cocktail party in the pool room, so maybe he thought she wouldn't mind.

Or maybe he was too drunk to realise what he was saying. Whichever it was she discovered that she was interested in hearing more.

'Not that I've slept with many women,' he continued. 'Only

three – that's not very many for a man of my age is it?'

'I'm not sure,' she said cautiously.

'Do you want to know who the first one was? It was my nanny. Not that she was *my* nanny by then of course – I was at school – but she was still with the family, looking after my younger sisters. I often used to go and chat to her when I was at home during the holidays – there wasn't a lot to do and I was often bored. Sometimes there were just my sisters, her and me in the house if my parents were away – this particular holiday they were in Paris.

'One evening I was in the schoolroom with her. She'd just put my sisters to bed and I asked if she'd play cards with me. She wanted to know what stakes we should play for and I suggested matches. She said that she had a better idea and we should play for forfeits. I wasn't sure what she meant but I was game for anything – it was just a way of passing the time – so I dealt the cards.

'That summer was the first time I'd seen her as a woman – if you see what I mean. Before that she was just nanny. But I'd started noticing what shapely legs she had and how her breasts pushed at the front of her uniform in a way that fascinated me. She wasn't particularly pretty, but she was very curvaceous with big, well-rounded hips.

'We played some silly game – I can't even remember what it was – but what I do remember what that when I lost the first hand she told me that my forfeit was to kiss her.

'The world suddenly stopped turning on its axis and I went brick-red and was immediately in an indecent state of arousal – a fairly frequent occurrence in those days. I leant across and kissed her rather clumsily on the lips and she pulled me closer and kissed me properly until I could barely breathe and the blood seemed to be pounding deafeningly through my body.'

There was a silence and Lucy glanced across at Edward to

see if he'd suddenly fallen sleep, but he was staring up at the sky with a reminiscent smile on his lips.

'I'm not sure how, because I certainly wasn't concentrating on the game, but I won the next hand. She asked me what her forfeit was and I blurted out that I wanted her to take her apron off. She laughed and asked me to undo the bow at the back. Even in her plain blue dress she looked infinitely desirable to me and it was hard to stay in my chair instead of taking her in my arms the way I wanted to.

'We played another couple of hands and she won both of them and asked me to take my jacket and then my shirt off. That made me bold and when I won the next hand I asked her to undo the front of her dress. She was wearing a cotton bodice with a little white satin bow at the neck and her full breasts were clearly outlined. I could even see the nipples, large like two acorns, and I just lost control.

'I'm embarrassed to say that I grabbed her hand and held it over my groin. She just smiled and said, "What have we here then?" She undid my fly and freed my painful erection from my underwear, but as soon as she took it in her hand, I came immediately.

'I was absolutely mortified but she didn't seem to mind, she just said, "I can see you've got a lot to learn, my boy," and led me down the hall to her bedroom.

'I was hard again almost instantly and this time she took her dress off completely and lay down on the bed. I can still see her in her cotton bodice and Directoire knickers, her lovely legs in black wool stockings. She pulled me down next to her and guided my hand to her breasts. Touching them felt like the best thing I'd ever done, they were so soft and cushiony and completely filled my hands.

'It can't have been much good for her – I hadn't a clue what pleased a woman – but I fondled them over her bodice

165

before eventually asking if she'd mind if I looked at them.

'She pulled her bodice over her head and let me gaze my fill. Her nipples were dark brown and I touched one with the tip of my finger and then kissed it. She seemed to like me nuzzling and kissing them but it was too much for me and I sensed I was going to come again. She must have realised it too, because she wriggled out of her Directoire knickers and guided me to the right place between her thighs. I'm ashamed to say that I ejaculated almost as soon as I entered her.'

Lucy was having trouble keeping her mouth from falling open at this frank and explicit description of Edward's loss of virginity.

He paused for so long she thought that might be it, but eventually he continued.

'We lay entwined on the bed, with me stroking her all over, unable to get enough of her. It was ages before I dared risk looking at her sex. I was startled – I didn't know women had hair down there. She let me examine her female parts and told me how to touch her to give her the most pleasure.

'As soon as I was hard again, I rolled on top of her and she told me to take the weight on my elbows like a gentleman, not just lie like a dead weight. I lasted a bit longer this time and it was even better – at least for me – but it still couldn't have been very good for her. I remember thinking that I could go on all night like that, but soon afterwards she sent me back to my room, saying she had to get up early in the morning.

'The following day I couldn't wait for her to put my sisters to bed so we could be alone. I even promised to read them a story to get them to go a bit earlier than usual. I'd been thinking about her all day and brought myself off at least half a dozen times. I was determined to last longer this time and I did. By the end of the holiday I considered myself very proficient in bed and couldn't bear the idea of going back to school and not being able to see her for weeks.'

He fell silent then said, 'Would you like a drink? I'm thirsty.'

'Some lemonade would be nice.'

'I'll go and see if I can find a steward.' He hauled himself out of his deck chair and left her. Lucy spread some cream onto her shoulders and turned onto her stomach. The sun and the wine she'd consumed at lunchtime were making her sleepy, but she was determined not to doze off and miss anything else he might have to tell her.

She'd actually found the story very arousing and she could tell that her bathing costume was slightly damp between the legs. But at the moment her body seemed to be in a perpetual state of readiness. Was it less than a week ago that she'd been driven to a frenzy of frustration by Boyd's refusal to make love to her?

It already seemed like another lifetime.

She raised her head and glanced cautiously around. There was no one in sight. Furtively, she slid her hand between her legs over her bathing costume and ran it over her vulva. Her clitoris was still fleshy and swollen – she wondered if it would ever return to being a tiny, flaccid sliver of flesh – it seemed to have been perpetually engorged for days.

Her own touch sent a jagged spike of arousal through her belly and she hastily removed her hand before she was tempted to continue and see if she could stimulate herself to a climax before Edward returned.

The sun, the constant sounds of the restless sea and the subdued throb of the engines, were all soporific and she began to doze off.

She was awakened a few minutes later by the return of Edward, followed by a steward carrying a tray containing a jug of iced lemonade and two glasses. The steward retreated and Lucy gulped thirstily at her drink.

'Did you ever see your nanny again?' she asked, eager to hear more.

'I ended up spending the next half-term with a school friend and his family. I didn't want to, but my parents arranged it with his parents. It was Christmas before I saw her again. I went up to the nursery, ostensibly to see my sisters, and there she was. They were nowhere in sight and I couldn't help myself, I grabbed her and started kissing and fondling her.

'After months without sex I just wanted to be inside her immediately, but she spoke to me very sharply and told me to let her go at once. She said that the under-nursemaid was in the next room with the children and any of them could come in at any minute. We arranged that I'd creep upstairs to her room late at night and that's what I did. It felt like really coming home to be welcomed into her bed again; my head pillowed on her soft, yielding bosom, my shaft deep inside her, where it wanted to be.

'I kept nearly being caught, although I tried hard not to be – I knew it would mean the loss of her job if anyone found us together. It was an ecstatic Christmas. It was Easter before I saw her again; I was sent on a school trip to Rome at half-term. I was devastated when she told me it was over, that she'd met someone who wanted to marry her. I didn't think I'd ever get over it, though of course I did.'

Edward's voice trailed off drowsily and they lay in silence for a while. Lucy half dozed off herself and they spent the rest of the afternoon alternately chatting and dozing.

Eventually it was time for her to return to her stateroom to prepare for the evening. There was a cable waiting for her.

LUCY HAVE GONE TO CORNWALL TO NURSE YOUR GRANDFATHER NOT SERIOUSLY ILL SO DON'T WORRY CAN YOU STAY WITH FAYES

SISTER UNTIL I RETURN LOVE AUNT SARAH

Lucy tapped on Faye's door and found her painting her nails with clear polish of the palest coral.

'Hi, where have you been all day?' Lucy greeted her, thinking that her friend was looking particularly pretty. Her chestnut hair was shining, her skin glowed and her china-blue eyes sparkled.

'Until just after lunch I was in here with Leo, but he was due back on duty in the early afternoon. I looked for you everywhere after he'd gone – where were you hiding?'

'Believe it or not I was on the second-class sun deck.'

'What on earth were you doing there?'

'Avoiding Andrei. This just arrived.' Lucy put the cable down in front of her friend. 'Will it be okay with Emily for me to stay there too, do you think?'

Faye scanned it swiftly. 'I should imagine so. It'll be pretty dull, Emily's one topic of conversation is her children, who incidentally are all ghastly. And all her husband talks about is the state of the economy. It'll be much better with you there, though.'

'I'm sure we'll still manage to have fun,' said Lucy doubtfully.

'Oh, Lucy!' wailed Faye suddenly. 'I won't be able to bear being back in London and having to stay with Emily. She'll want us to take an interest in the children and the cook's terrible. Everything she produces is steamed and stodgy. It'll be horrible after living like this.' She indicated the luxurious appointments of the stateroom.

'Let's enjoy it while we can,' said Lucy sympathetically. 'I agree – it'll be ghastly being chaperoned again.'

'Emily won't want to take us anywhere,' said Faye gloomily. 'So we'll always have to go with someone else's mother, which means leaving when they want to. It's enough to make me decide to get married as quickly as possible, just to get some freedom.'

'Only if you marry someone who'll let you lead your own life.'

'Amanda seems to manage.'

'I don't imagine all husbands are as tolerant as hers must be.'

'I'll look for one who is. I'll make it a priority.'

'Even over being extraordinarily good in bed? Anyway, I must go – it's time for me to transform myself for the gala ball. I'll see you later.'

Chapter Ten

The captain's gala dinner was the most formal and glamorous of the social events on the five-day Atlantic crossing. It was the occasion on which the women wore their most stunning gowns and sent their maids to get their most impressive jewels from the purser's safe.

The main lounge was already crowded by the time Lucy and Faye arrived, both of them keyed-up with anticipation. The air was filled with the mingled scents of dozens of different perfumes and the great banks of flowers which decorated the lounge.

Lucy was wearing a black, full-skirted Balenciaga gown made from stiff silk taffeta which left her shoulders and most of her back bare.

Around her slender throat was a diamond and emerald choker and a matching bracelet encircled one of her black elbow-length gloves at the wrist. She'd pinned the leopard brooch Andrei had given her to the front of her gown and it crouched there next to her right breast, emerald eyes gleaming.

After her afternoon on deck her skin glowed a warm honey, emphasising the grape-green of her eyes, and her old-gold hair had some lighter streaks in it from several days exposure to the sun and salt air.

Faye was equally stunning in a gown of amber *moiré* which now boasted a neckline which plunged much further than it had when she'd bought it. She'd persuaded Winnie to alter it for her by unpicking some of the stitching, although she knew that before the end of the voyage she'd have to get her to sew it up again and return it to its original more decorous state.

The amber watered silk was cinched in tightly at the waist and followed the curve of Faye's hips and legs down to her calves, where a series of kick pleats made it possible for her to walk unhampered.

Lucy thought she'd never seen her friend looking so sophisticated. The amount of creamy cleavage she was sporting was already turning heads and the cut of the gown emphasised her voluptuous figure in a way Mrs Faulkner must have been blind not to see. A large topaz dangled between her breasts on a fine gold chain and a ring set with an identical stone was on her right hand.

They both accepted a glass of champagne from one of the many circulating waiters and stood, trying not to be over-awed by the dazzlingly dressed, glitteringly jewelled guests. The men, all in sober black and white evening clothes, made a perfect foil for their colourful female partners.

'I wish this crossing lasted five weeks instead of five days,' said Faye vehemently, pulling her face slightly at the dryness of the champagne. She preferred sweeter wines but, like dry cocktails, she drank champagne when it was offered because it was the sophisticated thing to do.

Amanda came swanning up to them, her willow-slim figure shown off in a tight, indigo satin sheath dress cut on the bias. It had inset diamond-shaped panels in the skirt and a huge faux rose made from indigo tulle sprinkled with tiny beads at the bosom. The narrow shoulder straps were sewn with the same tiny beads, as was the hem. Her huge eyes looked as dark as pansies in her delicate face and she carried an ivory cigarette holder.

'Hello, darlings,' she greeted them affectedly. 'Isn't this fun? Have you seen Edward anywhere?'

'I saw him this afternoon,' said Lucy coolly, wondering if she'd just spent the last few hours in bed with Andrei.

'Where was that?'

'On the sun deck.' She didn't add that it had been the second-class sun deck.

'I'm sure he'll turn up eventually – after all, who'd miss the gala ball?' But Amanda's eyes continued to search the crowd as she chatted to them.

Leo came up, obviously intent on talking to Faye, but Amanda waylaid him and took his arm.

'Let's take a turn around the room and see who's here,' she suggested.

Leo shot a rueful look at Faye and led Amanda off into the crowd. Faye shrugged and accepted another glass of champagne from a passing waiter.

'I think she's just spent the afternoon sharing her charms with Andrei,' Lucy told her.

'Really?' Faye's china-blue eyes were startled. 'Andrei and Sonya spread themselves thin, don't they? Do you mind?'

'I don't suppose so. I strongly suspect that neither of them are people with whom it's possible to have a real relationship. They just absorb others into their own strange and rather fascinating world and then move on.'

'They've certainly made this voyage more interesting,' agreed Faye. 'Oh look, Sonya's just come in.'

Sonya paused just inside the door at the top of the flight of shallow steps and there was a distinct lull in the buzz of conversation as eyes turned to her.

Her gown of crimson chiffon clung to her so closely it might have been damp. From narrow shoulder straps it skimmed down her slender figure to her thighs, where it exploded into a delicate mass of separate handkerchief points which reached her ankles. There was a flamboyant ruby and pearl choker around the

173

slender ivory column of her neck and a matching tiara set among her glossy ebony hair.

'She knows how to make an entrance, doesn't she?' commented Lucy, as Sonya remained motionless, a faint smile playing around her lips. With her patrician poise and exotic beauty, it was easy to believe that she was related to the Tsars of Russia.

She slowly descended the steps and there was a faint murmur as the gossamer-fine points of her gown swirled around her thighs, half revealing, half concealing her shapely legs.

'Just imagine the effect of that dress when she's descending the sweeping staircase into the restaurant,' observed Lucy. 'Everyone will immediately suspend mastication and there won't be a mouthful consumed until she's reached the table.'

'She *is* striking isn't she?' sighed Faye wistfully.

The sun was setting on the horizon, a great ball of hazy flame which had been throwing rays of brilliant and rather lurid light through the windows at the far end of the room. Now it sank slowly out of sight making all the elegant Lalique lamps glow more brightly with the withdrawal of the competition.

Andrei appeared out of the crowd, impossibly attractive in his evening clothes, his tanned skin dark in contrast to the white of his shirt and tie. Lucy's stomach lurched with lust and she was struck again by how *foreign* he looked, with his wolfish profile, high cheekbones and opaque gold-green eyes.

Leo reappeared at the same moment, having left Amanda enjoying the compliments of one of her many male admirers, and immediately started talking to Faye in a low voice. Andrei drew Lucy to one side.

'It wasn't part of our agreement that you should hide yourself away from me, so I'm unable to enjoy the myriad pleasures of your fair, white body,' he murmured.

'What on earth makes you think I was hiding away?' she returned sweetly.

'I couldn't find you.'

'Then you can't have looked very hard.'

'I admit there were some places I didn't venture. The beauty salon for example, though if you did spend your afternoon there, the results are well worth it.'

He bent to take her hand, turned it palm upwards and kissed it, a long, hard kiss which seemed to brand her skin through the black silk glove. She felt her legs becoming weak and a slow gathering of heat deep in her sex.

He'd phoned her stateroom twice while she was getting ready for the evening. The first time she'd had Winnie say that she hadn't yet returned and the second that she'd just left. She knew it wasn't strictly adhering to the spirit of their agreement, but she wasn't prepared to be always available to him – particularly not just after she'd seen him with Amanda.

She raised one eyebrow quizzically at him and he met her gaze squarely. Something in his expression told her that he was remembering exactly how she'd looked when being paraded around the deck, her nether regions clad in a black leather girdle which rudely bisected her buttocks and placed the whole of her vulva on prominent display.

She hoped fervently that he wouldn't want her to wear it again.

But at the same time, she was aware of that giveaway moist heat between her thighs, a heat which reminded her how exciting she'd found it, even while feeling shamed and degraded.

She wondered if Sonya had ever worn it and whether she too had found it an arousing experience. Perhaps she should ask her.

People began to drift towards the restaurant, ready for the

sumptuous banquet which was to precede the dancing. It never failed to amaze Lucy how hungry the sea air seemed to make everyone, most of them usually only a few hours from their last substantial meal.

Sonya came strolling over to them, trailed by several men who had the single-minded air of dogs on heat. As soon as Lucy caught a whiff of her spicy perfume she was assailed by a vivid image of the other woman as she'd been last night in the sitting room of the suite she shared with Andrei.

She remembered opening her eyes to see Sonya, her black taffeta skirt pushed up out of the way, her camiknickers around her thighs, calmly masturbating to the spectacle of Lucy on her knees performing fellatio on Andrei.

But, because Lucy now realised that embarrassment was an alien emotion to Sonya, she didn't blush or avert her gaze as the other woman greeted her with a warm kiss.

'Lucy – how lovely you look. And what a gorgeous gown – Balenciaga?'

Lucy nodded. 'Yours is simply stunning, Sonya – you're going to cause a sensation when you glide down the staircase into the restaurant.'

'Which I am just about to do. I swam for quite a while this afternoon and it made me ravenous. Shall we descend the stairs together? Consider what a picture we will make, an English blonde in a black gown and Russian brunette in a crimson one.'

'I'm afraid you will have to go ahead without us,' Andrei interjected smoothly. 'I wish to talk to Lucy alone for a few minutes.'

'Then I'll see you at our table later.' With a smile Sonya left them and drifted elegantly towards the door.

Andrei drew Lucy's hand into the crook of his arm and led her towards the far end of the lounge and then out into the corridor.

'What do you want to talk to me about?' she asked warily.

'I don't want to talk to you at all at the moment,' he replied. 'I want to fuck you.'

Lucy flinched at his crudeness as he continued, 'What are you wearing beneath that dress?'

When she didn't reply he stopped and faced her. 'I have offended you, I can see. Would you rather I'd said I wanted to make love to you?'

'Yes, actually I would,' she returned coldly.

'There are many different sorts of sex, Lucy, as many as there are different types of love. There are times when I could fall to my knees and worship you and times when I wish to see you turned into a dishevelled, panting creature begging me to pleasure you again.'

'What a vivid imagination you have, Andrei. Either that or you must be confusing me with one of your other conquests – Amanda perhaps?' Her cool drawl was actually, she thought, a passable imitation of Amanda's affected one.

He started walking again, pulling her along behind him.

'I adore all English women, particularly when they forget about their breeding and their impeccable manners and let themselves go.'

He stopped, glanced around them and then opened a door in the corridor, pulling her in behind him. It was a storeroom in which the table linen for the first-class restaurant was kept. They were surrounded by rack upon rack piled high with tablecloths and napkins in pristine white, straw yellow, Wedgwood blue, dusky pink and mint green. It was warm in the room and the air was full of the clean scent of fresh laundry.

Without a word Andrei took her in his arms and kissed her, his hands warm on her bare back, his body lean and hard against hers. He kissed her gently at first, flicking his tongue teasingly between her lips, urging them apart so he could explore the soft contours of her mouth.

Part of her wanted to keep her mouth firmly closed and to refuse to respond, but it was difficult to resist him however much she wanted to, particularly since she'd promised to make herself available to him whenever and however he wished.

She compromised by allowing him to do as he chose physically, while resisting him mentally. So, although she let him hold her close and kiss her deeply, she pictured him with Amanda.

Nevertheless, she was still uncomfortably aware of the warm moisture gathering in her sex and a languid tingling sensation in all her limbs. He eased his hand into her gown and cupped her bare breast under the boned bodice. It was annoying to feel her nipple harden as he massaged it.

With his other hand he caressed the firm globes of her bottom, but the stiff fabric of her gown was too much of a barrier and he stepped away from her, swiftly dragging it up around her waist. The skirt, however, was too voluminous for him to keep it there and it started to fall again. Impatiently, he undid it and eased it down so it fell to the ground in a billowing rustle of silk.

He seized her by the waist and lifted her onto a pile of tablecloths on one of the racks, so she was at waist height to him. She was wearing a pair of camiknickers in black Brussels lace, the silken fuzz of her pubic hair a darker triangle beneath them.

Her black silk stockings were held up by matching lace garters and above the waist she was naked except for her elbow-length gloves and emerald and diamond choker and bracelet.

His face changed as he stood back and looked at her, his eyelids drooping, the lines of his face suddenly harder.

'You would drive a man to commit terrible crimes just to

see you like that,' he said at last. 'Touch me, Lucy, touch me with your long black gloves.'

She saw the beads of perspiration on his brow and realised that he was a man who was strongly visually stimulated. He undid his trousers and a massively engorged shaft sprang arrogantly out, marbled with purple veins. Lucy reached for it and ran her silk-encased hands caressingly down the full length, then cupped his heavy testicles.

A combination of the way she looked and the sensation of silk against his throbbing flesh seemed to send Andrei wild, because he groaned loudly and thrust his pelvis towards her. She took his member in both hands and squeezed and fondled it, rubbing it between her silk-clad palms.

His breathing became harsh and ragged and his eyes never left her, roaming over her pointed, naked breasts, then dropping to her lace-concealed mound.

'I must enter you – now,' he gasped and reached to slide her closer. He didn't wait to remove her lacy camiknickers, just thrust his shaft straight up the loose-fitting leg and directly inside her.

Lucy wriggled closer to the edge of the pile of tablecloths, so he could penetrate her more deeply, and hooked her legs around his waist. He plunged feverishly in and out of her in a piston-driven motion that emphasised the urgency of his need.

She wound her arms around his neck and he slid his hands under her backside, lifting her further onto him and rocking her strongly backwards and forwards with each determined thrust.

Lucy began to moan; low, heartfelt moans which, from fear of discovery, she tried to stifle without much success. She couldn't help it, she felt as though he was stoking a fire he'd lit in her days ago and which hadn't gone out since.

Her sex was a dripping, boiling, clutching part of her,

sending searing messages of jagged, gasping excitement to every nerve ending in her body.

She felt the thrilling, heart-stopping build-up of her climax and held him tighter, working herself against him, using him without compunction for the pleasure he was giving her.

She exploded into an orgasm which left her damp, breathless and invigorated. Her body went limp just as he gave three last convulsive thrusts and emptied himself into her in a series of dynamic spurts.

He rested his head on her shoulder while she held him close for a few moments. Then she leant back on her elbows, determined not to let him see how much he'd affected her. He withdrew from her and she felt his juices trickle into her lace camiknickers.

'Do I get to eat now?' she asked, as she picked up her dress and tried to decide the easiest way of getting into it without Winnie's help. He came to help and held it for her to step into, then fastened it.

He turned her towards him as they were about to leave the room.

'The memory of you wearing only your jewellery, gloves and lace drawers will stay with me until the day I die,' he said hoarsely.

Leo was not a happy man.

He was a shocked, disturbed and aroused man, but not a happy one.

He'd left Faye's cabin in the early afternoon, light-headed from lack of sleep, but deeply sated. They'd explored and enjoyed each other for hours at a time and he'd thought of little else all afternoon until he'd joined her for a drink in the lounge before dinner.

Happily, his duties included a considerable amount of

socialising, so he was able to escort her into dinner and sit next to her.

Her appetite for sex both excited and pleased him, even while part of him found it shocking. But he put a lot of it down to her innocence and thought that she was unaware that no decent woman, and certainly not an unmarried girl, ever took the initiative or displayed such abandoned enthusiasm.

He would have liked to indicate this gently to her, but couldn't think how to approach such a delicate matter without offending her.

He was also uneasily aware that if his liaison with Faye reached the ears of the captain, he'd lose his position. She was, however, making it very difficult for him to behave as though he was just doing his job by partnering an unescorted lady.

She kept leaning too close to him, whispering in his ear and touching his arm or hand as she spoke to him, making him glance nervously around to see if anyone had noticed what intimate terms they were on.

The amount of creamy cleavage alone she was displaying would have made perspiration stand out on his brow. Particularly since the topaz she was wearing on a fine, gold chain around her neck kept vanishing between her breasts, only to reappear tantalisingly as she moved or leant back on her chair.

He was finding it difficult to keep his eyes off the voluptuous swellings of her full orbs where they emerged from her amber silk dress. He'd look determinedly at the flower arrangement in the middle of the table, only to have his attention drawn to her breasts again as she leant forward to reach for her glass.

And as if that wasn't bad enough, as soon as she'd finished her first course – Ogen melon filled with summer fruits – she slid her hand onto his lap under the cover of the tablecloth and began to caress his cock through his trousers.

'Faye! Please stop that!' he hissed.

'Stop what?' she asked in an innocent voice, resting her elbow on the table and her chin in her other hand, looking at him beguilingly.

'This is neither the time nor the place,' he said in an urgent undertone.

'Mmm – are you sure?' Her hand moved persuasively over his throbbing member in a way which made him go dizzy with the effort of appearing unconcerned; when all he wanted was to grunt, groan and throw her on the table, to take her there and then.

Thankfully, at that moment the steward brought her turtle soup and she was effectively distracted from tormenting him – at least for a few minutes.

A conventional, rather reserved product of his class and upbringing, Leo had never met anyone like Faye. Her complete lack of guilt or remorse after they'd made love was puzzling to him. He was overwhelmed by both, and after the first time had castigated himself for taking advantage of her youth and inexperience.

He'd vowed not to let it happen again, but he'd been putty in her hands ever since, unable to resist her and hating himself for it. He could feel his already ruddy complexion going brick-red as she worked him up to boiling point.

The food at the gala dinner was magnificent. The chefs had surpassed themselves in both the variety and quality of courses prepared. Leo, who was accustomed to the cuisine on board and often ate it without really noticing it, found himself grateful for the expertise of the masters of the *Aphrodite*'s kitchens. It meant that as each course was served, Faye ceased fondling his manhood to concentrate on eating.

She felt as though she was storing up memories of sauces,

flavourings and textures to carry her through eating the stodgy nursery food served in her sister's house. She thought she must have died and gone to heaven as she ate her fillets of sole with asparagus in vermouth sauce, followed by *boeuf en croûte* accompanied by tender, stringless green beans, broccoli hollandaise and new potatoes.

By touching Leo under the table, she was also storing up more carnal memories for days when the most exciting thing on offer was a game of cards with her nephews and nieces.

She worked her way steadily through the five courses, savouring every bite.

'That was marvellous,' she said at last, laying down her spoon after scraping the last morsel of chocolate bombe from her dish.

Immediately, Leo rose to his feet.

'I have some duties to attend to,' he told her. 'I'll see you later at the ball.' He strode hastily off down the room, thankful that he'd managed to make it through the meal without coming in his trousers as a result of Faye's dexterous caresses.

She sighed in disappointment. As a finale to her erotic and furtive fondlings, she'd planned to drop something and then slide under the table and briefly touch him even more intimately. Oh well, she may as well order an ice before the coffee.

Seeing that Leo had deserted Faye, Sonya moved seats and came to sit next to her.

'How sad to think that tomorrow will be our last night together,' she said, picking up a chocolate truffle from the dish and popping it between her crimson lips. 'What will you be doing after the voyage is over?'

'Staying with my sister and her husband until my parents return from America,' Faye replied unenthusiastically.

'You sound as if that will not be very enjoyable.'

'It won't. What will you be doing?'

'Andrei has some business in London and after that we'll leave for the French Riviera, probably stopping in Paris for a few days.'

'The Riviera – how wonderful, though the season's virtually over, I believe.'

'Only the English think so. I know you all like to go and stay in draughty castles in Scotland in September, but Andrei and I prefer to remain where it is warm for as long as possible. The winters in Europe are so long and cold.'

Sonya shivered feelingly, although it was warm in the restaurant.

'I suppose they are,' replied Faye vaguely, who'd never really thought about it.

'We must make the most of each other while we can. Unless I can persuade you to change your plans and come with us.'

'Where? To the Riviera? Oh, if only I could, but I'm afraid it's impossible.'

'Why is that?'

'My parents wouldn't let me. I'm sorry – I'll really miss you.'

'And I you. What a pity you won't be able to join us. Will you miss Leo too?'

'Probably, though not as much as you.'

People began to leave the table in ones and twos to return to the main lounge where the dancing would shortly begin. There was no one left sitting close to them as Sonya pushed her chair away from the table and turned to face Faye, crossing her long, slim legs. Faye found her eyes drawn to the glimpses of silk-stockinged thigh visible through the layered points in the red chiffon.

'Speak to me of Leo,' urged Sonya, her silver-grey eyes fixed on Faye's face. 'Is he a good lover?'

Faye blushed and was annoyed with herself for appearing gauche in front of the sophisticated Sonya.

'Yes, he is,' she returned cautiously. Then, emboldened by the wine she'd consumed, she asked, 'Is Andrei?'

'The best.'

'Then why do you both take other lovers?'

Sonya laughed huskily, showing her perfect white teeth.

'How young you are. I suppose one answer would be that an individual's sexuality is multi-faceted and that no one lover can satisfy all aspects of it. There are things I like to do and have done that Andrei gets little pleasure from. The same is also true in reverse.'

'What would be another answer?'

'For the distraction. I have had many lovers, Faye, and I hope I shall have many more.'

'Do you remember them all?'

'Of course.'

'Tell me about them.'

Sonya laughed again. 'One perhaps. Which one shall it be?'

'One who stands out in your memory.'

'Very well. After we fled Russia we roamed around for a few years, then Andrei had word that a cousin of his was being held prisoner in St Petersberg by the Bolsheviks. He was determined to go back and see if he could free him. I didn't want him to go – I was certain he would be killed and I would be completely alone in the world.

'We were in Finland at the time and it was a bitter winter. I spent most of my days lying under a pile of fur rugs trying to keep warm, but it was only when Andrei held me in his arms that I didn't feel chilled.'

Sonya's face had clouded as she spoke and she reached for her glass of cognac and took a sip.

'He didn't want to leave me with only Marta to protect me.

He wanted to be sure I was safe, so he left his manservant, Boris, with us. I wanted Andrei to take him. It was a dangerous thing he was attempting and I knew that Boris, who'd been his father's manservant, would lay down his life for him.

'But he left in the night a couple of days before I expected him to and I was inconsolable. I thought I would never see him again and, other than the servants, there would be no link with the past. I cried and cried until Marta was at her wits' end. She sent Boris in to talk to me. He stood at the foot of my bed and told me he was sure Andrei would return to us unharmed. He was a huge bear of a man and had killed to protect us, but he was always gentle with women, children and animals.

'I was lying sobbing my heart out under about a dozen furs, with only the back of my head visible, when suddenly I felt his hand on my hair. He stroked it the way I'd seen him stroking horses to calm them down.

'It worked; it made me feel hope that Andrei might come back to us. I sat up and wound my arms around his neck while he continued to stroke and soothe me. When I'd stopped crying he tried to leave but I wouldn't let go – he was enormously strong and I felt so safe in his arms.

'I wanted him to get into bed with me and lie beside me just holding me. He wouldn't at first but I became distressed again and eventually he agreed, slipping in next to me. I slept for a while and when I awoke I thought it was Andrei beside me and began to caress him. It wasn't until Boris spoke that I realised my mistake. By then it was too late, I wanted him to make love to me.

'He kept trying to tell me it wasn't right, but Andrei and I had been lovers for some time and I already knew many ways to arouse a man. It had been a long time for Boris since his wife died and I don't think he'd had a woman since – a fact I took unfair advantage of.'

'After that, it was only when he made love to me that I could forget my fears for Andrei and we spent every night together under the pile of furs.'

Faye had been listening breathlessly to this account.

'But Andrei did come back to you – didn't he? How long was he away?'

'Four months.'

'And did he bring his cousin with him?'

'No, he died in prison before Andrei reached him. When he did return he was badly injured – a sabre wound. He lay near death for days while we nursed him. Since then we have been inseparable.'

'What happened to Boris?'

'He died in an accident several years later.' Sonya's tone was sombre as she spoke. 'Stephan is his son. Boris had left him with his sister, but he joined us when he was older.'

'Gosh,' breathed Faye, thinking about her own completely safe, uneventful childhood and adolescence. 'Nothing so exciting has ever happened to me.'

'Then think yourself lucky. I wish it had not happened to me.'

Sonya looked so desolate that Faye took her hand and squeezed it.

'Don't think about it. I wouldn't have asked if I'd realised it was going to upset you.'

Sonya raised her bleak eyes to Faye's face, then touched her gently on the cheek with her fingertips.

'Sweet Faye. Will you come to my room and make love to me now?'

'Oh, Sonya – of course I will.'

Sonya's bedroom was lit only by the light of two lamps, both with ruby chiffon scarves thrown over them to cast a warm, exotic glow. Slowly, she removed her red dress and then sank onto the bed wearing only her silk stockings, crimson camiknickers and matching suspender belt. Her small, perfect breasts looked rosy in the warm light filtering through the scarves, the nipples a rich brown.

She held out her arms and Faye sat down next to her, raising her hand to stroke her friend's cheek. Sonya lifted her head and kissed her gently on the lips, a feather-light caress which made Faye sigh and move closer.

For a while they stroked and kissed each other and then Sonya helped Faye out of her amber *moiré* gown, bending her head to kiss the valley of her cleavage.

Faye was wearing a wisp of black silk lingerie which fastened between her legs with two small ebony buttons. Her legs were encased in sheer black stockings held up by topaz silk garters sewn with tiny ribbons of the same colour. Her curvaceous figure looked almost indecently voluptuous in the frivolous underwear, which she had bought that afternoon in the expensive shop on the ship.

'How beautiful you are,' whispered Sonya, her hands at Faye's breasts, grazing over the nipples and kissing the swellings of the upper slopes where they spilled out over the top of the lingerie.

'You're too lovely to keep to myself,' breathed Sonya. 'I want others to admire you too. Would you mind if I asked Stephan to watch us?'

Faye gulped and tried to speak, but it came out as a dry croak. She minded a lot but, for some reason, the idea also made a hot little tongue of flame lick at her abdomen. And Sonya had just shared some of her terrible past with her and Faye would have done virtually anything to wipe that bleak look from her face.

'N . . . no, I don't mind,' she stuttered untruthfully. Sonya reached past her, picked up an intricately carved silver bell and shook it. A few moments later there was a tap on the door and Stephan entered. If he saw anything at all surprising in the sight of one of his employers, naked from the waist up, in the arms of another woman clad in the most diaphanous of underwear, he gave no sign of it.

His eyes flickered over them and then he said courteously, 'Yes, Princess?'

'Faye and I wish you to watch us.'

'Certainly, Princess. Will you be requiring any refreshment?'

'What a good idea – Faye?'

'Whatever you're having.'

'Then mix us some Bellinis please.'

While Sonya and Faye lay back and explored each other's bodies, Stephan left the room and returned carrying a tray containing two glasses and a jug of foaming champagne mixed with peach juice.

He placed the glasses on the bedside table and then withdrew to the other side of the room where he remained in the shadows, watching expressionlessly.

Sonya slipped Faye's shoulder straps over her arms, then drew the flimsy garment down to her waist, revealing her full, luscious breasts. She trickled some of her drink onto them and then bent her head to lap it up, her pointed tongue swirling erotically around Faye's coral nipples.

Faye felt her outer sex-lips distending and her tiny bud tingling in eager response. Sonya's mouth felt warm and soft as her lips tugged at the nipples, coaxing them into standing stiffly out from their puckered aureoles.

A little of the Bellini had run down to Faye's navel, where Sonya followed it with her tongue. She began to caress Faye's hips, smoothing over her belly, then following the line of her shapely thighs. Faye felt her sex moistening and expanding, the flame of heat becoming stronger by the moment.

When Sonya deftly undid the two buttons holding Faye's lingerie closed between the legs, Faye sighed and parted her thighs. Sonya lifted the flap of silk back to reveal the luxuriant dark red fuzz which partially concealed her friend's vulva.

On her hands and knees between Faye's thighs, Sonya bent her head and touched the rim of her friends outer sex-lips with her tongue. Faye shivered and Sonya licked her way around the outside, before probing gently and finding her inner sex-lips.

Faye felt awash with creamy moisture as Sonya pleasured her with her lips and tongue. She penetrated Faye's sex and explored every velvety fold, plunging her tongue deeply inside.

There was a sudden movement at the foot of the bed and, opening her eyes, Faye saw Stephan kneeling between Sonya's widely parted legs, his shaft a great knobbed, erect thing.

Startled, Faye watched him caress the lace-covered globes of Sonya's beautiful derrière, then saw him draw her camiknickers slowly down her thighs. Sonya gasped, her breath warm against Faye's vulva, as Stephan entered her and began a leisurely in-and-out motion.

She redoubled her efforts with her tongue, strumming and sucking the head of Faye's bud alternately until, suddenly, with a little 'oooh,' of surprise, Faye came in a hot flood of sensation which suffused her body in wave after delicious wave.

Her eyes fluttered closed and she could only hear Sonya's little moans of pleasure as if from a great distance. Stephan let out a sudden inarticulate cry, then the bed jerked – one, two, three times – as he enjoyed the release of a prolonged climax.

His last plunging thrusts must have sent Sonya toppling over the edge, for she too gave a soft cry and then lay still, her head resting on Faye's damp mound.

Chapter Eleven

The ball was in full swing when Lucy and Andrei returned to the main lounge after dinner. They danced together and, as she expected, Andrei danced as well as he made love, with the same thrilling combination of control and abandon.

The sensation of his arm around her, his body close to hers, made her feel breathless and giddy. Perhaps it was as well that the voyage would be over in only thirty-six hours. Lucy felt she'd become a slave to her own desires as well as his and she wasn't altogether comfortable with it.

But the prospect of parting from him and from Sonya also made her feel bereft – anything that happened to her subsequently was bound to pale in comparison to this erotic, exciting, voluptuous voyage.

She couldn't remember the last time she'd worn a pair of camiknickers which remained dry for more than a few minutes. She seemed to be permanently wet between the legs with the sodden crotch of her underwear always rubbing tantalisingly against her swollen clit.

Her lace camiknickers were damp now. She really should have gone back to her cabin to change them before dinner, but there was something pleasantly wanton about knowing that Andrei's juices had helped to soak them.

The dance finished and they joined Amanda, who was flirting rather desperately with one of the ship's officers by a massive pink and white flower arrangement. Lucy breathed in the mingled scents of carnations, blush roses and freesias and wondered how the flowers were kept so fresh. They'd been at sea for over three days but the flowers could have been cut an hour ago.

She joined in the conversation in a desultory way and then chatted to the officer while Andrei danced with Amanda. At the end of the dance she saw the two of them slip through one of the open doors at the far end of the lounge and out onto the deck.

Annoyed at being abandoned, Lucy excused herself and stalked back to her cabin. She ripped off the damp camiknickers and washed thoroughly, now anxious to cleanse herself of any lingering remnants of Andrei's lovemaking.

How dare he made love to . . . no, *fuck* her and then vanish with Amanda? He'd been yo-yoing about between the two of them all day and she wasn't going to stand for it. She didn't mind too much about Sonya – it was obvious that they shared a past and a closeness he probably never came near to with any other woman, but she found she did mind about Amanda.

She considered going to bed and getting an early night, but dismissed the idea. Why should she miss any of the fun just because Andrei was with someone else? There were plenty of other men who would be glad to dance and flirt with her.

She touched up her make-up, sprayed herself with scent and ran a comb through her gleaming hair, then looked at herself in the mirror. Even to her own rather critical eye she looked good.

She was just making her way along one of the corridors when she heard her name called.

'Lucy!' It was Edward, his hair rumpled, his evening dress slightly untidy, clearly the worse for drink. He stood in the doorway of one of the small lounges, glass in hand and said, 'I say – come and have a drink with me.'

She smiled at him and went into the room, taking a seat in

one of the high-backed, chintz-upholstered armchairs. There were only two other people in the room and they were absorbed in each other, talking in low voices. Edward rang the bell for the steward.

'Havin' a good time?' he asked her while they waited for him.

'Wonderful,' she returned brightly and not altogether truthfully.

The steward arrived and Edward ordered drinks for them. 'I'm not,' he continued, as soon as the man had left them. 'I'm havin' a terrible time because Amanda is with that Russian bastard again.'

Lucy knew just how he felt, but she wasn't about to let it show.

'What's wrong with that?' she asked. 'There's no harm in dancing, is there?'

Edward buried his face in his hands and said in a despairing voice, 'I've lost her, I know I have. In two days she'll be gone from my life forever.'

'Nonsense – you don't know that for sure,' she replied bracingly.

The other couple left the room, their arms around each other. Lucy moved to sit on the arm of Edward's chair and tentatively stroked his crisp, tow-coloured hair.

'Come on, Edward – you mustn't let it get to you like this. You should let her see that you can play her at her own game.'

Edward raised his head to look at her hopefully and say, 'How do I do that?'

'Dance with other women, flirt with them – particularly the younger ones. At best it might make her jealous and at worst it'll be fun.'

He reached up, hooked his arm around her waist and pulled her onto his lap. Before she could protest he covered her mouth with his and kissed her. He tasted faintly of whisky and toothpaste and his lips were gentle. At first she let him kiss her because she wanted to comfort him, but as it continued she found herself aroused.

She remembered the story he'd told her that afternoon about his nanny and how exciting she'd found it. Of their own volition her arms wound themselves around his neck and she kissed him back. Even through the stiff skirts of her black gown she could feel the rapid hardening of his manhood and it gave her a heady feeling of power to know that she'd been responsible.

She didn't object when his hand closed on her breast and caressed it fervently through her stiff bodice. His touch sparked off a reckless desire to feel him inside her. She wriggled her bottom against his shaft, wishing her skirts weren't in the way.

Hot spirals of lust were uncurling from her groin, sending hectic messages to all her nerve endings. Her vulva began to throb urgently and suddenly she knew that she had to have him, there and then.

Edward's chair had a high back which was towards the door. Glancing that way, Lucy realised that anyone walking past the open door wouldn't be able to see them. It was the work of a moment to stand up, deftly undo his trousers and flip her skirts up around her waist.

She sank hastily back onto his knee, her skirts settling decorously around her. Now, even if anyone came right into the room and around the chair, to all intents and purposes she was just sitting on his knee. Anyone with any delicacy would immediately withdraw, leaving them to carry on.

She could tell that Edward was too drunk and excited to have any reservations about having sex with her in a public place. She doubted if he even knew where they were. She shifted position so that his engorged rod lay against her sex-valley and murmured, 'You'll have to help me.'

She raised herself as he took his shaft in his hand and, after a couple of abortive attempts, managed to push it up the loose-fitting leg of her camiknickers. It butted up against the swollen tissues of her vulva and she parted her thighs invitingly under the concealing cover of her skirts.

It took a few moments and she had to raise herself slightly, but then he was inside her with a sudden jolting thrust. It pushed her off balance and she sat down heavily, so that he was immediately sheathed up to the hilt in her moist, velvety core.

His eyes glazed, his breath coming in harsh gasps, Edward began to move his hips beneath her, while continuing to caress her breasts. Lucy found that if she held onto the arms of the chair she could lift herself slightly and move up and down on the engorged shaft which was giving her so much pleasure.

She controlled the rhythm of their reckless coupling, moving to give herself the maximum pleasure, not letting him speed up and end it too soon.

She was just rising and falling on him with the smoothness of a fairground ride when, to her horror, the steward came back into the room.

'More drinks, sir?' he asked, pausing just inside the doorway.

Edward's face went stiff with shock, but Lucy managed to say, 'Not at the moment thank you – we'll ring if we want you.' The man nodded and vanished.

They were both too far gone for the interruption to put them off and Lucy continued to ride Edward faster and faster until, with an inarticulate cry, he clutched her breasts convulsively and came.

Her own climax was only a second or two later; a whooshing cascade of sensation which rippled over her, leaving her hot, breathless and trembling.

She eased herself off him and smoothed her skirt back down,

not a moment too soon. A large party of revellers surged into the room, taking a respite from the festivities in the main lounge.

'Edward,' she urged him in a low voice, 'do yourself up before anyone notices.' He looked vaguely around, apparently puzzled by the sudden appearance of all the other people, then furtively fastened his fly.

'That was marvellous,' he breathed. He seized her hand and kissed it. '*You're* marvellous,' he added.

Faye wandered back into the main lounge just in time for the ribbons holding the nets of balloons against the ceiling to be untied, releasing bobbing clouds of pink and white spheres onto the heads of the revellers.

Many of the more boisterous passengers began to burst them as they wafted down, and soon the highly polished parquet floor was covered in deflated scraps of coloured rubber.

Faye hadn't really wanted to leave Sonya, but the older woman had said she'd see her later for a drink, making it politely clear that she expected her to go, even if she had kissed her fondly before she left.

Faye was mildly shocked that Stephan had joined them on the bed. She wasn't sure exactly what it was that had shocked her. It couldn't just be because Stephan was a servant – after all, Sonya had earlier confided her affair with his father Boris and she'd felt sympathetic, not shocked.

Perhaps it was because Sonya had slept with both father and son. Not many women could claim that – or at least Faye didn't think so, but she realised they'd hardly be likely to advertise it if they had. Maybe it was because she'd got the distinct impression that Sonya and Stephan were about to do something together that they didn't want her around for.

Whatever it was, she wouldn't have missed the last hour for the world.

Faye couldn't see either Leo or Lucy anywhere in the main lounge, so she strolled into the bar which was in a room to one side. After ordering a sweet Manhattan she stepped through the open door at one end of the room and onto the terrace.

A solitary man was leaning on the rail, smoking. He started when he saw her and then immediately looked away.

'I'm sorry,' she said diffidently. 'Did you want to be alone? I can go back inside if you do.'

'No, it's alright,' he muttered. He looked vaguely familiar, so she assumed she'd met him at some stage of the voyage.

She stepped up to the rail and took a sip of her drink.

'Lovely night,' she ventured, gazing up at the dark sky where only a few stars were visible. The rest were concealed by drifting swathes of cloud which moved restlessly above their heads.

'I suppose so.' His accent, with its slightly flattened vowels, wasn't one she was used to hearing and she wondered if he'd managed to infiltrate the first-class section from second or third class.

'I can't believe that tomorrow will be our last night at sea,' she continued. 'I think I'd like to stay on board forever.'

'Really? I'd like to disembark in Southampton and never set foot on a ship again as long as I live.'

'Will you have to? Set foot on a ship again, I mean.'

'You could say that.'

'Why?'

She thought he'd reply that he had family or business interests in America, so she was surprised by his answer.

'Because it's my job.' Startled, she looked at him more carefully, wondering if he was a steward she'd mistaken for a passenger, though surely no steward would risk his job by standing around smoking on the terrace of one of the bars. But he was wearing evening dress, so he *must* be a passenger and he must be travelling first class. 'I'm the band leader,' he added.

Of course, now she recognised him. She just hadn't looked at him carefully enough. A rather bitter smile flitted across his face and she realised that he was half expecting her to demand to know what he was doing in an area reserved for passengers.

'That must be interesting,' she said brightly.

'It's okay, but I'd rather work on terra firma. I hate being cooped up on a ship.'

'I'd hardly call it cooped up,' she said in surprise, looking at the massive expanse of deck in front of them.

'I'm sure you wouldn't. But then you're not sharing a windowless cabin the size of a dog kennel with three other musicians, and you don't have to spend the time when you're not playing in the evenings cooped up in a poky hole behind the stage. Sometimes I just can't breathe. Tonight I couldn't stand it any longer so I came out here for a few minutes, but this will be my last voyage if anyone sees me.'

'Why do you do it if you hate it so much?'

'Something you probably wouldn't understand – for the money.'

'Of course I understand. What I meant was, why not play in a hotel or nightclub if you hate being on board a ship so much?'

'This was the only job I could get. They're not that easy to come by you know.'

Faye was silenced. How easy jobs were to come by wasn't something she knew much about. In fact, this voyage seemed to have shown her that there were an awful lot of things that she didn't know much about.

'I'm sorry,' she said eventually.

He flashed his teeth at her in a sudden disarming grin.

'Don't be. It isn't your fault. I'm probably lucky to have a job at all.' He glanced at his watch. 'I'd better get back. We're due on again in a few minutes.'

'You're very good,' she told him uncertainly. 'Everybody says so.'

He grinned again. 'I should hope so. Got to go. Bye.' He dropped his cigarette, ground it out with the heel of his shoe and slipped silently away.

Faye wondered if either Lucy, Leo or Sonya had returned to the main lounge yet. She drifted back in there and watched the dancing for a while, but strangely she saw no sign of anyone she knew. Several men asked her to dance, but she didn't feel like it and politely refused.

The band came back on and she listened to them for a while. They played very well and no one would have guessed the bandleader was hating every minute.

She lifted her drink to her lips and then noticed to her horror that her topaz ring was missing. She stood frozen to the spot while she tried to recollect where she'd been when she last remembered having it on.

Of course, she'd taken it off in Sonya's bathroom while she was washing her hands – she must have left it there.

Anxious to retrieve it – her mother would be furious if she lost it – Faye hurried back towards Sonya's suite. She was quite pleased to have an excuse to return there. Perhaps Sonya would be ready to come back to the ball with her by now. It felt a little lonely to be in the middle of all those people and not have anyone she knew to talk to.

She tapped gently on the door but there was no reply. Cautiously she tried the handle and the door opened. There was no one in the suite's sitting room and she was reluctant to knock on the door of Sonya's bedroom in case she was still engaged in some carnal activity with Stephan.

A sudden hoarse cry came from the bedroom and echoed through the suite. Without considering the consequences, Faye threw open the door and then stood rooted to the spot in shock at the scene that met her eyes.

Stephan lay strapped spread-eagled to the bed, naked except for a blindfold and a leather belt which was fastened around his neck. Marta, Sonya's maid knelt beside him, her mouth around his shaft, one hand cupping his testicles. Marta wore her usual uniform of a navy-blue dress with a white collar and cuffs, but the dress was unbuttoned at the front and her large, full breasts were hanging out of it.

Sonya herself, naked except for her shoes, stockings, crimson suspender belt and a pair of leather gauntlets was kneeling on either side of Stephan's face, wielding a whip.

Stephan's face glistened with her juices and he was straining eagerly upwards with his tongue to where she was poised above him, her thighs wide apart, her deep-pink vulva on full display.

With an inarticulate cry, Faye raised her hand to her throat, too shocked to do anything but stand there staring at the strange and terrible scenario, then she turned on her heel and fled, her ring forgotten.

She was sitting trembling on the edge of her bed when there was a gentle tapping on the door.

'Faye – it's Sonya. Please let me in.'

She didn't reply, even though Sonya remained there for a while, knocking on the door and repeating her request to be allowed to enter. A few minutes later Faye heard voices in the corridor and then a key turned in the lock and a stewardess looked in, with Sonya just behind her. She'd obviously persuaded the woman to use her master key.

'Thank you,' Sonya said in a low voice and pressed some

money into her hand. 'I'll ring if I want you.' She closed the door and advanced into the room, then perched on the edge of the dressing table. She was fully clothed, her crimson dress clinging tightly to her slender figure, her hair and make-up perfect. 'I told her I feared you were ill,' she explained to Faye.

'Well I'm not,' she muttered.

'No, perhaps so, but I can see that you're very shocked. Why is that?'

Faye wasn't going to reply, but Sonya fixed her with her brilliant silver-grey eyes and Faye found herself saying, 'He was tied up and you were *whipping* him.'

'That's right I was. But please rid yourself of any idea that what I was doing was against Stephan's wishes, he was a willing participant.'

'He was crying out – I heard him.'

'Believe me, that was a cry of pleasure.'

'How *could* it be?' asked Faye furiously.

Sonya sighed and came to sit next to her on the bed.

'My dear Faye, I think you've already discovered that there are many ways to heighten pleasure. Stephan and I share a fondness for just a little pain to render it more intense.'

'And does Andrei share your fondness?' demanded Faye coldly.

'Not really, although he indulges me from time to time. I may have been whipping Stephan, but only very gently. What I was doing didn't even break the skin and isn't any more painful than the spankings I gave you after I tied you up. Didn't you find that enjoyable – at least on one level?'

'I suppose so,' replied Faye reluctantly.

'By tomorrow any slight marks I may have left will have faded and he'll be ready at any time for some more. If he found it distasteful do you think he would have been so aroused?'

'I don't know,' admitted Faye.

'Men can't fake arousal – they either are or they aren't and the evidence is unequivocal. I would hate you to think I mistreated those who work for me, Faye. Would it make you feel any better to come back to the suite with me now and ask Stephan about it yourself?'

Faye shuddered at the idea. 'What was your maid doing there?' she asked. 'Does she like to be whipped too?'

'No, Marta likes only pleasure and Stephan is more than willing to provide it.'

'Why did you send me away?'

'Because I knew it was something you were not ready for. And I was right, wasn't I?'

Faye sighed. This was all too complicated for her.

'Why did you come back anyway?' asked Sonya curiously.

'I left my ring in your bathroom.'

'I'll have Marta bring it at once.' Sonya left the bed and moved towards the phone.

'No, it doesn't matter – it will do in the morning,' said Faye hastily, unwilling to face the maid after seeing her in such a compromising position.

'Very well. Shall we go and sit in the verandah café and have a drink together?'

'If you like,' replied Faye ungraciously.

Sonya bent and kissed her softly on the cheek. 'Poor Faye – you still have so much to learn.'

When Andrei and Amanda reappeared in the main lounge, Edward and Lucy were dancing. Amanda spotted them and immediately headed in their direction.

'Edward! Lucy!' she called, waving. Edward took one look, then turned his back, gathering Lucy more tightly in his arms.

'Don't want to see her,' he slurred. 'Don't love her any more. Love you now.'

'I'm sure you don't really mean that,' murmured Lucy as Amanda reached them, Andrei just behind her.

'Edward – I've been looking for you all evening,' she greeted him. 'Dance with me; Lucy can dance with Andrei.'

'Don't want to dance with you,' he said truculently. 'Want to dance with Lucy.'

The last thing Lucy felt like doing was spending any time with Andrei, but she was keen to avoid a scene and said hastily, 'I've danced long enough. I'll see you later.'

She made her way across the crowded dance floor, not pausing to see what happened next. Andrei caught up with her as she reached the perimeter.

'Why are you dashing off like that?' he asked.

'I'm not *dashing* anywhere. I'm just leaving them to it. They're obviously going to row and I don't want to be caught in the middle,' she said offhandedly.

'The upright Edward seems to have transferred his affection from Amanda to you very suddenly,' he commented, looking at her closely. 'Why is that?'

She shrugged indifferently and turned to walk away from him, but he followed her through the open doors at the far end of the lounge and out onto the deck.

'Why is that?' he repeated.

'Why are you asking me?' Lucy continued to stroll away from where the noise and lights of the ball were spilling out through the doors. There were couples dotted here and there, enjoying the cool evening breeze or indulging in some furtive fondling.

'Because I think you know.'

'Really?' She yawned affectedly and then said, 'If you don't have anything more interesting to do than interrogate me about

Edward and Amanda, I wish you'd go away and leave me to enjoy a stroll before I turn in.'

In the shadows of one of the ventilators he caught her wrist and pulled her close to him.

'You've had sex with him – and recently,' he said slowly. 'I can smell him on you.' Lucy tried unsuccessfully to pull away from him, not sure whether to tell him to mind his own business, deny it or brazen it out, but he held her tightly. 'I thought we had an arrangement,' he continued.

'What does that have to do with anything?' she demanded.

'I thought we'd agreed that you were to be my sexual plaything for the duration of the voyage.'

'That's right.'

'Then what were you doing with another man?'

She looked up at him. His face was in shadow, but she could see his eyes gleaming a feral gold in the dark.

'I don't recollect agreeing to you having the *exclusive* use of my body,' she pointed out tauntingly.

How dare he start behaving possessively when he'd probably just bedded Amanda?

'It was implicit in our agreement.'

'Not as far as I'm concerned.' His body felt as hard as iron against hers as he backed her up against the ventilator and held her there.

'I don't think I like the thought of you with Edward.'

'Really? Well, that's just too bad.'

'I think I'm going to have to punish you for this,' he said thoughtfully.

At his words, a hot little snake of lust whipped through Lucy's body, but she managed to say, 'And just how are you planning to do that?'

'Maybe I'll parade you through the ball dressed as you were in the linen cupboard, in just your underwear, gloves and jewellery.'

The thought made Lucy go cold. She shivered as she imagined the music coming slowly to a halt and everyone turning to stare at her. She saw herself, head held high, as she stalked through the crowded room looking to neither left nor right, her naked breasts on display for every man in the room to ogle. Suddenly, instead of feeling cold she felt hot, in fact virtually molten at the idea of all those men seeing her, lusting after her.

Even so she managed to say dismissively, 'I think the captain might have something to say about that.'

'Possibly. We'll go to your stateroom instead.'

'And what if I don't want to go to my stateroom?'

'You have no choice in the matter. I'm choosing to exercise my right to take you when I want you, where I want you, how I want you. I should be careful, Lucy, or I may decide to have you here and now, up against this ventilator where anyone might see us.'

To Lucy's shame the idea made a little tongue of flame lick at her sex as she envisaged the sort of gasping, urgent coupling they might have, right there on deck. Andrei stepped away from her and took her arm.

'Your stateroom then,' was all he said.

Once there, Andrei threw himself down on the bed and said casually, 'Undress.'

There was a hot spot of colour on each of Lucy's cheeks as she slowly obeyed him. Sometimes he brought to mind some sort of eastern pasha treating her as if she were a member of his harem.

'You'll have to undo my dress,' she reminded him. 'I can't manage on my own.'

'Perhaps you should ring for you maid.'

'Don't be ridiculous,' she said coldly, aghast at the idea of the rather strait-laced Winnie witnessing the sort of decadence Andrei obviously had in mind.

She went over to the bed and presented him with her back. He undid the gown's tiny fastenings with the deftness borne of practice. She let it fall to the floor, then slowly removed her bracelet and gloves. Her stockings followed and then her camiknickers.

'The choker too.'

She raised her hands to her throat and removed it, then stood naked as he silently appraised her.

'Take a bath,' he ordered her. 'I've no wish to smell Edward on you.'

'Then you'd better have one too,' she retaliated, 'or Amanda might as well be in bed with us.'

'That certainly presents an interesting scenario which may be worth exploring at some future date. However, I don't need to bathe because the only woman I've had carnal knowledge of tonight is you.'

She must have looked sceptical because he said lazily, 'I've no need to lie to you, if I'd had Amanda tonight I'd admit to it – after all, what could you do about it? Now go and bathe – and leave the door open, I wish to watch you.'

Watch her? Lucy flushed and protested, 'I prefer to bathe in private, thank you.'

'What you prefer or don't prefer is of no interest to me at the moment. Run your bath.'

Fuming, Lucy went into the bathroom, being careful not to trip over the raised sill between the two rooms, and turned on the taps. She added some bath salts and soon clouds of scented steam began to waft into the bedroom. Without once glancing at Andrei, she began her preparations, pinning up the golden waves of her hair on top of her head and laying one of the huge, fluffy towels within reach.

She could feel his eyes burning into her as she stepped into the scented water and lay back. She picked up the cake of pink soap and lathered one arm dreamily, then the other. She took a long time over her ablutions, working up lots of rich lather and eventually emerging pink and glowing.

She returned to the bedroom draped in the towel and looked at him enquiringly. He swung his long legs off the bed and asked, 'Where do you keep your lingerie?'

She indicated one of the chests of drawers. He began to rifle through the scraps of silk, satin and lace he found in there, occasionally holding a garment up and then discarding it. Eventually he settled on a slate-grey charmeuse slip which was split to the hip on one thigh. He threw it to her together with a pair of grey stockings and a matching suspender belt.

'Here – put these on.'

The idea of dressing for sex was a new one to Lucy. Before she'd met Andrei she'd always imagined that sex with a lover would take place between the sheets with both of them naked. Instead, she usually seemed to be in a state of semi-undress, her clothing dishevelled and in disarray, which was obviously how he liked it.

She pulled on the underwear, then slipped her feet into a pair of high-heeled grey suede shoes. He walked over to her and said, 'Place your hands on your hips and stay silently in that position until I tell you to move.'

The increasingly familiar feeling that she was a creature he used for his pleasure assailed her as he began to touch her, more in the way of an owner examining his property to see if it had been damaged than a lover caressing his mistress.

His hands followed the curve of her stomach and hips, smoothing over the sensuous fabric of her slip, then slid over her thighs, moulding and caressing them. Despite herself, Lucy could feel her arousal mounting, even at this impersonal handling.

He touched her all over, dropping to his knees and encircling her ankles, then her calves with his long fingers, before kissing her thigh where it was visible through the slit in her slip.

Her breasts were subjected to a long, tactile exploration, the nipples teased and coaxed into swollen points which thrust against their satin covering and sent urgent messages of excitement to her throbbing sex.

But even though she could feel her body gearing up to accommodate him, eager and ready for penetration, her warm juices gathering in her velvet-lined core, this wasn't what she wanted.

She wanted to wind her body around his, pull his head down and have him kiss her. She wanted him to whisper words of adoration, admiration, even love; she didn't want to stand like a statue while he coldly, skilfully brought her to a point of readiness.

He covered her mound with the palm of his hand and massaged it through the slippery satin. She felt herself parting her legs slightly and hated herself for it. But she ached for him to touch her there, burned for the pressure of his cool fingers against her throbbing vulva.

He slid his hand between her legs and massaged her with the tips of his fingers, gently and teasingly. A faint dew of perspiration broke out on Lucy's upper lip as she willed herself to remain still and not spread her legs as far as she could, grab his hand and thrust it upwards to work her to a climax.

This was all wrong. She wanted some say in the way things progressed. She wanted to tell him how she needed him to touch her; she wanted to touch him. The self-control required to stay quiescent was too much. A tiny moan escaped her lips and he smiled grimly.

The teasing pressure against her labia and clitoris was driving her wild. It wasn't hard enough to bring her the release she was starting to need so desperately, it was just spreading a tickling, itching, throbbing fire in her sex.

She stood there for what felt like an eternity while he continued caressing her through the rich Charmeuse of her slip, until her legs trembled and she'd bitten her lip quite badly with the effort of remaining motionless and quiet.

At last she couldn't help herself.

'Andrei . . .'

'Shhh.' He pinched the soft fold of one of her outer sex-lips and then resumed his tantalising fondling.

She was reminded of the first time they'd met. That was the very thing he'd said to her as she'd leant in a similar state of desperate, inconvenient arousal against the rail of the observation platform. But then he'd worked her swiftly to two hot, gasping climaxes, not teased her the way he was doing now.

The satin under his fingers was soaked with her juices and still her honey flowed. She could hear her own breathing – shallow, ragged – as she fought to retain some measure of self-control.

At last he stepped away from her and walked over to the table where he removed the large vase of white orchids and placed them on a chest of drawers.

'Get on the table on your hands and knees,' he ordered her calmly.

She didn't want to get on the table, she wanted him to take her to bed and make love to her properly, not couple with her like an animal on all fours.

But she wouldn't debase herself by pleading with him. Instead, she did as he ordered and then had the additional humiliation of having him walk around her considering her from all angles, before rearranging her so her spine dipped, her bottom was high in the air and her legs widely parted.

He lifted her slip and folded it over her waist, exposing the perfect ivory swellings of her pert buttocks and the whole of her slick, crimson vulva. She gritted her teeth as he caressed her rump lingeringly, then without warning shoved his hand between her legs, squashing her swollen clitoris up between her labia and rubbing hard with a practised circular movement.

The result was electric. Her body seemed to be swept by a fire of pins and needles, half burning, half numbing, then there seemed to be an explosion of heat in her belly and she came in a jarring, crashing wave of pleasure.

As she gave herself up to it, he grabbed her hips and plunged into her, spearing her instantly on his swollen rod, shafting her in smooth, deep thrusts.

His hands clasped her breasts as he drove in and out of her and she felt another climax building swiftly, even before the previous one had receded.

She worked her hips in time to his thrusts, meeting each one, jamming her derrière back against his groin, feeling his heavy testicles slapping against her as they moved together. She came again in a gasping, choking spiral of pleasure, just before Andrei reached his own climax and erupted strongly into her, shouting out his own satisfaction in a hoarse cry.

Chapter Twelve

Amanda was in the back of an open-topped car being driven along a winding coast road high above the sparkling blue waters of the Mediterranean. It was a glorious day, warm and sunny, the air fragrant with the scents of the wild flowers which rioted down the cliffs.

Far below them, the tranquil sea washed lazily against the rocks, breaking in lacy waves at the foot of the cliffs, tracing their rugged contours with tiny, white frills.

Her face shaded from the sun by a wide-brimmed hat and a pair of dark glasses, Amanda studied the broad shoulders of her driver, a blond Russian with a spectacular physique. He'd come with the car and she enjoyed looking at him almost as much, if not more, than the breathtaking scenery. She particularly liked the set of his well-shaped head under his chauffeur's hat and the competent way his large hands held the wheel.

'Find somewhere for us to have our picnic,' she ordered him. 'I'm getting hungry.'

'Yes, madam.' His accent was earthy and guttural and it made Amanda's stomach lurch. Eventually he pulled over to one side of the road and stopped the car.

'Will this do, madam?' he asked, indicating a grassy, flower-strewn plateau about a third of the way down the cliff.

'I should think so.' He held open the door and Amanda stepped gracefully from the car, not missing the way his eyes lingered on the swell of her breasts, then dropped to her thighs

211

as the fine silk of her crocus-yellow striped dress tautened over them.

He took the picnic hamper and a rug from the boot and then followed her as she picked her way delicately down the rocky path that led to the plateau. He spread the rug on the rough, tussocky grass and then busied himself unpacking the hamper, while Amanda sank gracefully down and propped herself up on one elbow.

'The champagne first,' she directed him. It had been packed in ice and the bottle was running with condensation as he deftly wrapped it in a starched, snowy napkin and popped the cork.

The foaming golden liquid tasted wonderful and she lay back and sipped it, watching him from behind her dark glasses as he unpacked plates, cutlery and innumerable savoury delicacies from the wicker basket.

'That tunic looks rather hot,' she commented, as she saw the beads of sweat standing out on his forehead.

'It is, madam.'

'Then I think you'd better take it off.'

'Very well, madam.'

He unbuttoned the thick serge tunic to reveal his undershirt and braces.

'The undershirt too, but keep your hat on.'

Without a word he let the braces dangle by his sides and stripped off the undergarment, then replaced his hat. His torso was a rippling mass of finely muscled planes adorned by a thick mat of blond chest hair. Amanda studied it and slowly licked her scarlet lips with the tip of her pink tongue.

'You'd better remove the trousers too.'

In reply he undid the laces of his shoes, tugged them off and then removed his trousers and socks. Amanda's eyes were drawn to the huge bulge of his groin concealed under the rough cotton of his remaining garment.

She stretched across and laid her hand on it, it was already semi-erect and it hardened rapidly as she gave it an experimental squeeze.

He continued to unload the hamper, his face impassive, his eyes averted from her. Amanda slipped her hand inside his waistband and sought out the hard, smooth shaft of his manhood. It throbbed in her hand, hot and heavy. She could feel an answering throbbing in the moist tissues of her sex and the slow rise of the tide of her arousal.

Her thumb found the glans and rubbed it, spreading the drop of liquid she found there with a circular movement. He was kneeling as he went about his task and with her free hand she drew his undergarment down over his muscular buttocks, her breathing quickening as she did so.

The cotton caught on his rearing shaft and she freed it impatiently, then sat back and stared at where his huge, tumescent member jutted arrogantly out from its thick nest of blond hair.

'Stop doing that and come here,' she ordered him, patting the rug next to her. He sat beside her and she ran her hand down his chest, toying with his chest hair and raking his nipples with her long nails. She stroked the flat planes of his belly, then felt his muscular thighs, before sighing with satisfaction.

'Before you serve lunch I'd like you to service me,' she told him. 'You may do as you please with me – just don't treat me like a lady.'

There was a long-drawn-out pause, then he turned his head and looked at her. His ice-blue eyes were brilliant and unfathomable as he reached out a hand and jerked her hat from her head, tossing it carelessly to one side.

'You cheap little whore, you've been like a cat on heat since I picked you up from the hotel,' he said slowly, his voice harsh, his accent giving the words an additional rough edge.

'You've been sitting in the car in your expensive silk dress thinking about what you'd like me to do to you.'

One large hand covered her breast and squeezed it, while she stared at him mesmerised, her breath coming in short gasps. With a swift movement he wrenched the front of her yellow-striped dress, tearing it down to her waist and ripping her camisole at the same time so that her breasts were bared.

He pushed her back on the rug, bending his head to suck hungrily on one jutting nipple, fondling her other breast with a large hand and then burying it in her crotch through the tattered silk.

She moaned and spread her legs for him, feeling a raw, desperate heat which threatened to overwhelm her growing in her belly. He pushed his hand up her skirt, then froze when he realised she was naked below the dress except for a wisp of a suspender belt and her pale stockings.

'Only a dirty little slut goes out without camiknickers,' he growled, his fingers probing the moist, swollen folds of her vulva. 'You're hot and wet for me already – *aren't you*?'

Amanda's head rolled from side to side as he explored her dripping sex with rough fingers, pushing them inside her, pressing against the velvety walls of her inner chamber.

He knelt between her thighs, pulling her legs up over his shoulders, his member poised at the entrance to her quim as he lowered himself onto her. She wriggled her bottom down the rug, her sex-lips widely parted, her clitoris a swollen red bud.

He paused above her, making her wait, then gradually slid the first inch or so of his shaft between her inner labia and into the whorled entrance to her sex. She clutched at it with her internal muscles, trying to draw more of it in, her hips raised off the ground.

With a sudden thrust he entered her completely, his huge

member filling her up, stretching her to capacity.

'Yes . . . yes . . .' she moaned, as he commenced an athletic, rhythmic pumping, while continuing to accuse her of the most wanton, depraved behaviour in his harsh, foreign accent.

Amanda was being driven wild by it. She scratched his chest so hard with her long nails that he seized her wrists with one hand and held them above her head without pausing in his exertions. She writhed and bucked beneath him, the rags of her silk frock soon damp with her perspiration.

The sun beat down on them, bees buzzed among the sweetly-scented flowers and the waves made a distant whooshing sound at the foot of the cliff, but they were both oblivious to it all as they moved frantically, feverishly together.

The whooshing of the waves became a thunderous hammering in Amanda's ears as she approached a climax of earth-shattering proportions. The bright sunlight was blotted out and became total blackness as she thrashed and flailed beneath him. Then somehow she wasn't lying on her back on a rug any more; she was in bed between rumpled sheets and there was a deafening banging coming from somewhere.

Dazed, bewildered, Amanda sat up, feeling her climax slipping away. In the dim light filtering through the curtains she realised she was in her stateroom on the *Aphrodite* and someone was knocking on her door.

She switched on her bedside lamp, then stumbled out of bed.

'Edward!' she exclaimed groggily. He lurched into the room, slamming the door behind him.

'Where is he?' he demanded, throwing open the wardrobe and then looking into the bathroom.

'Who . . . what are you talking about?' she asked dazedly.

'That Russian bastard!' roared Edward.

How had he known about Stephan – it had just been a dream,

hadn't it? A wonderful, delicious, erotic dream from which Edward had just rudely awakened her.

Edward looked at Amanda for the first time. Her *eau-de-Nil* satin nightgown was damp and clung so closely to her slender figure that even her mound was clearly visible. One shoulder strap had slipped down to reveal a puckered-nippled breast, a gleaming ivory in the lamplight.

'I know he was here!' he yelled.

Without a word Amanda sank languidly onto the bed and delicately touched her own swollen nipple with her slender fingers, stroking it gently. Edward stood stock-still and stared at her, a muscle working in his jaw.

Her sex began to pulse again, a soft insidious tattoo of desire.

'Edward,' she murmured, 'shut up and come here.'

After Leo crept out of her cabin at the break of day, Faye was unable to go back to sleep. She tossed and turned for a while and then decided to get up and go for a swim – she could always have a nap after lunch to catch up on her sleep. She pulled on a towelling robe over her swimming costume and walked through the silent ship to the sun deck.

The breeze was still cool but the sun was just putting in an appearance on the horizon, washing everything in hazy primrose light. The ventilators looked like giant saxophones and cast long, irregular shadows; while the funnels towered high above the deck, trailing puffs of grey smoke behind them.

Faye paused on the edge of the pool to shed her robe, then tentatively walked down the first three steps until she was knee-deep in the water. It felt cold, much colder than in the afternoon when the sun was high in the sky. She hesitated, wondering whether to forget about her swim and go and see if coffee was being served anywhere yet.

A sound just behind her made her turn. The band leader

she'd spoken to last night had appeared and it was obvious that he'd been planning to swim too.

He looked annoyed when he saw that the pool was occupied and that his swim was probably no longer on the agenda, but then he obviously recognised her.

'Morning,' he greeted her.

'Hello there – you're up early.'

He pulled a wry face. 'I need to be if I want a swim before the early risers appear, but you've beaten me to it this morning.'

'I couldn't sleep. Go ahead, I won't tell anyone.'

He nodded at her, threw his towel down on a chair and dived in. He began to swim up and down the pool employing an efficient crawl, his body cutting sleekly through the water like a seal. Faye remained on the steps wishing she could swim like that, but she'd never mastered the crawl. The best she could do was a rather lethargic breaststroke with her chin well up to keep her face out of the water.

Her new acquaintance clearly liked living dangerously. Using a pool reserved for first-class passengers would mean instant dismissal if any of the ship's officers spotted him or anyone travelling reported him.

He paused at the bottom of the steps and stood up, slicking his dripping hair back from his face.

'Aren't you coming in?' he asked.

'It's a bit chilly for me, but I was enjoying watching you.'

'Come on – it only feels cold for the first few seconds, after that it's glorious.'

Reluctantly, Faye took another step in and then shivered as the water lapped at her thighs.

'Just dive in,' he encouraged her. 'It's better to get it over with at once.'

Not wishing to appear feeble, Faye took a deep breath and launched herself into the water, gasping with shock as it closed around her. She swam sedately up and down for a while and then climbed out and sat on the steps, wrapped in her robe. The sun had risen high enough to shed some welcome warmth and she was glad she'd made the effort to come and swim.

The sky was already a cerulean blue and it promised to be another hot day. She gazed up at it thinking that the sky in London was never quite so intensely blue. A movement on the deck above caught her eye and she saw Leo, dressed in a fresh set of immaculate whites looking down at her. She waved cheerfully and he waved back, heading for the steps leading down to the deck she was on.

It suddenly struck her that Leo would certainly recognise the band leader and take exception to him being in the pool. She threw off her towelling robe and swam as quickly as she could towards him. She didn't dare call out and risk Leo hearing her.

In her haste she forgot to keep her head well up and got her face wet.

'Quickly – get out of the pool,' she spluttered. 'The first officer's heading this way.' He glanced up, saw Leo striding towards them, and swam swiftly to the far end, where he hauled himself out and headed off down the deck.

'Who was that you were talking to?' asked Leo, leaning down to help her out of the pool.

'I don't know his name,' she said truthfully.

'It looked suspiciously like the band leader to me,' he retorted, 'and if it was, he shouldn't have been here.'

'No, he's one of Sonya and Andrei's friends,' she told him mendaciously. 'I danced with him at the ball last night.'

'What you find so fascinating about those two I'll never know,' he replied, effectively distracted. 'It'll be a relief to me when I see them leave the ship.'

Faye shivered, partly from cold and partly from the

depressing thought of never seeing them – or Leo – again. Leo picked up her towelling robe and wrapped it around her tenderly.

'You'd better go and get a hot shower. I'll see you later.'

The cable was waiting for her when she returned to her cabin.

FAYE CHILDREN HAVE MEASLES CAN YOU STAY WITH LUCYS AUNT UNTIL PARENTS RETURN EMILY

Faye ran herself a hot bath wondering who on earth they could both stay with now. It was a huge relief not to have to stay with Emily, but it didn't leave them with many options. She would have liked to go and tell Lucy, but it was much too early to disturb her friend, particularly as she was probably still with Andrei.

Pondering the situation she sank gratefully into the scented, steaming water and began to consider who might invite them to be house guests for a while.

When Winnie arrived to tidy her stateroom and hang up her clothes from the night before Faye asked, 'Is Lucy awake yet?'

'Yes, Miss Faye – she's just rung for the stewardess to order her breakfast.'

Still in her silk robe, Faye hurried next door to show her the cable. Lucy was sitting up in bed brushing her golden hair and yawning. She greeted Faye affectionately and studied the cable with a furrowed brow.

'Goodness, aren't we the orphans of the storm,' she commented. 'Whatever shall we do now?'

'I've been trying to think and although I've various cousins and uncles and aunts, there isn't a single one I'd actually like to stay with.'

'Let's draw up a short list,' suggested Lucy. 'There's a pad and pen over there.'

The stewardess arrived with her tray so, while she tucked into a fresh fruit salad of nectarines, strawberries and bananas, followed by toast and marmalade, Faye jotted down a few names.

'I've listed all my possibles,' she said. 'What are yours?'

Lucy paused in the act of spreading marmalade and said, 'Well, there's Uncle Matthew, but he's a bachelor, he hates women and he won't have them in the house, so he's no use. Cousin Betty would take us in but she breeds bull mastiffs – the house absolutely reeks – so forget her. Then there's Great Aunt Anne, but she's a member of some strange spiritualist sect and they hold seances in the dining room, which would be too depressing for words. Whom have you put down?'

'My Uncle Hugh, but Maisie, his wife, is unlikely to agree to have us because they have two daughters who unfortunately look like Hugh.'

'And what does Hugh look like,' asked Lucy with interest.

'All whiskery and gingery with massive hands and feet and the biggest nose you ever saw on a human being.'

'Why does that mean we can't stay?'

'Because Maisie is desperate to get my cousins married off – they've been out for years. And it's not just that they're rather plain; the older one sniffs all the time and the younger can't sing but insists on doing so on every possible occasion. Maisie spends all her time trying to inveigle eligible men into the house under all sorts of pretexts. I'm not being vain, but she'd consider us unfair competition and refuse to consider it. If she sees me coming at a dance or something, she shepherds them off rather than risk me hanging around and showing them up. Well, that's what Mother thinks anyway.'

'Oh dear – who else do you have on the list?'

Faye consulted it again. 'Cousin Dickie and his wife Eliza.'

'Are they a possibility?'

'They'd be delighted to have us, I'm sure, but Mother would have a fit because Dickie is a notorious womaniser and the only person who doesn't know it is Eliza. I'm afraid that rumour has it that no woman is safe in that house. Apparently Dickie spends the nocturnal hours creeping around in his nightshirt trying doors. They get through maids like other people get through packets of tea.'

Lucy brightened up. 'That needn't affect us, need it? We can lock our doors or put a chair behind them. If he did manage to get in, whoever's room it was could just scream the house down and embarrass him.'

'Mother,' said Faye firmly, 'wouldn't hear of it. I'm not allowed to stray from her side if he's anywhere around.'

'Who does that leave then?'

Faye sighed. 'My grandmother.'

Lucy pulled a face and pushed her tray away from her. Faye's grandmother's vile temper and sour disposition were notorious. A stay with her was out of the question – even if she'd have them, which was doubtful because she couldn't stand any of her family, said so often, and only saw them rarely.

'What about Amanda?' Lucy suggested. 'If we explained the problem, do you think she'd invite us to stay with her?'

'Have you forgotten? She's going straight up to Scotland to stay with her husband's parents.'

'Oh, yes, that's right.' Lucy sipped her coffee thoughtfully. 'Faye . . .' she began at last.

'Uum?'

'We could just book into a hotel.'

'A hotel?' Faye brightened considerably, then her face fell. 'We can't really though, can we? Not on our own – it would be all over London within days.'

'It's the nineteen-thirties, not the eighteen-nineties. It's only because both our families are old-fashioned that we're treated like children.'

'We'd get a reputation for being fast,' pointed out Faye.

'So? Let's face it, Faye – we *are* fast. Particularly the way we've both been behaving for the last few days.'

'No one knows about that, do they? We've been discreet.'

'Probably not discreet enough. You know how people like to gossip.'

'We need to sort something out,' said Faye. 'We'll be back in England by this time tomorrow. Couldn't we just go down to Cornwall and stay with your grandfather?'

'It wouldn't be very fair as he's ill. He probably needs peace and quiet. And his house is miles from anywhere – we'd be very bored.'

Faye rose to her feet and tightened the belt of her silk robe.

'Give it some more thought – there must be somewhere we can go. Maybe I'll ask Amanda, there may be some distant relative she knows better than I do.'

Faye found Amanda reading the lastest copy of *Vogue* on deck, Edward next to her absorbed in a detective novel. Amanda looked as stunning as usual in a pair of navy-blue linen trousers with a red-and-white-striped top. On her perfectly pedicured feet were a pair of cork-soled sandals which showed off her toenails, newly painted to the same scarlet as her fingernails.

She raised her sunglasses and surveyed Faye with her pansy-dark eyes while the younger woman told her about their dilemma.

'Darling, that's terrible. I only wish I could invite you up to Scotland. It would be infinitely less grim if I had some fellow souls to talk to. Sure there must be someone you could foist yourselves on? You can certainly stay with me tomorrow night

– I won't be leaving for Scotland until the following morning.'

'Thanks, Amanda, that'll be a big help. I'm sure we can come up with someone if we think hard enough.'

'Don't you have any friends you could try?'

'Probably. We just don't know who's in town and who isn't at the moment as we've both been away.'

'Well, that's settled then. You can stay with me tomorrow and telephone round. Lot's of people should be back by now.'

Faye wasn't so sure. It would be the end of September before London filled up again properly and, as far as she knew, most of her friends were still holidaying somewhere. Nevertheless, at least they had a roof over their heads tomorrow and, as Amanda had nominally been in charge of them on the voyage, neither her mother nor Lucy's Aunt Sarah could object to that.

'I think I'll go and play shuffleboard, for a while,' she said more cheerfully. 'Will you both join me?'

'Edward will,' said Amanda immediately. 'He wanted me to play earlier, but it's just too energetic for me at this time of day.'

Edward put down his book and leapt to his feet.

'Sounds just the ticket. See you later, darling.'

As soon as they'd gone, Amanda picked up her bag and headed back towards her cabin. The erotic dream she'd had about Stephan had left her with an itch that only he could scratch. Edward had satisfied her briefly, but he was too gentlemanly, too restrained, to give her what she wanted at the moment.

Once in her cabin she picked up the phone and dialled Sonya and Andrei's suite, praying Stephan would answer. Instead she got Sonya.

'Amanda – how are you today?' Sonya greeted her. They chatted for a while and then Sonya suggested meeting in the verandah café for coffee.

'Why don't I come to your suite,' suggested Amanda, trying to sound nonchalant. 'The verandah café may be crowded at this time of day.'

There was a pause and then Sonya said lightly, 'Very well, I'll have Marta prepare a pot of coffee. It's a beautiful day – we can have it outside.'

Amanda hastily scribbled a note for Stephan and put it in her pocket, hoping she would get the opportunity to deliver it. She checked her appearance, patted some more powder from her gold and mother-of-pearl compact onto her nose and then left her cabin.

Sonya was lounging on a deck chair on the suite's private verandah, but sadly there was no sign of either Stephan or Andrei. She was coolly elegant in an ivory satin robe with an embroidered peacock on the back, her feet in a pair of high-heeled, ivory satin slippers. Marta brought a tray of coffee and then vanished, leaving Sonya to pour.

They chatted casually for a while and then Amanda said, 'Meeting you and Andrei again on board certainly made this a much more interesting voyage than I'd anticipated.'

Sonya smiled enigmatically.

'I hope you will find it even more interesting tonight.'

'Why? What's happening tonight?' drawled Amanda.

'Andrei and I are throwing a farewell party. You will be receiving an invitation later.'

'Really? That's wonderful. Where are you holding it?'

'The gym,' said Sonya dreamily.

'The gym?' echoed Amanda startled.

'Yes, it was Andrei's idea – isn't he clever? And – even better – it's a masked costume party.'

'Fancy dress? I don't think I've got anything I could wear,' said Amanda doubtfully.

'It's a costume party with a difference,' Sonya tantalised her.

'Really? Do tell.'

Sonya told her. Amanda's eyes widened and then she laughed throatily. 'Surely not everyone will want to do that?'

'Then they need not come. All costumes will be inspected before entry will be allowed.'

'Who will be carrying out the inspections?'

'Stephan.'

Amanda felt a wild, snaking lash of lust between her thighs and stirred slightly on her seat. Tonight promised to be *very* exciting.

'I haven't forgotten our first evening at sea,' she said, lifting her cup to her lips.

'Nor have I.'

'Tell me, Sonya, is Stephan often part of these scenarios of yours?'

Sonya smiled showing her perfect, white teeth.

'As often as he chooses to be.'

'Do you and he ever . . .'

'Frequently.'

'Doesn't . . . doesn't Andrei mind?'

'Why should he?' Sonya stirred her coffee gently, a slight smile playing around her lips. When there was no reply she asked, 'Did you enjoy Stephan?'

'Very much.'

Sonya left her own seat and came to join Amanda on hers. 'Tell me what you thought . . . what you felt that evening,' she murmured. She raised her hand to stroke Amanda's hair, then her cheek and then her shoulders. While Amanda talked of that dinner they'd had together, Sonya caressed her gently, smoothing over the slim curves of her waist and belly, then her breasts.

The lash of lust between Amanda's thighs was fanned into a fire and she fell silent, waiting eagerly for Sonya's next move. The Russian princess drew Amanda's striped top over her head and then dropped the rolled-ribbon straps of her pearl white camisole down her arms so her breasts were bared. She bent her sleek, dark head and took one distended nipple in her mouth, sucking and tugging it softly with her lips.

Amanda's back arched and her head dropped back, displaying the graceful column of her neck. Sonya skilfully undid her linen trousers and the note Amanda had written to Stephan fluttered out.

About to push it back into the pocket, Sonya's eyes were caught by her servant's name and, to Amanda's consternation, she coolly read the message. Smiling, she placed it on the table and slipped her hand inside Amanda's trousers where she wriggled her slim fingers inside the other woman's camiknickers and dabbled them in her dripping vulva.

With her free hand she picked up a small silver bell and rang it. Stephan appeared in the doorway, reminding Amanda so vividly of her dream that she instantly spasmed into a tiny, liquid orgasm, helped by the insistent pressure of Sonya's fingers on the hood of her clit.

'You wanted me, Princess?'

'Yes, Stephan. Our guest has brought you a note, would you care to read it.' Stephan picked up the scrap of paper and perused it expressionlessly. 'Also, I wanted you to see how wet she is – come and feel.'

'Yes, Princess.'

Amanda almost forgot to breathe as Stephan squatted beside the chair and pushed his hand inside her trousers next to Sonya's. Suddenly there were two hands exploring her quim, then she felt three of Stephan's fingers thrust inside her, while Sonya tickled her clit.

'She is *very* wet, Princess,' he agreed, just as Amanda was racked by another, stronger climax which made her internal muscles clutch at his fingers.

'I think she'd like you to fuck her, Stephan. Would you like to perform that service for her?'

'Very much, Princess.'

'Take her into the bedroom and I'll come and help you make her comfortable.'

Amanda almost swooned with sheer carnal anticipation when Stephan lifted her into his arms and carried her into the suite, fondling her bottom and breasts as he did so.

He dumped her on the bed and stripped off her trousers before pulling her to her feet again and positioning her with her back to one of the tall bedposts.

Amanda was startled when, watched by Sonya, he lashed her wrists around the post behind her with a supple leather strap.

Her camisole was still rolled down around her waist and her only other garment was her loose-legged camiknickers.

'I'll just make her come one more time, Stephan, and then I'll leave her alone with you for a while,' Sonya promised him, finding Amanda's swollen bud again. She rubbed it skilfully and quite hard with her forefinger, while Stephan swiftly divested himself of his clothes.

The sight of his ramrod-hard shaft rearing towards the ceiling, combined with Sonya's almost painfully arousing friction, was too much for Amanda. She convulsed into what was to be just one of the large number of climaxes she would sustain that day.

Chapter Thirteen

'A costume party?' said Lucy, pleased. 'That should be fun.' She and Andrei were in the verandah café having coffee after taking a stroll around the deck. He was looking darkly handsome in his open-necked white shirt and flannels but, despite the fact that his clothes had obviously been made for him in London, no one would ever have made the mistake of thinking he was English.

In direct contrast, Lucy looked like the archetypal English rose in a sea-blue linen dress with elbow-length sleeves and a broad black patent-leather belt cinching in her narrow waist. When she'd looked at herself in the mirror before leaving her cabin, she'd thought that she appeared to be thriving on a diet of sea air, sex and very little sleep. Her grape-green eyes were clear and sparkling, her skin tanned to a warm honey and her golden hair shining and sun-streaked.

'What are you going as?' she continued.

'I haven't decided yet.'

The last night of the voyage was traditionally fairly quiet because everyone had to be up early the following morning to disembark. Lucy had assumed that the evening would be pretty much an anti-climax after the captain's gala dinner and was delighted to discover that the festivities – at least among their set – would continue.

'I'll have to give my own costume some thought,' she said, pouring more milk into her coffee. 'I'm not sure what I'll be able to throw together.'

'There's no need for you to do that,' he said softly. 'I have a costume for you.'

Lucy raised her eyes to his and her stomach kicked with apprehension tinged with anticipation. The expression on his face was similar to the one it had borne when he'd paraded her around the deck in the leather suspender belt.

'Wh . . . what sort of costume?' she asked nervously.

'You may see it this afternoon.'

'Thanks all the same, but I think I'll have a look through my wardrobe and get Winnie to adapt something for me.'

His heavy eyelids drooped briefly over his eyes and she had a sudden sense of his iron will as he said, 'Perhaps you would like to see the costume before making that decision.'

There couldn't be any harm in that, she supposed.

'Okay,' she said lightly.

They were partially hidden from the other people in the café by an ivy-covered trellis and he placed his hand briefly and meaningfully on her mound. She knew that this was to remind her of the hold he had over her and she felt a tiny spasm of excitement high up in her sex. He withdrew his hand but his touch served to remind her again of their strange and decadent liaison.

To stop the swift rise of colour in her cheeks, she glanced around the room. The overall effect was that of a winter garden with great tubs of exotic plants and flowers artfully arranged at intervals. A tall palm tree overhung their table and great swathes of trailing creeper hung from the nearby wall.

'I find it quite hard to believe I'm on a ship when we're in here,' she said lightly, changing the subject.

'I think that's the general idea. Some people don't like to be on board a ship and if they sit in here, or the library, they can pretend they're in a hotel because, other than the throbbing of the engines, there's nothing to indicate that we're at sea.'

'I love being on board a ship, or at least I do on this voyage. The journey out was a nightmare and both Faye and I were seasick all the way.' She shuddered at the memory. 'Thankfully it's been fairly calm this time.'

She was immediately assailed by the memory of the one rough evening when she'd lost to Andrei at cards. She'd been so engrossed in trying to beat him that she'd barely noticed the rolling of the ship. It was interesting to speculate whether the sexual thrall Andrei had her in would have been strong enough to prevent seasickness if the weather had remained really rough.

Andrei drained his coffee cup. 'Do you shoot?' he asked her casually.

'Only clay pigeons. The idea of hunting anything living disgusts me.'

'Are you a good shot?'

'Only average,' she replied cautiously. 'Why?'

'I thought perhaps we might compete against each other shooting clay pigeons,' he said smoothly. A warning spark ignited in Lucy's brain.

'What would we play for?' she asked with feigned innocence.

'If I lose I will forfeit my rights to your sexual favours. You will be free to refuse me or take anyone else as you please.'

'And if I lose?'

'You will wear the costume I have chosen for you to the party tonight.'

Lucy gave him a long, level look, then she laughed out loud.

'I wouldn't be so foolish twice, Andrei – my guess is that you're a crack shot and I'm not about to be taken again. No, we'll play for who buys the pre-lunch drinks.'

She smiled at him disarmingly but, although he smiled back,

she could sense his determination to bend her to his will.

Sonya found Faye browsing through the magazines in the library. The older woman was wearing a severe black linen dress of impeccable cut worn with black gloves, a small black hat trimmed with black and white braid and black kid-leather shoes. Her only jewellery was a single strand of pearls which cast a soft glow on her pale, ivory-skinned face.

Looking at her, Faye thought that never in a million years would she be able to achieve that effortless elegance.

'Hello, Faye, I've come to return this,' Sonya greeted her, handing over Faye's topaz ring. Remembering the circumstances under which she'd tried to retrieve it last night, Faye flushed.

'Thank you,' she muttered.

Sonya perched on the arm of one of the leather chairs and crossed her slim legs.

'Are we still friends?' she asked, tilting her head quizzically.

'Yes, of course,' replied Faye, without looking at her. Then she felt her own china-blue eyes drawn to Sonya's silver-grey ones and when they met all her doubts melted away.

'I also came to deliver this in person,' Sonya told her, handing over a stiff, white envelope.

'Another party,' said Faye, when she'd read the invitation. 'I suppose it's a farewell party,' she added sadly.

'Will you come?'

'I'd love to but I don't know what I'll wear.'

'Why don't you come and rifle through my wardrobe this afternoon? I've collected many costumes from different countries on my travels, I'm sure we could find you something.'

'That would be lovely. Will you be able to lend Lucy something too?'

'I think Andrei already has a costume in mind for her.'

'I love parties. What time will it start?'

'After dinner. People can eat at their leisure and then go and change before coming. I'm going for a stroll along the deck before lunch – will you join me?'

As Lucy had suspected, Andrei was an excellent shot and easily beat her, although he appeared to be preoccupied as he expertly shattered clay pigeon after clay pigeon. He left her somewhat abruptly, saying he would see her in the afternoon, not giving her the chance to buy him the drink he'd just won from her.

Shortly afterwards she bumped into Faye and Sonya and all three went for a glass of champagne which they drank in the shade of a yellow-and-white-striped parasol at a white-painted table set out on the deck.

Leo came and spoke to them briefly, then as he walked away Sonya said, 'He reminds me of one of my lovers from several years ago.'

'Really?' asked Faye with interest. 'Who was that?'

'A German baron I met while in Munich. He was very much of that type – so stiff, so correct, so formal. He quite disapproved of me, but his desire for me overcame that and he pursued me vigorously.'

'Were you lovers long?' Lucy wanted to know.

'A couple of months perhaps. He had a castle in Bavaria – a very small castle – but very beautiful. I stayed there with him for a while.'

'Why did you stop seeing him?'

'He couldn't accept Andrei as a part of my life. He wanted me to cut loose from him, give up my travels and become his mistress.'

'His mistress?' echoed Faye. 'Didn't he want to marry you?'

'No. He was of the type who would only marry a virgin he had courted from her parents' home. I had a past, I kept company with people he could not approve of, I was fit only to be his mistress. Nevertheless, he was a pleasing lover once I'd shown him what I liked.'

Faye wondered if the baron had also liked a little pain with his pleasure, and the idea made a shiver ripple down her spine. Had Sonya punished him for his arrogance? Had he enjoyed being humbled?

Sonya sipped her champagne dreamily and continued, 'He became angry when I told him I was leaving for Vienna the following day. He threatened to keep me prisoner in his castle, he said that no one but him would ever have me again, then he locked me in a suite of rooms high up in a turret.'

'Really? Like in a fairytale,' breathed Faye. 'Did you sit and gaze out of the window and wonder if Andrei would come to your rescue?'

'No. I waited until the baron came to me that night and I feigned acquiescence. I pretended I found his masterfulness exciting and we made love for hours. I drove him to further and further excesses until he was exhausted and drained. When he eventually dozed off to sleep I tied him to the bed, took his keys and borrowed one of his cars to drive back to the hotel in Munich where Andrei and I were staying.'

'Did you ever see him again?' Lucy asked.

'Yes. I took Andrei back with me and we made him watch while Andrei had me in front of him. I wanted to make it clear that I hadn't appreciated his threats or his imprisoning me and that in no way did I belong to him. Then we returned to the hotel and left Munich that day.'

'Did you leave him tied up?'

'Oh yes, certainly. I'm sure one of his servants would have found him eventually.'

Lucy and Faye exchanged glances. This was a long way from their own rather uneventful lives to date.

'My story about how Duncan Stewart kept me prisoner in the gun room until I'd kissed him under the mistletoe last Christmas, hardly compares does it?' sighed Faye. 'Another glass of champagne?'

Lucy was sunbathing on her verandah when Andrei brought her the costume to look at that afternoon.

It was really rather lovely, she thought, holding it up and examining it. It was a harem girl's outfit, the top part of which was made from cloth-of-silver. It was lavishly embroidered in pinks, purples and mauves and stopped just above the navel. The accompanying pair of filmy, lilac silk trousers were shot with silver thread and the soft fabric billowed out from the waist to where it was softly gathered at the ankles.

'Shall I try it on?' she asked.

'Please do.' She was about to take it into the bathroom but he stopped her. 'I wish to watch you trying it on. No objections please, Lucy, I shall make love to you in a short while and this will whet my appetite.'

'I wouldn't have thought that your appetite needed any whetting,' she retorted sweetly, but stayed in the room nevertheless.

With her back to him she undressed, then pulled on the top. It fitted perfectly, moulding itself to the contours of her breasts and emphasising her narrow waist. Still in her camiknickers she picked up the trousers and prepared to step into them.

'No self-respecting odalisque would wear camiknickers beneath her harem pants,' he told her. She hesitated, then pulled them off before stepping into the trousers.

'Oh, Andrei, they've come apart at the seams,' she exclaimed. From just above her pubic floss at the front to just below her anus at the back, the material was not sewn together. 'Don't worry,' she told him cheerfully, 'I'm sure Winnie will be able to sew it up before the party.'

An expression of mild impatience crossed his face.

'My dear Lucy, they're meant to be worn like that.'

Shocked, she stared at her reflection in the mirror. If she kept her legs together the material met at the front, giving the illusion that she was decently dressed. If she took a step or moved at all, the material drifted apart to reveal all her golden floss at the front and the cleft between her buttocks at the back. Andrei came up behind her and tapped her gently on the bottom.

'Open your legs.' Automatically she obeyed him. Immediately the whole of her vulva was on display too, so that even the most casual observer could see the intricate folds of her sex-valley and sex-lips and gauge her level of arousal. Andrei ran the tip of his finger down the furrow between her buttocks.

'This is how I like to see you,' he murmured, 'open and ready for me at any time.'

With his other hand he stroked her golden fleece briefly, before tracing the rim of her labia with his forefinger. To her shame a few drops of moisture trickled from her sex and gleamed there in a shaft of afternoon sunlight.

'If you think I'm wearing this to a party you must be out of your mind,' she said caustically. 'I'll wear it for you now, while we're alone, but you'll have to be content with that.'

He continued to stroke her sex-lips with soft, insidious strokes.

'Perhaps I should have explained before – no one will know who you are. This is to be a masked costume party and everyone's identity will be concealed.'

'That doesn't make any difference,' she flashed. 'I'm not parading my private parts through a crowded party.'

'The other stipulation is that all guests will display some

part of their sex-organs, both men and women. It will be interesting to see who is recognisable and who is not.'

'I should think half the women on the ship will know who you are if you display your . . . your manhood,' she retorted.

He smiled at her unperturbed.

'You obviously have an overrated idea of my stamina if you think that. Nevertheless, you will wear this costume tonight, if only to please me.'

'And why would I wish to do that?'

He didn't reply, just kept up his insidious stroking until her clitoris stood out from her labia like a tiny ship's figurehead.

Lucy's legs began to feel weak and she felt a hot, tingling itch in her groin which made her want more than this light, teasing stimulation. She moaned slightly and changed position, mentally willing Andrei to shift into the next gear.

He stroked the shaft of her swollen bud and the sensation of heat which suffused her body increased. She didn't dare move in case he stopped before she reached the dizzying explosion of pleasure he was so adept at bringing her.

Her breathing quickened and she was virtually on the point of coming when he stepped away from her.

'If you don't want to wear the costume then take if off,' he told her. 'Someone else may wish to borrow it.'

Lucy could barely believe that she'd been left high and dry on the brink of climaxing, but she was reluctant to let him see how frustrated she felt.

She pulled the silver top over her head and handed it to him, then pushed the harem pants down her hips and thighs and stepped out of them. She could feel the tide of her arousal receding and it left her feeling irritable and edgy. Why couldn't he have continued for a few moments? Her body knew his touch now and responded to it eagerly, it wouldn't have taken long.

'Aren't we going to . . . you know?' she heard herself saying. He threw himself on the bed, lit a cigarette and then picked up a magazine from the bedside table and began to flick idly through it.

'Do you wish to?'

'I . . . I don't know,' she said untruthfully. Andrei appeared to become absorbed in an article and, rather bad-temperedly, Lucy pulled on a silk robe and turned her back to him. She fastened a white lace suspender belt around her waist and then sat at the dressing table to roll a pair of stockings up her long legs.

'Don't bother with the camiknickers,' he said without looking up as she prepared to don a pair. Her stomach immediately lurched and the walls of her velvet inner-chamber clenched and unclenched with anticipation.

She replaced the camiknickers in the drawer and began to attend to her make-up, although it was actually perfect and had only been applied an hour before.

When she'd done that, she brushed her hair and then began to buff her nails, determined not to sit there just waiting for him to finish reading. At last he looked up and threw the magazine to one side.

'Come here,' he ordered. She went over to the bed and allowed him to help her out of her robe. He laid her on her back and pushed a pillow under her hips, then he took one of her silk scarves and tied her hands to the headboard.

'I don't want to be tied up,' she protested.

'Remember our agreement? This is part of it,' he said dismissively.

She was seething with a combination of anger and apprehension as her ankles were similarly tied to the corners of the bed, so she was held in position with her thighs widely spread. She could see herself in the tilted pier glass directly opposite, her breasts thrusting upwards, a hectic flush already on her cheeks.

Andrei sat beside her on the bed and kissed and caressed her breasts, tugging gently on her nipples with his lips, moulding them in his hands and tonguing her aureoles until she found it hard not to squirm around on the bed.

When he picked up another scarf and bound it around her eyes, she was driven to protest again.

'Don't blindfold me – I don't like it.'

'Not being able to see will heighten your sense of touch,' he said soothingly, 'as you'll soon discover.'

She heard him moving around the room and then she nearly jumped off the bed – or at least as far as her bonds would allow her to – as something soft and downy was drawn across her breasts.

It took her a few moments to identify it as her powder puff, as he dabbed delicately at her nipples and tickled her cleavage with it, then stroked her belly. He worked it in swirling circles up her stocking-clad thighs, then dabbled it voluptuously against the bare skin above her stocking tops.

It was a sublime feeling and she began to relax, sighing as he dabbed at her vulva with it, stimulating every inch of her sex-flesh. It was almost painfully arousing to have it make fleeting contact with her clitoris.

She was less keen on his next choice – her hairbrush. Although the bristles were only soft, it still felt scratchy and stiff as he drew it over the firm, high orbs of her sensitive breasts. It was more enjoyable as he brushed his way over her thighs, although she suspected her stockings would be ruined. Having her golden floss brushed was a novel experience but she winced in anticipation as he approached her labia.

Thankfully he didn't linger in that area. Instead, he turned her partially onto her left side, though it was an uncomfortable position as there wasn't enough play in the scarf holding her right leg to enable her to lie fully on her side.

He used the hairbrush to stroke her buttocks quite roughly, so that after a few minutes the tender skin of her bottom felt as though it was on fire. It was a relief when he finally let her fall onto her back again.

Lucy couldn't tell how long she lay there while he touched, stroked and tormented her with a variety of objects until she was dazed and disoriented, never knowing whether the next thing to make contact would be soft or hard, hot or cold.

Every nerve ending was jangling with alarm and anticipation and she jumped whenever he touched her.

It was then that he turned his full attention to her sex-delta. She gradually relaxed again as he used his hands and mouth to turn her private parts into a yielding, pulsing dripping jungle of desire, until the need to have him bringing her to a climax, enter her, fuck her, was overwhelming.

He worked on her in silence and as she was still blindfolded it was as if all her senses were centred on the sensations he was coaxing from her overflowing quim.

Her arousal mounted and mounted until she felt it would be impossible to climb any higher and that she would black out if she didn't climax soon. But somehow Andrei never lingered on her throbbing bud quite long enough to push her over the edge. She tried to press her thighs together but the silk scarves kept them wide apart. She tried to will herself into orgasm but it didn't work.

'Andrei,' she gasped at last, 'let me come!'

There was no reply, then the bed rocked as he stood up and she heard him walk across the room. Lucy simply couldn't believe her ears when she heard him pick up the telephone and order tea.

'What the hell are you doing?' she demanded, barely able

to speak for the urgent, frustrated throbbing in her sex. When he didn't reply, she shrieked, 'Andrei! Let me go at once! Do you hear me! *Let me go!*' She yanked wildly at the silk scarves holding her prisoner, but they merely tightened over her wrists and ankles.

'If you shout like that again I may have to gag you,' he threatened pleasantly. 'Surely you wouldn't deny me the refreshment of tea after all the time I have just spent pleasuring you?'

'You haven't pleasured me yet,' she ground out through gritted teeth. 'I've been hovering on the brink of coming for hours now. Please, Andrei, just let me climax and then we'll have tea together.'

'If that's what you want.'

'It is, it is,' she moaned as the bed sagged under his weight.

'I wish to please you in all things carnal,' he told her, sliding two fingers inside her and simultaneously circling her clit with his thumb. She waited breathlessly for the few deft strokes which she knew was all it would take to send her into ecstasy, but they didn't come.

'Andrei – please,' she begged, hating the imploring note she could hear in her voice.

'I will do exactly as you desire,' he said softly, 'if . . .'

'If what?' she said desperately, wondering why he was tormenting her like this.

'If you agree to wear the harem costume just as it is at tonight's party.'

Lucy went rigid on the bed.

The bastard. The absolute bastard.

As if her blindfold had suddenly been removed and her sight restored, she saw his plan. He was going to keep her suspended in purgatory until she acquiesced to his demand.

'Go to hell,' she said icily. 'Now let me go or when your

tea arrives I'll scream my head off and you can spend the last afternoon and night in the hold or whatever passes for the cells on this ship.'

There was a knock on the door and to her amazement he said, 'Go ahead. If you don't mind being seen in that rather unusual state by the steward and you don't mind the entire ship knowing about it within the hour.'

He walked unhurriedly down the short corridor to the door and opened it.

'I'll take it in,' she heard him say, while she bit her lip and tried to decide whether to scream or not. Too late, the door closed and she heard the steward's footsteps fade away.

'I will *never* forgive you for this,' she said in a low, distinct voice as she heard him pour his tea.

It seemed like a lifetime before he returned to the bed. By this time her frustration had ebbed slightly, but when his hand closed over one breast, she knew he would have her reduced to the level of a cat on heat again within a few minutes.

She tried to resist his skilfully arousing hands, lips and tongue by making her mind go blank, but it didn't work. When he climbed astride her supine body and she felt the smooth glans of his penis nudging between her thighs, she thought he'd relented.

But his hard rod remained poised at the entrance to her yearning, clutching, aching sex-valley as he said, 'Just agree to wear the harem costume and I'll spend the next hour satisfying you in any way you wish.'

In a fever of desperation she wriggled her body frantically down the bed, trying to get more of him inside her. But her bonds allowed for very little play and she was unsuccessful. Teeth clenched, she called him every vile name she could think of as he rolled off her and began to fondle her inner thighs.

'I wouldn't have believed you would know such words,' he

observed mockingly, slipping two fingers inside her and moving them around. 'Your friends would be shocked to hear you now.'

Driven to distraction, Lucy opened her mouth and screamed as loudly as she could – anything to end this torture. He clamped his hand over it and squeezed her clit teasingly with the finger and thumb of his other hand.

'Just agree and I'll fuck you to a dozen orgasms,' he breathed against her ear.

His hand lifted from her mouth and against her will she heard herself saying, '*Yes! Yes!* I'll wear your wretched costume, just don't torture me any more.'

It took only a few seconds before she climaxed; an explosive, gut-wrenching, endless spiralling into ecstasy, which left her weak, trembling and spent.

Andrei removed her blindfold, undid the silk scarves binding her to the bed and mounted her, his shaft in his hand. He slid it smoothly inside her sopping quim and bent to kiss her, then reared back in shock as she thumped him as hard as she could on the side of his head.

She'd actually been aiming for his chin, but the removal of her blindfold had left her dazzled by the light streaming in through the windows and she was slightly off target.

He swore and grabbed her wrist as she attempted to follow it up with another blow, so great was her fury at the way he'd treated her. She hit him on the chest with her other fist and he grabbed that wrist too, holding them over her head while she struggled wildly to free herself so she could vent more of her rage.

But even as she twisted and turned beneath him, he continued to thrust in and out of her and very quickly she felt another climax building.

Of their own volition her hips were moving against his,

meeting each thrust, slamming up against him, demanding more. She came again, a powerful, piercing, jagged climax which spasmed through her body leaving her like a limp doll impaled on his still plunging shaft until, with a hoarse groan, he erupted inside her in a great surge of release.

He lay to one side of her, panting, until she hit him hard across the buttocks.

'I hope you don't think that's it,' she said coldly. 'You promised to satisfy me for as long as I liked if I agreed to wear your obscene costume. Well I've agreed, so get busy again.'

Chapter Fourteen

Faye was shaking as she tried her costume on again before dressing for dinner. She could only be devoutly thankful she would be masked if she was going to attend a party dressed in the Marie Antoinette costume Sonya had lent her.

It had been fun at first. She'd enjoyed rifling through Sonya's wardrobe, thrilled by the variety of costumes the other woman had picked up on her travels. She'd felt spoilt for choice as she'd stroked the rich material of one, admired the delicate embroidery of another.

It was only when she'd begun to try them on that she'd realised what they all had in common.

They all left some part of either her breasts, bottom or mound on display. Under Sonya's ironic gaze she hadn't felt able to say what she really thought. Her friend had gently made it clear that anyone attending the party had to do so with some intimate part of their body exposed, or they wouldn't be admitted.

Faye had been tempted to say that she wouldn't be going, but she couldn't bear the idea of being left out, particularly on the last night.

She'd tried on five different outfits, tugging furtively at them in an attempt to see how decent she could make them, but they'd all remained obdurately revealing. She'd eventually chosen the Marie Antoinette costume as the least of several evils because it exposed only her breasts. When she'd tried it on she'd thought it was lovely – except for that one detail.

Of Wedgwood-blue silk, trimmed with clusters of matching blue ribbons and white lace, it had several stiff underskirts which made it stand out several feet around her. It suited her doll-like beauty, the tight lacing emphasised her narrow waist and she loved the full spread of her skirts and the way they rustled as she walked.

But the tight lacing also pushed her breasts up and they spilled out above the intentionally low-cut bodice in a spectacular display of creamy flesh, tipped by coral nipples. No matter how much she tugged, the bodice remained determinedly below her breasts.

It had another feature she wasn't keen on, but thankfully this one was hidden. Two be-ribboned panniers covered her buttocks and hips, but the material beneath them had been cut away, so if anyone raised them the full swell of her ample bottom was exposed.

'You look so beautiful,' Sonya had told her softly, standing behind her and stroking Faye's breasts with her slender hands. Faye had stood mutely in front of the mirror watching as the coral nipples grew hard and sensitive under Sonya's caresses.

She'd succumbed of course, but now she wasn't sure she had the courage to go through with it. She smoothed the blue silk of the skirts and adjusted the fall of delicate white lace from the elbow-length sleeves, but nothing she did could detract from the fact that she was virtually, and very obviously, naked from the waist up.

If only the costume had been decent she would have loved wearing it – it was perfect for her. Perhaps she could arrange a white chiffon scarf over her breasts, but even as she tried it she knew that it wouldn't work.

Stephan would be manning the door and, as each masked and cloaked guest arrived, they would be subjected to an inspection to ensure that they'd complied with Sonya and Andrei's rules.

Faye had asked Sonya what she would be wearing and she'd produced a Cleopatra costume which had taken Faye's breath away.

Authentic in every detail, the dress was made from white linen so fine that it was virtually transparent and the fabric was woven with gold so it shimmered softly in the afternoon sunlight. Gathered under the bust in soft pleats, the dress had a deep neckline with two wide shoulder straps and fell open from above the navel to the ankles.

Faye had goggled at it, speechless.

'It's lovely,' she had managed at last, thinking that at least no one would be looking at her if Sonya was in the room.

Now, staring at her exposed bosom, Faye wondered if she'd be able to keep her cloak on – at least for a while. She picked up the black silk mask which came with the costume and pulled it on.

That was much better – at least the brazen hussy she saw reflected in the mirror was an anonymous brazen hussy. As far as she was concerned she was planning to remain masked all evening.

It was a curiously subdued couple of friends who went into the terrace grill for a drink before dinner. Both wearing cocktail dresses – no one dressed for dinner on the last night – they ordered a bottle of champagne and went to sit at one of the tables by the curving wall of windows.

Lucy broached the subject that was on both their minds.

'I hardly dare ask,' she said, after taking a reviving gulp of her drink and then coughing as the bubbles caught the back of her throat, 'but what costume are you wearing?'

'Marie Antoinette,' replied Faye self-consciously. 'What about you?'

'A harem dancer.'

They were both silent for a minute and then in reply to Faye's unspoken question, Lucy blurted out, 'The pants are virtually transparent and split between the legs. Honestly, Faye – it's horrific, you can see everything when I walk.'

'That sounds like an improvement on mine – a topless Marie Antoinette. It doesn't matter whether I walk, stand or sit – my breasts stand out in front of me like ripe grapefruit on a shelf.'

She looked so comically put-out that Lucy couldn't help herself and burst out laughing.

'Of course, we don't have to go,' continued Faye.

'I do – I've promised Andrei.' Both women drained their glasses as if on a single string and Lucy poured two more. 'The champagne should help,' she said hopefully.

'And the fact that we'll be masked,' added Faye.

'This is ridiculous,' said Lucy suddenly. 'No one will know who we are and, even if they do, everyone else will be in the same position. It will be fun, something to remember when we're back on what I'm afraid will seem like the very dreary debutante circuit. Let's have lots to drink and try to enjoy ourselves.'

They clinked glasses and smiled at one another.

Unusually for her, Faye couldn't eat much at dinner and merely toyed with her food. It was probably as well, the tight lacing of the dress would be unbearable if she had a full stomach. Leo came to chat to her for a few minutes as she drank her coffee.

'I hope you aren't thinking of going to the private party being held in the gym tonight,' he said austerely.

'We . . . we thought we'd just look in for a few minutes,' replied Faye lamely.

'I don't think you should go at all.'

'We've been invited – it would be rude not to,' she murmured.

'There won't be any of the ship's officers or crew there,' he pointed out. 'I don't like the sound of that at all. Things could easily get out of hand and who'll be there to put a stop to any trouble?'

'I promise that if there's any trouble, I'll leave at once.'

'Come and find me if there is – I won't be far away, but I wish you'd change your mind and not go.'

Lucy joined them at that moment.

'Don't be a spoilsport, Leo – it's the only thing of any interest happening tonight,' she told him.

'There'll be dancing in the main lounge,' he said defensively.

'That won't be as much fun as a party,' Lucy asserted. 'Drink up, Faye – it's time we went to change into our costumes.'

With an apologetic look at Leo, Faye allowed herself to be borne away.

'I hope he doesn't take it into his head to insist on looking in,' she said. 'He'd pass out from shock. Will you come and lace me into my costume later? I can't manage it by myself.'

'Just as soon as I've got into mine,' Lucy assured her.

Faye had a vague recollection of reading somewhere that women in the eighteenth century powdered their hair. In a determined attempt to disguise herself she went into the bathroom and emptied virtually a full tin of talcum powder on her chestnut waves. She pinned it up as best she could, looked at her reflection doubtfully in the mirror and then went to pull on the underskirts.

When Lucy arrived, her cloak around her, her mask in hand, she was startled.

'What on earth have you done to you hair?'

'Covered it in talcum powder.'

'I thought you must have gone prematurely white from fear.'

'No, but when I wash out the powder it may have turned white underneath from shock. Have you thought what the men will look like?'

'Let's hope they'll all be so conscious of their own semi-nakedness that they won't notice ours.'

Lucy laced Faye into her dress, then slipped off her cloak and stood with her legs apart. They both burst out laughing at the same moment.

'We look like a couple of . . . I don't know what we look like!' gasped Faye. 'Quick, let's go before we lose our nerve.'

They donned their masks and cloaks and made for the gym. Someone's valet was standing at the end of the corridor which led there and he checked their invitations before he allowed them past.

There was a small ante-room to each side of the double doors leading into the gym. Stephan was in one inspecting each female guest in turn and Marta in the other inspecting the male guests.

Lucy went first and at his request removed her black silk cloak. His cold blue eyes surveyed her dispassionately and then he gestured at her to open her legs. Her face burning under her mask she did so, then had to suffer the indignity of him walking around her, observing her naked sex from all angles.

She jumped when she felt his hand on her fleece and he said, 'It is the wish of the Princess and the Count that all guests must be in a sexually aroused state before joining the party. I must satisfy myself this is the case and, if not, take the necessary action.'

His hand slid downwards and he dipped his fingers into the groove between her labia. It was slick and wet. Her afternoon with Andrei had ended with her sustaining several more climaxes and her body, even several hours later, was still in an excited state.

Stephan ran his fingers around her sex-lips, slid briefly into her moist quim and then thumbed her clit before saying, 'You may join the party.'

Thankfully, Lucy started to pull her cloak back on but he stopped her. 'All cloaks must be left in here,' he told her, indicating the line of hooks on the wall where many were already hanging.

Lucy was nonplussed – she hadn't bargained for this, but she didn't seem to have much choice and having come this far she wasn't about to back out now. She left her cloak, then taking a deep breath slipped back outside, trying to take tiny steps so her costume didn't reveal too much.

Faye's eyes widened when she saw her, 'I thought we were keeping our cloaks on,' she hissed, as Stephan beckoned her into the ante-room.

'So did I,' returned Lucy. 'I'll wait for you out here.'

Nervously, Faye opened her cloak to reveal her full, naked breasts to Stephan. He looked at her long and hard and then whisked her cloak from around her.

'It is necessary that all guests are in a state of arousal before joining the party,' he said. 'I must check this myself and if they are not, as part of my duties I must remedy the situation.'

Faye was so embarrassed to be standing there in her revealing costume that she barely heard him. She was too busy wondering whether to grab her cloak and flee back to her cabin and was startled when he moved behind her and she felt him lift one of the panniers of her dress.

A moment later she let out yelp of surprise as she felt his hand on her bare bottom. Her legs tensed automatically as Stephan groped between them to find her dry and tight.

'You are not sexually excited,' he told her. 'This must be attended to immediately.'

'Wh . . . what . . . how?' she stuttered.

'Open your legs.'

Accustomed from childhood to being obedient, Faye did as she was told. The hand between her legs began to caress her vulva, massaging it and pressing upwards, stimulating the tight knot of her clit with the pad of his thumb. With his other hand he fondled her breasts, weighing them like the grapefruit she felt they resembled, stimulating her nipples by moving the palm of his hand over them in a circular motion.

Faye stood stock-still and let him handle her, glad she was masked. She pretended to herself that this wasn't really happening, that it was just an erotic dream.

It was very erotic in a way. He touched her impersonally, like a man doing a job, but glancing downwards she saw that there was a large bulge in his trousers and his breathing wasn't quite even.

For a short while she thought his ministrations weren't going to have the desired effect and that she would remain dry and tight.

What would happen then?

Would she be sent away, forbidden to join the party? Or would he send for Sonya to come and attend to her? Or perhaps Andrei?

The idea, combined with Stephan's practised stimulation began to have the desired effect and a few moments later she heard him grunt with satisfaction as her labia and sex-valley became moist and slippery.

'You may join the party now,' he told her, withdrawing his hand and letting the pannier fall back into position to conceal the cut-away part of her skirt.

In a daze, Faye stumbled outside to find Lucy chatting to

Amanda, whom she recognised instantly, despite her black velvet mask.

Amanda had already removed her cloak to show that she was wearing a white Grecian gown which fell in elegant folds around her bare feet in their gold, thonged sandals. The gown was pleated and draped to emphasise her tall, slender figure, leaving one shoulder and one breast bare. Her dark hair was piled on top of her head and there was a narrow band of black ribbon around her forehead.

Stephan appeared in the doorway and his usually impassive face hovered for a moment on what might have been the hint of a smile, then he indicated she should enter the room. Amanda obviously had no inhibitions about what was to come. She glided after him and as she moved her gown fluttered around her, revealing that it was split to the waist over one hip to allow alluring glimpses of her ivory limbs.

'Don't wait for me,' she called over her shoulder as the door closed behind her.

A man came out of the ante-room opposite and Faye clutched at Lucy's arm when she saw that he was displaying a huge, erect penis which rose from the folds of a tiger skin tied around his waist.

'That maid of Sonya's just pulled my . . . my penis out and rubbed it,' he told them in a strangled voice which she recognised as Edward's, despite the fact that it seemed to be an octave higher.

He was masked too, but she could see that his cheeks were flushed beneath it. He noticed Faye's naked breasts for the first time, gulped and then said questioningly, 'Faye?'

'I thought no one would recognise me,' she said disappointed. 'Particularly not with white hair.'

'Don't worry, I wouldn't have done,' he assured her. 'But Lucy recognised Amanda and as soon as I heard her voice I knew who it was, so I expected her to be with you. If you see what I mean . . .' His voice trailed off.

'Amanda said not to wait for her, so let's go inside,' Lucy encouraged them. 'I don't know about you two, but I'm ready for another drink.'

'Rather,' agreed Edward fervently, trying without success to tuck his rearing member back inside the tiger skin.

Inside the ante-room Amanda leant back against the wall and wound her arms around Stephan's neck, her eyes glittering behind her mask.

'I think you'll find I need a lot of attention,' she purred. 'Far more than any of the other guests.' He slid his hand under her gown to discover that she was naked beneath it. He stroked the silken skin of her hips, then burrowed between her thighs to find that the tissues of her vulva were hot, swollen and sopping wet.

'A little more stimulation would not go amiss,' he agreed, pushing three fingers inside her and exploring the velvety walls of her inner chamber. He bent his blond head to take the distended nipple of her naked breast between his lips and flicked his tongue over the swollen point.

Amanda moaned and bore down on his hand, opening her legs wide.

'You'll need to be very thorough,' she gasped, reaching for his fly. Two of his buttons flew off as she dragged his trousers around his thighs. He pushed her back against the wall, withdrew his hand from her sopping quim and substituted the massive column of his manhood in one smooth thrust.

Amanda groaned and pulled his head down to fasten her mouth to his. His hands found her hips and lifted her off the floor so she could wrap her long legs around his waist, jamming herself as far onto his rod as she could. He supported her with his hands under her bottom and they commenced an urgent, frantic coupling against the wall.

She rose and fell on his pistoning member, her moans and cries of pleasure audible to the people in the corridor outside.

The hours she'd spent with Stephan earlier in the day had been among the most exciting in her life, particularly when she'd been tied helplessly to the bedpost.

The knowledge that by this time tomorrow her sexual idyll would be over, increased her determination to milk every drop of carnal gratification from the party. She could tell by his quickening thrusts that Stephan was on the verge of release and rocked herself wildly on the shaft which was impaling her so pleasurably.

Her climax shattered through her slender body, causing her legs to tighten convulsively around Stephan's waist as he erupted into his own release.

It was a trembling and sated Amanda he lowered to the floor a few moments later. She smiled at him as she rearranged her costume and tidied her hair in the mirror.

'I think I'm ready to join the party now,' she told him. 'I'll probably see you later.'

Faye was in a state of shock and Lucy only marginally more in control. Neither woman would ever forget the sight of so many male members displayed in varying stages of erectness.

'I can't look,' Faye said weakly when they walked into the gym.

It was a bizarre spectacle.

Standing in groups around the various vaulting horses, benches and exercise machines were figures from every era of history, each of them partially naked. The array of male genitalia, buttocks, breasts and mounds was staggering.

Edward grabbed three glasses from a tray and handed

two of them to his female companions.

'What is it?' asked Faye in a trembling voice.

'Who cares,' returned Lucy, draining half her glass in one gulp. It was chablis and although Faye would much have preferred hock, she nevertheless gulped it gratefully down. Edward downed his in one and then muttered something about whisky and vanished in pursuit of one of the waiters.

Faye envied Lucy – when she was standing still her costume was reasonably decent, but half the men in the room appeared to be ogling her own full breasts.

A slim and regal figure in a gauzy gown of flimsy gold and white came across the floor to speak to them. Faye would have known Sonya anywhere, even if she hadn't already seen the costume she was wearing.

The Russian princess made a convincing Egyptian queen. Under her painted mask they could see that her eyes had been outlined with kohl, the lids heavily made-up with green malachite powder. Around the slender column of her ivory neck was a gold sunburst necklace and her upper arms and wrists were weighed down by several heavy gold bangles.

But the most arresting part of her appearance was the way her dress fell open from the navel downwards to reveal a smooth, shaven mound.

Even Faye, who'd seen the costume earlier that day, was unprepared for the overall effect. She'd never seen a woman without a pubic fleece before and thought how erotically vulnerable Sonya's delicate mound and vulva looked without their usual triangle of silken hair.

The blunt arrow of her deep crimson clit protruded from her outer sex-lips and Faye wondered whether Stephan had been instrumental in her obvious state of arousal.

'Welcome, both of you,' she greeted them, leaning forward to kiss Faye's cheek and then Lucy's.

Faye couldn't take her eyes from Sonya's sex.

'When . . . why did you do that?' she blurted out.

Sonya laughed huskily.

'My appearance is authentic in every detail. Egyptian women removed all their body hair with pumice. Andrei removed mine with a razor just a few hours ago.'

Lucy had a sudden vivid picture of Sonya, perhaps sitting on her *chaise longue* on a towel, her legs apart, her eyes half closed as Andrei bent over her, razor in hand.

Lucy knew that she herself would be terrified in case he cut her, but something told her that Sonya would have no such fears. She imagined him deftly working up a lather first, then skilfully removing the dark, silken fuzz an inch at a time. When he'd finished and had rinsed away the foam, had he bent his dark head to kiss the newly revealed whorls of Sonya's vulva? Or had he been too tired?

She had, after all, kept him in her cabin until it was time to dress for dinner, making him pleasure her again and again until she was completely satisfied. She had to admit he had stamina.

Faye was still staring raptly at Sonya's bare mound.

'Would you like to touch it?' asked Sonya invitingly.

In response Faye stretched out a tentative hand and ran her fingers over the whole area. It felt soft and smooth to the touch – Andrei had obviously done a very thorough job.

'It feels lovely,' said Faye. 'Touch it, Lucy. Should we try it, do you think?'

Lucy in turn traced the contours of Sonya's mound and replied, 'I wouldn't dare.'

Noticing their empty glasses Sonya gestured to a waiter who proffered foaming flutes of freshly poured champagne.

'There are several things to remember while you are here,' she told them as they sipped their drinks. 'The first is that if you see a man in a detumescent state, you are at liberty to arouse him in any way you choose. The converse is also true, but as long as you remain aroused no one may touch you without your permission.

'Soon there will be dancing to break the ice and after that . . . who knows? When you leave here, please remember to don your cloaks as I've no doubt that the charming, but disapproving first officer who is so enamoured of you, Faye, is somewhere in the vicinity just waiting for the opportunity to crash in and break up the party. Above all, enjoy yourselves.'

She glided away to greet more new arrivals.

'Do you see Andrei anywhere?' Lucy wanted to know.

'Difficult to tell. Could he be the Roman soldier, do you think?' Lucy studied the tall, lean figure leaning against the wall. He was the right height and his shoulders had the same spread, but the way he held himself wasn't familiar. She glanced down to where the man's member reared parallel to his spear and shook her head. It was much shorter and thicker than Andrei's.

'No, I don't think he's here yet.'

'Let's walk around – I feel conspicuous just standing still,' suggested Faye. She was eager to stop people looking at her and thought they might be distracted by the sight of Lucy's golden-fleeced vulva when the thin lilac silk of the harem pants drifted apart as she walked.

'Who's that, do you think?' asked Lucy, indicating a Josephine Bonaparte with no back to her dress from the waist down.

'The French industrialist's wife from the next table, I think.'

They were both intrigued by the fact that many of the guests were totally unrecognisable, despite the fact that they'd undoubtedly met them all during the voyage.

'Amanda's taking a long time,' commented Lucy, who'd noticed she hadn't entered the gym yet.

'Stephan must be having difficulty getting her in the party mood,' said Faye, remembering her own body's initial reluctance to respond to the Russian's impersonal handling.

'I'm not sure about that. She seemed keyed up with anticipation when she was waiting to go in. I just hope Edward hasn't noticed how long she's taking.'

'Edward's too busy chatting to Elizabeth the First.' It was true that he seemed to be deep in conversation with a petite redhead whose hair was threaded with pearls and who was wearing a rich brocade dress and a stiffly starched ruff, beneath which her breasts protruded rudely through two large, circular holes.

Andrei entered the room at that moment and Lucy recognised him immediately despite his mask. He was wearing a wide-sleeved white shirt and a pair of skintight fawn breeches which were tucked into a pair of soft black leather boots.

A crimson sash around his waist and a sheathed sword by his side indicated that he was a buccaneer. The only unorthodox aspect of his costume was a cut-away oval in the front of his breeches from which his rampant phallus reared arrogantly ceilingwards.

He paused just within the doors and scanned the crowd. Lucy felt her already moist sex-valley becoming drenched by a sudden rush of her juices as his eyes met hers across the rapidly filling room.

He strode across, pulled her into his arms and kissed her. She could feel the heat and iron hardness of his manhood pressed against her stomach and longed to feel it forging inside her, eagerly welcomed by the soft folds of her pulsing sex.

Suddenly it seemed like a waste of time to be at a party when they could be in her stateroom, their bodies moving against each other in an urgent striving for satisfaction.

She felt his hand cupping her silk-swathed buttocks, then

his fingers slipped inside the split in her harem pants.

'So wet and ready,' he breathed, probing the cleft of her buttocks, then sliding down between her legs. She was immediately receptive to his touch and her breath caught in the back of her throat as he brushed the bud of her clit with his finger. Like a tiny electric shock, she felt a sudden charge of lethal sexuality jab through her body.

She pressed against him and her slender hand closed around his manhood, feeling the heat of it searing against her palm. She was assailed by the determined thought that if all she had left was one more night with Andrei, she was going to enjoy it to the full, regardless of who might be watching.

Chapter Fifteen

Sonya ascended the low platform at one end of the room and clapped her hands together for silence. Regretfully, Lucy stopped fondling Andrei's throbbing member and turned to face the Russian princess as she addressed the gathered revellers.

'Welcome everybody, we're so glad you could attend the last night of festivities on board the SS *Aphrodite*. To begin the evening, there will be dancing – but it will be dancing with an unusual twist.'

She went on to explain that they should form a large double circle, men facing women. They were to follow the usual steps of an old-fashioned dance but, instead of taking each other by the hand, or in the traditional waltz hold, they would each clasp their partner rather more intimately.

When the music struck up, Lucy was opposite Andrei and they were to walk twelve paces forwards and then twelve paces back, before waltzing in tight circles within the large circle.

His hand smoothed over her bottom, then she felt two fingers pushing inside her from behind until she was effectively impaled by him. As they walked forward Lucy could feel his fingers moving within her and her muscles clenched welcomingly around them.

It was a strange and sweetly deviant sensation to be steered through the motions of the dance like that, rather than with Andrei's arm around her. She found it extremely arousing and adjusted her movements to obtain the maximum pleasure from the penetration.

When it was time to turn and retrace their steps, Lucy reached for his member and squeezed it gently as she led him back down the room.

For a while she was much too intent on her own pleasurable reaction to take any notice of the other dancers but, as they waltzed, fondling each other openly, she couldn't help but notice the lewd and inventive ways in which the rest of the guests were touching each other.

Faye's partner, a slim, fair-haired pilot in a brown leather jacket, his face partially masked by his goggles, was clasping her by the breasts, while she had her hand rather diffidently on his bare buttocks.

Amanda, who had at last joined the party, was leaning back against the broad chest of a Breton fisherman, her arm bent behind her and her hand busy stimulating his shaft. He had one hand pushed through the slit in the side of her costume and over her mound, his fingers splayed across it beneath the thin covering of cotton.

Her mouth below the black silk mask looked swollen and very red and Lucy saw her suddenly bite her lip in an attempt to suppress a moan.

Goodness – she wasn't going to come in front of everyone was she? But it seemed she was because her eyes fluttered closed, her back arched and Lucy saw her body racked by a series of spasms.

The erotic dance came to an end and was followed by several others, all designed to encourage lewd behaviour. After about an hour Andrei suggested a glass of champagne. He kept his hand buried in her sex, propelling her across the room before him, his thumb pressed tantalisingly against the furled bud of her anus. They were sipping their drinks when Sonya announced the next event of the evening.

Everyone in turn had to work their way around the gym, using each piece of equipment briefly and as best they could if hampered by a particularly restricting costume. Lucy could see that this would be supremely exhibitionist and waited with interest to see who would lead the way.

The Roman soldier volunteered and showed off his superbly muscled body as he vaulted over horses, climbed ropes, hung upside down on the wall bars and lifted weights.

Faye watched in dawning horror from the other side of the room. Never very athletic, she doubted if she'd be able to do a circuit of the gym in sports gear, let alone in a Marie Antoinette costume.

Now seemed as good a time as any to take a breather from the party and return to her stateroom to freshen up. She also wanted to check that the powder hadn't worn off her hair – she didn't want the slightest hint of chestnut to show through. She planned to rise early the next day to wash it and by doing so expunge any trace of the brazen creature who'd spent the evening at a party with her breasts on full display.

She slipped out of the gym and hesitated outside the anteroom where she'd left her cloak. What if Stephan was 'inspecting' a late arrival to the party? It would be too embarrassing for words. But she could hardly make her way along numerous ship's corridors dressed as she was.

Nervously, she poked her head around the door and was relieved to find the room deserted. She took her cloak from its hook and tied it around her, then set off for her cabin.

She was just passing the main lounge when, to her horror, she heard her name called. Looking huntedly over her shoulder she saw Leo coming towards her. How had he recognised her in a mask, cloak and powdered hair?

For some reason she panicked, thinking she couldn't let

him see her like this, and turned into the lounge, hoping to lose him in the press of people. But as she exited by a door at the other end of the room, she saw he still had her in sight. Not only that, but all the people in there seemed to be looking at her. She supposed she did stand out as everyone else was in cocktail wear.

She fled hastily along the corridor but, glancing behind her, she saw that he was gaining on her, an expression of confusion on his face, so she lifted her skirts and ran faster.

She dived into a narrow passage opening off the corridor and it was only when she was halfway along it that the realised it was a dead end.

'In here,' a voice said and a door opened. She shot through it and found herself behind the stage in a small space cluttered with musical instruments. The band leader closed the door behind her and said, 'You'd better duck down behind the piano in case he comes in here.'

Faye picked her way as quickly as she could through the clutter, narrowly missed putting her foot through a double bass and was pulled up short when her cloak caught on the corner of a packing case.

'Quick!' the band leader, who was listening at the door, urged her. She wrenched at her cloak but it remained caught fast. She hastily shed it and then crouched in the narrow space behind the piano. A second later the door opened.

'Where did she go?' she heard Leo ask.

'The woman with the cloak? Through the curtains and onto the stage. What's going on?'

Faye heard Leo cross the room, swear when he walked into something, then there was a brief flare of noise from the main lounge as he parted the curtains and then he was gone.

'You're probably safe to come out now,' the band leader told her. He was lounging on a battered kitchen chair when she peered huntedly over the top of the piano.

'Th . . . thank you,' she stuttered.

'My pleasure. I don't know who you are or what you've done, but anyone who's fallen foul of our overly officious first officer is okay in my book. Drink?' He produced a hip flask from his pocket.

'Please. Could you just pass me my cloak first?'

'He took it with him.'

Faye stared at him aghast. 'Wh . . . what?'

'He took it with him,' he repeated patiently. 'So, beautiful lady, why was he in such hot pursuit? Are you a stowaway?'

'No, I'm not.' Faye's tone was indignant in the extreme.

'Are you coming out from behind that piano? It's a bit disconcerting to be able to see only your mask and wig.'

'I . . . I can't.'

'Why not?'

Faye was too mortified to reply. She bit her lip and stared at him. Puzzled, he rose to his feet and crossed to the piano, then his mouth fell open as he took in her state of undress.

'Would you mind awfully lending me your jacket?' she asked.

'Do I have to? This is the best thing that's happened to me all year. In fact, I know you don't I? You're the beautiful passenger with the chestnut hair I've talked to a couple of times.' He pulled off his jacket and handed it to her.

Faye scrambled thankfully into it and then emerged from the shelter of the piano.

'How did you recognise me?' she asked in dismay.

'Your voice mainly. But it would be difficult to forget a spectacular figure like yours, even if I've never seen quite so much of it before.'

He passed her the hip flask and she gulped down several

mouthfuls of neat whisky and then coughed as it hit the back of her throat.

'So tell me, why is one of the first-class passengers running around the ship wearing a wig, a mask and a fancy gown with no top to it?'

'It's not a wig,' said Faye, sinking onto the edge of a packing case. 'I emptied a tin of talcum powder on my hair. And I've been at a fancy-dress party in the gym. It's a very . . . adult . . . fancy-dress party,' she ended lamely.

'I can tell that. You mean there's a roomful of women with their breasts on display. This I've got to see.'

'You wouldn't be allowed in without an invitation,' she told him hurriedly.

'Pity. I couldn't persuade you to open the jacket for a bit, could I? It would give me great pleasure just to sit and look at you.'

Faye wasn't sure why, but somehow she found herself opening the jacket. He sat and gazed at her openly, then said in a strangled voice, 'You'd better close it again, this is giving me ideas I'd be better off not having.'

A lock of his dark hair fell forward across his forehead and as he brushed it back he looked tired and vulnerable. He also looked very attractive. She felt a rush of sympathy for him – it couldn't be much fun having to work for a living when you were constantly surrounded by people who dedicated their lives to enjoyment.

She left the jacket open.

As he devoured her with his eyes, she felt a slow, hazy warmth rising over her body as inexorably as the tide, until even her milky breasts were flushed with heat.

Slowly, he rose to his feet and crossed to the packing case, then stopped in front of her, a question in his eyes. In reply, she took his hand and raised it to her breast. He let our a hoarse groan and caressed it fervently, nuzzling its twin with his mouth. They fell backwards onto the packing case, kissing feverishly, their hands roaming freely over each other's bodies.

'How do I get you out of this thing?' he muttered in her ear as he tried to find the fastenings.

Faye thought about the tight lacing it had taken Lucy ages to do up and murmured, 'You don't – it would take too long.' He began fumbling with her skirts, but there were too many layers for him to lift with one hand.

'This is more effective than a chastity belt,' he grunted, reluctantly using both hands to try to get them above her waist. It proved impossible, however hard he tried.

Faye was struck by a sudden thought. She rose from the packing case and tugged at the panniers of her skirt. They lifted to reveal her creamy buttocks.

'Now that,' he said admiringly, 'is what I call a costume.' She bent over the packing case and her bottom jutted alluringly through the hole. The band leader sank to his knees and laid his cheek against the smooth, ivory flesh. She could feel the slight rasp of his stubble as he rubbed it against her, before kissing his way over the full globes.

When the muscular thrust of his tongue entered her vulva and began exploring every moist fold and crevice, Faye sighed with pleasure and opened her legs wide for him. He lapped, licked and probed her until she was sucked into a dizzying spiral of pleasure which made her eager for more.

He traced erotic swirls and circles around her sex-lips, teased her swollen clit and flickered along the groove of her sex-valley until, with a gasping little cry, she came.

He entered her then; a smooth, satisfying slide into her welcoming quim until he was sheathed right up to the hilt. He started slowly, moving steadily in and out, giving her time to begin the slow build-up of pleasure again.

Faye forgot where she was, forgot that at any moment anyone, including Leo, could burst through the curtains from the stage and find them at their impromptu coupling over the packing case, her breasts thrusting out over the top of her tightly laced bodice, her buttocks protruding through a large hole cut out of the back of her skirt.

The band leader moved faster and faster inside her, clasping her breasts, his heavy testicles swinging against the full swell of her rump. Finally in a boiling surge of long-denied release, he came, collapsing on her just as her second climax erupted through her body.

There was a long silence, broken only by their ragged breathing and the muffled hum of conversation from the main lounge, then the band leader pushed himself upright and fastened his trousers.

He glanced at his watch and said, 'Oh no – we're on again in five minutes. The rest of the band will be back from supper at any moment.'

'Can I keep your jacket until I get something else from my cabin?' she asked frantically.

'Sorry – I need it. Hang on a sec.' He burrowed in a curtained-off alcove but couldn't find anything suitable. In a flash of inspiration he ripped the curtain from its hooks and threw it to her – not an instant too soon as the door was suddenly flung open and the rest of the band trooped in.

There were a few raised eyebrows and knowing looks, but Faye was beyond caring, and she was still masked so they wouldn't know who she was.

The band leader followed her outside and put his hands on her shoulders.

'That was undoubtedly the best bit of this or any other crossing I can remember,' he said simply. 'Thanks.'

She hurried back to her cabin and, with fumbling fingers,

undid the gown. She wasn't going to wear it a moment longer and risk any more embarrassment. If that meant she wouldn't be allowed back into the party, then it was just too bad.

She was going to wash her hair too and return to being a normal passenger.

It was over an hour later, after a lengthy shower, that she was ready to return to the party. After some thought she dressed in a brightly patterned satin kimono over a decorous amount of underwear and set off back to the gym, her mask dangling over her wrist. If asked she would say she was a geisha girl and if anyone objected to her being fully dressed she could always display more of her bosom.

She wasn't surprised to see Leo positioned near the gym and this time she didn't mind him seeing her.

'Hello,' she greeted him, 'still on duty?'

'Just for another hour,' he said, looking at her costume with a puzzled expression. 'Why aren't you at the party?'

'I wanted something from my cabin,' she said glibly. 'Have you been standing here for long?'

'Only a few minutes, there was a problem in the terrace grill I had to deal with.' He stared at her kimono, 'Have you been wearing that all evening?'

'Yes,' she said, 'why do you ask?'

'I thought I saw you earlier in a wig and a cloak.'

'Really? It can't have been me then.'

'Is it a good party?' he asked.

'Yes, I'm having a great time.'

'Is there anything going on in there I should know about?'

Faye met his gaze innocently. 'What on earth do you mean?'

'Are they gambling or anything like that?'

'Absolutely not,' she assured him. 'Just dancing and a few games.'

Leo took a quick look around and then pulled her into his arms. 'I thought when I came off duty, we might go to your cabin.'

'Okay – I'll meet you there in an hour.'

He kissed her briefly, then she continued on her way.

The party was still going strong, but no one took any notice of Faye as she slipped in through the doors, her mask back on. She soon bumped into Edward, who didn't even notice she'd changed her costume as he swept her off to dance.

Lucy and Andrei were leaning against the electric horse, taking a breather from dancing.

'I've never tried one of these,' Lucy told him, patting the leather saddle. 'Have you?'

'Only once I think,' he said. Then he grinned at her, his teeth very white against his black mask. 'Let's ride it together.'

'I don't think I want . . .' but Andrei had seized her by the waist and lifted her onto the saddle before she'd finished protesting. He swung one of her legs over so she was sitting astride, making her costume open around her private parts. The leather felt warm and smooth against her bare bottom and vulva as she held onto the handle. She felt a long way off the ground and was glad when Andrei swung himself up to sit behind her.

He leant over to flick the switch that would start the horse moving and then put his arms around her.

Lucy was totally unprepared for the arousing friction the leather of the saddle made against her vulva. It felt wonderful, stimulating her almost to the point of climax within only a minute or two. She bore down on it, holding on tightly, afraid she would become so excited her grip would loosen and she'd be thrown off.

She could feel the leather becoming slick and slippery with

her juices and wondered if any other woman had ridden the horse with a naked sex. Her climax built more swiftly than she would have believed possible and she let out a loud cry as she came, dozens of searing spikes of pleasure jabbing through her slender body.

Andrei held onto her and then she felt him lifting her up and backwards until his shaft was directly beneath her throbbing, tingling quim. She sat down on it heavily, thrown off balance by the movement of the horse, prolonging her climax as he penetrated her deeply.

It was a sticky, breathless, exciting ride. Lucy felt her body could barely sustain so much pleasure as they were rocked up and down. The horse might have been designed to heighten intercourse, drawing them into its rhythm, allowing them to stimulate each other in ways not usually possible.

When they'd both enjoyed the ride to the full, Lucy, rather regretfully, allowed Andrei to lift her down. He paused for moment to look around at the revellers, many openly copulating, and smiled a satisfied smile.

'Shall we return to your stateroom?' he asked. 'I'd like to enjoy you to the full as it's our last night together – unless of course I can persuade you to come with us to the Riviera.' They left the gym and walked hand in hand along the corridor.

'I only wish I could,' said Lucy regretfully. 'I've enjoyed these last few days more than any other period of my life.'

He stopped and turned to face her. 'Then why not come?' he said urgently.

'Just the three of us?'

'And Faye if she wants to.'

'What if I said I'd come if it were just the two of us?'

Andrei looked at her sombrely, his eyes opaque and gleaming with gold lights through the slits in his mask.

'That is not possible – it will never be possible. Sonya and

271

I will always be together. We will never leave each other – but that does not affect my relationship with you.'

They reached her stateroom and went in. Several of her cases were standing open, already half full of her clothes, and Winnie had efficiently packed the steamer trunk during dinner and that was sitting in the corridor outside.

'Now,' said Andrei quietly, 'I wish to take you in a different way, a way I think perhaps you have never been taken before.'

Several hours later Lucy awakened from a brief, exhausted doze, slid silently out of bed and went into the bathroom. She felt stiff, but not unpleasantly so, and her body was suffused by a deep-seated languor.

She splashed some water on her face and then stared at herself in the mirror. She wondered if anyone would be able to tell how much she'd changed in the last few days just by looking at her.

Did her descent into debauchery show on her face?

In only a few hours they would be docking at Southampton and the voyage would be over. She glanced through the open door at the slumbering Andrei, one arm flung back above his head, and wondered if many women had such ambivalent feelings about their lovers.

On one hand he'd shown her pleasure she could never have imagined, on the other he'd humiliated and degraded her, using her for his own ends and to satisfy his own aberrant desires.

The memory of the way he'd tormented her only that afternoon came back to her, filling her anew with lust and fury in equal parts. She glided softly back into the cabin and stood watching him for a moment and then a slow smile spread over her face.

Slowly, stealthily, she picked up two silk stockings from a chair and went over to him. Holding her breath she wound one around the wrist of his outstretched arm and secured it to the headboard. His other arm lay by his side and it seemed to take an eternity to draw it above his head and secure that one too.

His feet were next. She'd lashed the left one to the bottom of the bed with another stocking before he stirred and his eyes opened. She seized his right ankle and yanked it down the bed, tying it before he had chance to come round properly.

Lucy was shrewd enough to realise that Andrei would never have voluntarily allowed her to tie him up – he was a man who liked to call the tune and stay in control.

But during the next few hours he was going to learn that he couldn't always have it his own way. She was going to spend her remaining time on board making sure that she repaid him for every moment of shame and helplessness he'd put her through, while pleasuring herself selfishly and determinedly.

He raised his head and their eyes met.

'Untie me,' he directed her tersely.

Lucy smiled at him triumphantly but didn't reply. Instead she moved over to the dressing table and picked up her hairbrush. She drew it through her tangled golden curls as he said, 'Lucy, release me at once!'

'Why should I?' she asked dreamily.

'I think you're forgetting that it is I who decides what takes place between us.'

'Oh, I think you've had more than your pound of flesh, Andrei. From now until I decide to let you go, the tables are turned and I'm taking charge.'

She dragged the sheet from him so he lay naked before her. He yanked at his bonds with enough strength to make the headboard bend, but it didn't give and neither did the silk stockings. For all their delicacy they were strong enough to keep him firmly bound to the bed.

After a few more futile tugs he lay back and said calmly,

'Very well, do as you please. But do not be surprised if I fall asleep – it has been a full night.'

'Not as full as it's going to be.'

Lucy went over to the wardrobe and selected a black lace basque because she knew Andrei found it more arousing when she was partially dressed.

The basque, newly purchased from the ship's expensive shop, came down almost to her golden fleece at the front and just above her pert buttocks at the back. Four small suspenders dangled from it and she sat on the chair in front of the dressing table facing him as she rolled a new pair of sheer black stockings up her legs.

She made sure that he caught several glimpses of her swollen vulva as she did so, spending a long time over the simple procedure, smoothing the stockings upwards from ankle to thigh with long, lingering strokes.

As she fastened the last suspender she glanced at him through her lashes and saw that his previously slumbering manhood was stirring. With her back to him she bent down to lift a pair of high-heeled black kid shoes from the wardrobe, well aware that her naked derrière was on provocative display.

When she turned around his face was impassive, but his member was semi-erect. She got lithely onto the bed and sat astride his strong thighs. With gentle fingertips she set out to coax him into a full erection, circling his glans with a teasing motion, then running down his shaft to feather around his testicles.

It didn't take long before his manhood towered impressively up between his thighs, a drop of clear liquid already forming on the end. Lucy bent forward and took the glans between her lips, drawing it into the warm velvet of her mouth where she sucked and licked it until she heard him emit a heartfelt groan.

He was obviously annoyed with himself for letting it escape, because after that he remained determinedly silent. She let his shaft slip from her mouth and then nibbled and kissed her way along the full length of it, squeezing it rhythmically, until she could sense his urgent desire to come.

She knelt above him, his rod in her hand, and slowly lowered herself onto it. She could feel the hot throbbing against her silk-lined sheath as she took all of it inside her and began to clench and unclench her internal muscles.

As soon as she sensed his release was imminent, she knelt up, letting it slip out of her to land with a soft thwack on his stomach. She lay down beside him and kissed his chest.

'So impatient,' she murmured, 'but not just yet.' To keep him in a state of arousal she whispered the most exciting and arousing things she could think of in his ear, occasionally stroking his organ with a slender hand.

She mounted him again, this time pulling the front of her basque down to expose her firm, high breasts to his hungry gaze. She caressed them herself, toying with the swollen rose-pink nipples, tracing the circles of her aureoles. He remained resolutely silent, but his eyes never left her.

She bent over him and offered one swollen nipple to his lips. He took it and sucked on it, flicking at it with his tongue until she felt an answering heat building in her groin. She knew he was hoping to excite her to the point where she'd mount him again and perhaps this time ride him until he climaxed, but he wasn't getting away so easily.

She sat up and moved up the bed until she was astride his face.

'I want you to bring me to a climax with your lips and tongue,' she told him. 'If you do that to my satisfaction, I may let you go.'

She lowered herself onto his face and immediately felt his muscular tongue stabbing voluptuously at her clit. Andrei was skilful and practised at this particular way of giving pleasure and she was ready to come within a couple of minutes. Every time she felt close she shifted position slightly and broke the rhythm he kept assiduously setting up.

But it was too much like torturing herself and very soon she gave way to her body's urgent clamouring, allowing the waves of convulsive pleasure to spasm through her. When she rolled to one side and lay on the bed she saw that his face was glistening with her juices. She waited to see if he would now beg or demand to be released, but he remained silent.

At last she said, 'That was very good, but on balance I don't think I've *quite* finished with you yet.'

She sat astride him again and this time used his cock to bring her to a climax by rubbing it backwards and forwards over her swollen, sensitive bud. The sense of power it gave her to see him lying helplessly bound and forced to pleasure her, acted like a strong aphrodisiac and even after she'd come again she couldn't bring herself to untie him.

She must have dozed off because the dim light of dawn was just beginning to filter in when she next opened her eyes. The bed seemed to be shaking and she wondered dazedly if they'd run into another storm before she realised that it was Andrei wrenching with all his might at the stockings securing him so humiliatingly to the bed.

She felt a pang of remorse when she saw the red weals his struggles had made on his wrists and ankles, but she determinedly suppressed it. After all, had he been moved to release her when she'd begged and pleaded with him yesterday?

Instead she knelt astride him again and touched herself between the legs, forcing him to watch while she masturbated to a climax so strong that warm honeyed juices ran down her thighs, soaking her stocking tops.

She wondered why he didn't close his eyes to shut out a

sight which must be torture to him, but instinct told her that it was pride, the same pride which made him refuse to plead with her.

She could already hear sounds which indicated that the ship was stirring and knew she didn't have much time left. She took his ramrod-hard shaft and eased it into her dripping quim. This time she didn't hold back. She rode him hard, rising and falling on him with a ferocity which surprised her as much as it obviously surprised him.

His hips bucked wildly beneath her as he thrust upwards to meet each downward movement of hers. It was a wild, rough ride, each of them intent on their own satisfaction.

At last with a hoarse groan which echoed around the cabin, Andrei erupted into her in a seemingly endless torrent of release. Lucy was almost too weak to enjoy her last and strongest explosion into ecstasy and slumped onto his hard chest, her ragged breathing echoing in her own ears.

As soon as she had the strength, she tugged weakly at the knots in the stockings, but they had tightened too much for her to undo them. She eventually gave up the futile struggle and went to get her nail scissors.

Remembering how she'd hit him when he'd eventually released her, Lucy prudently freed his ankles first and left one wrist still secured, then hesitated, wondering if he was planning to inflict some form of bodily harm on her in retaliation.

He must have read her mind because he smiled sardonically and said, 'Have no fear. I have never used violence against a woman in my life and despite the extreme provocation I'm not about to do so now.'

Relieved, she cut the last bond and then stepped backwards, hovering nervously near the bathroom door, ready to dive in and lock it behind her.

He rubbed briefly at his wrists and ankles, then reached for his clothes and dressed silently before turning to face her.

He caught her chin in his hand and said softly, 'I wish you would reconsider, Lucy, and come with us to the South of France – what an asset you would be to our party.'

His gold-green eyes bored into her, then he bent his head to kiss her hard on the mouth and left without another word.

Lucy stood on deck, light-headed from lack of sleep and a surfeit of sex. She'd showered and dressed, then rung for Winnie to come and finish packing. She'd found Faye already on deck and, if appearances were anything to go by, her friend was feeling just the same way.

Silently, they watched the lush, green shore of the Isle of Wight slip by as they steamed past it on the very last lap of the journey.

'Sonya came to my cabin first thing this morning,' said Faye tonelessly. 'She wants us to join them on their travels.'

'Andrei does too.' There was a prolonged pause and then Lucy said slowly, 'If your sister thinks you're staying with me and my Aunt Sarah thinks I'm staying with you, doesn't that give us *carte blanche* to do anything we like – at least for a few weeks?'

'We might get away with it, but what if we're found out?' Faye wanted to know.

'I think it would be worth it. After all, can we really face returning to our old way of life after all we've experienced for the last few days?'

'I don't suppose we can.'

They turned to look at each other.

'If we're careful, and cover our tracks, it may work out,' was Lucy's view. 'I'll tell Winnie I don't need her and let her go back to the house, so she won't be able to tell on us, then I'll get a new maid from an agency.'

'I'm sure Amanda will help cover for us if we ask her to,' added Faye.

The decision made, they hugged each other gleefully. Then Lucy said, 'Let's go and tell them the good news.'

Arm in arm, they strolled along the deck, the salt breeze fresh in their faces.

A Message from the Publisher

Headline Liaison is a new concept in erotic fiction: a list of books designed for the reading pleasure of both men and women, to be read alone – or together with your lover. As such, we would be most interested to hear from our readers.

Did you read the book with your partner? Did it fire your imagination? Did it turn you on – or off? Did you like the story, the characters, the setting? What did you think of the cover presentation? In short, what's your opinion? If you care to offer it, please write to:

> The Editor
> Headline Liaison
> 338 Euston Road
> London NW1 3BH

Or maybe you think you could do better if you wrote an erotic novel yourself. We are always on the look-out for new authors. If you'd like to try your hand at writing a book for possible inclusion in the Liaison list, here are our basic guidelines: We are looking for novels of approximately 80,000 words in which the erotic content should aim to please both men and women and should not describe illegal sexual activity (pedophilia, for example). The novel should contain sympathetic and interesting characters, pace, atmosphere and an intriguing plotline.

If you'd like to have a go, please submit to the Editor a sample of at least 10,000 words, clearly typed on one side of the paper only, together with a short resumé of the storyline. Should you wish your material returned to you please include a stamped addressed envelope. If we like it sufficiently, we will offer you a contract for publication.

Adult Fiction for Lovers from Headline LIAISON

SLEEPLESS NIGHTS	Tom Crewe & Amber Wells	£4.99
THE JOURNAL	James Allen	£4.99
THE PARADISE GARDEN	Aurelia Clifford	£4.99
APHRODISIA	Rebecca Ambrose	£4.99
DANGEROUS DESIRES	J. J. Duke	£4.99
PRIVATE LESSONS	Cheryl Mildenhall	£4.99
LOVE LETTERS	James Allen	£4.99

All Headline Liaison books are available at your local bookshop or newsagent, or can be ordered direct from the publisher. Just tick the titles you want and fill in the form below. Prices and availability subject to change without notice.

Headline Book Publishing, Cash Sales Department, Bookpoint, 39 Milton Park, Abingdon, OXON, OX14 4TD, UK. If you have a credit card you may order by telephone – 01235 400400.

Please enclose a cheque or postal order made payable to Bookpoint Ltd to the value of the cover price and allow the following for postage and packing: UK & BFPO: £1.00 for the first book, 50p for the second book and 30p for each additional book ordered up to a maximum charge of £3.00. OVERSEAS & EIRE: £2.00 for the first book, £1.00 for the second book and 50p for each additional book.

Name ....

Address ....

....

....

If you would prefer to pay by credit card, please complete: Please debit my Visa/Access/Diner's Card/American Express (Delete as applicable) card no:

Signature .... Expiry Date ....